CW00375520

Written in Blood

Inspector Ted Greening is in a bad mood – he has a splitting headache, his whisky bottle is empty, and a body has just been dug up in the grounds of a local mansion. There is only one thing to do – pass the buck.

Detective Inspector Harry Timberlake and Detective Sergeant Darren Webb are assigned to the case, and their suspicion immediately falls on the formidable Sophie Pusey and her son Charles, the owners of Towers Hall, now living in France. Could the dead woman be Betty Lock, Charles's pregnant girlfriend who disappeared fifteen years ago?

Sophie arrives back in Terrace Vale accompanied by her step-son Jean-Louis, the Comte de Gaillmont. She is cold, haughty and decidedly unhelpful. Timberlake and Webb breathe a sigh of relief when their investigations seem to point them away from the sinister Towers Hall.

Especially as Harry's private life is becoming rather complicated. He's recently been reunited with his former lover, Dr Jenny Long – so why can't he get Woman Detective Constable Sarah Lewis out of his head? Sarah, in the middle of a disturbing rape case, is equally confused: she just can't forget that year she spent with Harry . . .

Then another body is found shot dead at the gates to the great house, and Timberlake and Webb are drawn once more into the dark, murderous world of the de Gaillmonts and their deadly secrets.

Written in Blood

Max Marquis

MACMILLAN

First published 1995 by Macmillan

an imprint of Macmillan General Books
Cavaye Place London SW10 9PG
and Basingstoke

Associated companies throughout the world

ISBN 0 333 64426 3

9 8 7 6 5 4 3 2 1

A CIP catalogue record for this book is available from
the British Library

Phototypeset by Intype, London
Printed by Mackays of Chatham PLC, Chatham, Kent

For Margaret

Chapter 1

James Michael Kinnell was normally a fairly quiet sort of person, hardworking and frequently sober, not given to raising his voice except when discussing football; but he had a very loud voice when put to it. His sudden high-pitched yell, followed by 'Jaysus Chroist Almoighty!', and then a more restrained 'Holy Mary, mother of God!' repeated several times while he crossed himself, made his workmates stop work quicker than if the union shop steward had shouted, 'All out!'

Kinnell's bad day began when his spade scraped on something round and hard. As a frequent victim of Sod's Law, he guessed it wasn't buried treasure but an old drainpipe, or a sewer pipe which would stink the place out if he broke into it. He wasn't even that lucky.

He gingerly scraped away more of the heavy, sodden earth – gingerly, because once he had driven a pneumatic drill through a mains electric cable, extinguishing the lights in a large office block as he was sent flying through the air smelling faintly of singeing. His life was saved because he was wearing his working wellies. This experience had made him understandably circumspect. He uncovered the object a little more, stopped, peered closely, and let out his terrified yell.

Since he had started work digging the trench for new drainpipes in the grounds of Towers Hall that morning, James Michael had felt a pricking of the thumbs. Despite his rugged appearance and a hairline that struggled to keep above his eyebrows, he was highly sensitive to ambiences and auras, and he hated being at the Hall. It gave him clammy shivers even in the warmest weather, but these days a job was a job.

The house was large, by far the largest in Terrace Vale and one of the largest in London. It was situated at the bottom of a cul-de-sac on a sort of peninsula projecting into the adjoining Metropolitan Police area of Southington. The cul-de-sac was named Willow Square, although, typical of the names of Terrace Vale streets, it was neither square nor were there any willow trees, weeping or laughing.

The house at the end of the square dated from the 1860s, and looked as though the architect of the Albert Memorial had designed it while smoking something illegal. Its largely castellated exterior was a mass of convoluted ornamentation and small towers of flagrantly phallic form, innocently designed long before Freud was in long trousers. It was the sort of home where Bram Stoker might well have written *Dracula* – if he'd had the courage to live there.

The place had a sinister reputation locally, with a history of more than a fair share of accidents, tragedies and premature deaths. The extensive grounds were made dark and uninviting by nasty spiky trees, fleshy-leaved laurel bushes and relentless ivy. Mothers used to frighten naughty children by threatening to take them to Towers Hall and leave them there.

Now, after fifteen years of being uninhabited and closed up, it was being totally renovated and redecorated, although the exercise was rather like trying to make a mausoleum look cosy.

The foreman, Gerry McGrath, followed by most of the other members of the outside working gang, hurried over to Kinnell, who was still crossing himself. He stopped long enough to point into the trench he had dug.

Emerging from the boggy earth at the bottom like a swimmer breaking the surface of the water was the head of a woman, her long hair still attached to it.

'Terrace Vale Police,' Sergeant Rumsden answered, in his this-is-your-friendly-local-police voice. 'Sergeant Rumsden, station officer. Can I help you?'

'Southington nick here, sarge,' replied his opposite number there. 'Somebody's found a body. It's yours.'

'We haven't lost any bodies,' Rumsden answered, switching off his nice-to-the-public tone. 'You can keep it.'

'Somebody dug it up in the grounds of Towers Hall in Willow Square. That's your area. We've got enough of our own work to do without doing yours for you. Cheers.'

'They *will* be pleased upstairs,' Rumsden said to the wall.

Upstairs, Detective Chief Inspector Ted Greening sat at his desk and swore. He had just found that the half-bottle of whisky in the bottom drawer was empty. There was an emergency bottle in the glove compartment of his car, but that was down in the station yard. He weighed the effort of going to his car against the need for a drink, and reluctantly decided against moving. Later the scales would tilt heavily in favour of his going to get the bottle.

Mornings were never his best part of the day. It took him a couple of hours for the effects of the excesses of the previous night to drain away, but he had learned to live with that, after a fashion. Mornings were when he had to struggle out of bed and face his wife across the breakfast table – breakfast, in his case, being laced black coffee and two paracetamol.

Marjorie Greening was forty-eight, and looked as if she had been so for the past ten years. Her mouth was a thin, pallid line set in a permanent scimitar-slash of disapproval. She hadn't always been like that. If she hadn't been strictly religious, she would have divorced Ted Greening decades earlier; as it was, she accepted him as Her Cross.

When the then dashing young Ted Greening had met Marjorie Spinks, a nineteen-year-old Woolworths shop assistant, she was attractive with a seductive figure and an inviting manner. But soon after his marriage Ted Greening began to ask himself why he had married her. One of the reasons was that she steadfastly refused to allow Greening any pre-marital sexual liberties whatsoever, which was so stunningly unique in his experience that it totally derailed his judgement.

It was only after some months of spiritless wedlock that it dawned on him that her air of awkward sexual provocation had been copied from film stars in the belief that it would make her appear adult and sophisticated. He soon discovered that her reluctant approach to sex wasn't maidenly timidity: she genuinely had an eyes-closed, teeth-clenched, white-knuckled approach to *It*.

Marjorie dutifully bore her husband two children early in their marriage, then developed a permanent bedtime headache that had lasted for a good twenty-six years. For twenty-four of them Greening hadn't cared. The moment that the children were legally old enough to leave home they left like hungry greyhounds.

There were two possible means of surviving life with Ted Greening. One was the bottle, but living with him and his thirst was enough to scare anyone off liquor. So Marjorie Greening opted for Plan B. She Got Religion.

Greening was just over fifty; he, too, looked older. He was putting on weight faster than he was replacing his wardrobe. He could have gone to a costume party in his ordinary clothes as the Michelin Man. He was a glad-hander, back-slapper, knowing winker and a bad dirty story-teller. All he wanted now was a life with no waves: his eye was firmly fixed on his retirement. The pity of it all was that once he was a first-class copper, a successful thief-taker. He had several commendations for his work and his bravery, but the last one was a long time ago.

When Sergeant Rumsden appeared in Greening's office he knew it was trouble.

'Oh, gawd, what is it?' he asked.

'Somebody's found a body in Towers Hall.'

Some of the gloom lifted from Greening's face. 'Hold on. That's the bloody great pile just off Southington Close, isn't it? It's not our problem.'

'Sorry, Ted,' Rumsden replied, without the least hint of regret. Sergeant Anthony C. Rumsden was something of an institution at Terrace Vale, and was the only one of his rank who called Greening 'Ted' – and that was only when the wind was in the south. 'It's in Willow Square, which is just inside our patch.' Before Greening could find another straw to cling to, Rumsden added, 'I checked.'

'Is HT in?' HT was Detective Inspector Harry Timberlake.

'Yes. I just saw him go into his office.'

'He can deal with it, then,' Greening said, his brow lightening a little. 'Give him the details, and make sure the doc's told. And the pathologist. I'm up to my eyes with work at the moment.' He indicated the pile of dossiers on his desk that he always kept for camouflage. Rumsden smiled a knowing smile and left.

About half an hour later Harry Timberlake and Sergeant Darren Webb were by James Michael Kinnell's neatly dug trench, looking down at the top of a woman's head. Beside them were the Scene of Crime Officers, or SOCOs, ready to make a microscopic examination of the area surrounding the body.

In a case of suspicious death the very first thing that must be done, even before the SOCOs get to work, is for a doctor to pronounce the victim dead. So the normal procedure is for the

4

police to keep everyone well back from the immediate vicinity, and for the SOCOs to lay down tapes to mark out a pathway for the police doctor to approach without leaving any false clues from his shoes or clothes near the body.

The area around the trench was hidden from public view by a large canvas tent-like structure, with a temporary canvas roof. This didn't discourage the workmen on the site, kept at bay by a barrier of broad tape, from staring at the blank walls as if they were waiting for a film to start, and speculating on what was going on behind them. They had been quick to seize the opportunity to lean on their spades instead of using them.

James Michael Kinnell, who had recovered from his initial shock, was animatedly explaining for the fifth or sixth time to anyone who would listen how he had discovered the body – that is, if there *was* a body attached to the head he had uncovered.

The near-static human tableau came to life with the arrival of the local police surgeon, Dr Lawrence Pratt. It was really stretching things to wait for him to turn up and pronounce that a body buried under four feet of earth was dead, but going by the book often avoided providing loopholes for wily lawyers. Even if the head is a couple of feet from a body, the doctor must confirm that the body is a *dead* body, not just someone with a bad headache.

Dr Lawrence Pratt was just under six feet tall, which meant he had to look up to Timberlake. His long hair, such of it as remained, was dyed a highly improbable black and combed carefully into a complex whorl from the back, then carefully plastered down with some sort of unguent that smelled like a tart's boudoir. It made him look as if someone had painted his head with black gloss paint, and anyone talking to him needed a great deal of will power to avoid staring at his hair.

Dr Pratt wore a fawn-coloured three-piece suit; no one had ever seen him in anything else. If someone had told Timberlake the doctor went to bed in that suit he would have believed them. Despite his appearance, however, and the fact that he could fool himself he didn't look bald, Dr Pratt was a good police surgeon and a better-than-average GP. Unfortunately he thought himself something of a wag. The sad truth was that fate had played an ironic trick on the doctor with his name: in all matters outside his considerable professional competence, Dr Lawrence Pratt was indeed a prat.

He borrowed a spade from one of the onlookers and eased

5

himself down into the trench, using it as a sort of makeshift alpenstock. With rubber-gloved hands he gently moved earth from the top of the head. When he had uncovered something that looked like a face he said, 'He, she or it is dead. That's official.' A determined wag to the last he added, 'I'll stake my reputation on it.' No one laughed.

'Any idea of the time of death?' Darren Webb asked with an innocent expression. There were a few snickers. Timberlake gave him a reproving glance.

Dr Pratt climbed out of the trench. 'You lot can dig it out now,' he said grumpily. Two SOCOs exchanged glances. They knew whose job that would be.

There followed two developments which deepened the cheerlessness of the scene. It started to rain, and the pathologist, Professor Peter Mortimer, arrived, accompanied by his assistant, Miss Gertrude Hacker. Mortimer looked like one of Stephen Lowry's stick figures brought to something approaching life. He moved with all the natural grace of Frankenstein's creation as played by Boris Karloff, although Mortimer looked a little better. Gertrude Hacker was about fifty-five, dressed in her usual formless tweed suit, hat and woollen jumper. From his car, an old Rover shaped rather like an upright piano, Mortimer pulled an ancient black umbrella tinged with green, and a leather bag that looked as if it might have served during the Jack the Ripper investigations. He put up the umbrella and set off for the screen, leaving Gertrude Hacker to trail wetly behind him with the bag. Mortimer rarely had any consideration for the living. He nodded minimally in reply to the greetings of the detectives, and peered into the trench. Gertrude Hacker stood beside him, dripping stoically. The now half-revealed body could be seen, wrapped in the vestiges of some sort of material.

Mortimer put up a hand in the direction of Gertrude Hacker, who without a word handed him a pair of rubber gloves from the bag. He put them on and started to let his angular frame down into the trench. Timberlake was irresistibly reminded of an aged camel reluctantly going down on its knees.

Mortimer straddled the body and held out a hand behind him. Gertrude Hacker silently passed him a large plastic bag. He fitted it over the head and sealed it under the chin. After that he cleared away the earth and mud from the hands and bagged them in turn.

He straightened up with an almost audible creak. Sergeant Burton, the senior SOCO, and Darren Webb each took a hand and helped Mortimer out of the trench.

'Dig it out *carefully*,' Mortimer told Burton unnecessarily. 'We don't want it coming apart in your hands.' Webb looked at some distant trees. 'Get a stretcher or a ground sheet under it to lift it out. Leave it here under cover until the undertaker's men arrive, then make sure they treat it *carefully*,' he repeated. 'See it's properly covered and don't let them take it out while it's raining. And be sure to get adequate samples of the soil,' he said – quite unnecessarily, for Johnson knew his job as well as anyone.

Having given a comprehensive lecture to grandmothers on how to suck eggs, without further word Mortimer left the tent, raised his umbrella and made for his car. Gertrude Hacker squelched behind him, the rain pelting down on her.

'Lovable, isn't he?' commented Sergeant Johnson.

'Not my idea of cuddly,' Timberlake replied. He walked over to the group of workmen standing in the rain, still waiting vainly for something to happen.

'Who's in charge here?' he asked.

'I'm the clerk of works,' said the man whose authority was underlined by a bowler hat, collar and tie. 'Martin Stubbs.'

'Mr Stubbs, is the owner at home?'

'No, sir.'

' "Inspector" will do. Who's the owner, and where is he?'

'Now you're asking,' Martin Stubbs said portentously. 'That's a bit of a puzzler, that is.'

The telephone rang in the editor's office of the *West Thames Times*, which carried in smaller type beneath the masthead *and Southington, Wallsend and Terrace Vale Messenger*. West Thames itself and these three other districts were all part of the London Borough of West Thames. The *WTT*, as it was called locally, was one of the best known and most interesting local papers, with a healthy advertising revenue and a paid circulation of 20,000.

'Editor's Office,' announced Iain Logan. In fact he *was* the editor, but he never admitted it on the phone before he knew who was calling. That way he avoided a lot of explanations, arguments and threats.

7

'Horace Bean here, Mr Logan.' He could have announced himself PC Bean, No. 293, Terrace Vale station, but Iain Logan knew him all right.

'What have you got for me, Horace?'

'Towers Hall. They've just dug up a woman's body.'

'Whose? How long has it been there?'

'Don't know yet. They've taken it for tests and that.'

Iain Logan thought rapidly for a moment. 'Who else knows?'

'Only the workmen. I don't suppose they've thought of calling anyone.'

'Right. See you at the pub tonight. This one could be worth a bit extra for you.'

The name Towers Hall rang two bells in Logan's head: the first a loud, close one about the house's reputation; the second, a more distant bell that interested Logan more. He was sure someone had mentioned something about the place that happened before he joined the paper twelve years ago.

Although the *WTT*'s resources didn't stretch to a computerized cuttings library like those of national newspapers, they did have an extensive card index of stories with a local interest. Iain Logan looked up Towers Hall. The writing on the card made him utter something obscure in Gaelic. He hurried to the store-room where bound copies of the *WTT* were kept. He selected the volume for July to December 1979, he found the date he wanted. He read the story with increasing excitement, referring from time to time to the filing card.

When he had finished, he shut the book noisily, leaned back in his chair and said, 'The bastards! They murdered her!'

Chapter 2

Ted Greening was feeling even less human than usual as he parked his car, which looked as badly used as its owner, and walked carefully across the station car-park to the back entrance of Terrace Vale nick. He had spent most of the previous evening with one of his informants, a young woman who earned her very good tax-free living on her back, staring at the ceiling over men's shoulders. Greening put his feet down with great care so as not to shake his head. He had the weird sensation that his eyeballs were loose in their sockets and if he lowered his head they might drop out. What he wanted now was a large black coffee with a generous measure of whisky in it.

He was not going to get it.

'Guvnor!' Sergeant Rumsden called out when he caught sight of Greening. One glance was enough to tell him this was not the day to call him Ted. 'The Chief Super wants to see you as soon as you come in.'

Greening mentally ran through all the swear words and rude expressions he knew but couldn't find one strong enough. He was forced to settle for a defeated 'Oh, bugger.' Greening didn't like the chief superintendent: he was too aware, too efficient and, in Greening's view, too much of a slave-driver. He turned to Rumsden. 'Just turn your back for a second and let me nip in without you seeing me.'

'I'd like to help, guv,' Rumsden replied with monumental hypocrisy, 'but it wouldn't do any good. The Super can see the car-park from his window.'

Greening belched sourly, failed to do it silently, and wished he hadn't tried.

'Harry Timberlake's already with him,' Rumsden reported to Greening's retreating back. Now Greening knew he had to see the chief superintendent: he didn't want Timberlake to drop him in it while he wasn't there to flam his way out of any trouble. He was being grotesquely unjust. If anything, Timberlake was liable to help cover for Greening, but he was judging Timberlake by his own standards.

The chief's office was on the first floor, up twenty stairs covered with frayed linoleum marked with a moonscape of small indentations dating from the days of stiletto heels. Before he was three-quarters of the way up them Greening had to pause for breath; he paused again outside the door to gather himself as much as possible, and try to think.

'Good morning, Ted,' Chief Superintendent Gregory Marlow greeted him in a neutral tone that did nothing to put Greening's mind at rest.

'Morning, sir,' he replied. He nodded at Harry Timberlake, who was sitting near the chief super's desk.

Greening wasn't pleased to see Timberlake, for if there was going to be any blame flying around, he couldn't divert it in Timberlake's direction without his knowing it.

Chief Superintendent Gregory Marlow was new to Terrace Vale. Three months earlier he had been promoted from Detective Superintendent to take over command of the station from Bernard Liversedge, a slack, buck-passing politician of a policeman who had found his proper place in a back office at Scotland Yard, as Officer in Charge of Paper Clips or something. Marlow, however, was Harry Timberlake's kind of policeman. He was decisive, had been a working detective – a good one – and he understood the pressures and difficulties of the job. He appreciated good work; and he also knew all the dodges and devices of the column-dodgers, skivers and corner cowboys. Greening was afraid of him.

'Have you seen the local rag this morning?' Marlow asked. He handed over a copy of the *West Thames Times*, observing Greening with a certain amount of sympathy. 'Cigarette, Ted?' He offered one from a box on his desk although, like Harry Timberlake, he didn't smoke himself.

Greening clutched at it as if he were drowning, lit it and took two deep drags before looking at the paper.

The *WTT* editor had been very busy the previous evening and night. It was the day before press day, and Iain Logan calculated that if he worked hard enough he could prepare an entirely new

10

front page for the typesetters the following morning. He ran through the roll-call of the editorial staff in his mind before settling, a little reluctantly, on the reporter who had written the original stories fifteen years ago. She was now freelance, but he phoned and asked her to come in to help him write a new splash – the lead story.

It took a lot of persuasion. Logan tried cajolery, flattery, *bonhomie* and appeals to her professionalism. At last he pushed the right button: he offered money. While he waited for her to arrive he downgraded the original lead, which was about a government decision to close a local hospital, supposedly to give patients a better service. The *WTT* thought it was a totally daft idea.

All the front-page stories were typed on the paper's computers and then sent by modem to the typesetting company at Watford, who faxed the proofs back to the paper for checking. Finally, when the *WTT* okayed them, the typesetter's copy was taken from the Watford office by courier to the printing works, to arrive half an hour before the works' deadline. It was this revised edition of the paper that Greening was studying through a haze of tobacco smoke. 'Bloody hell,' he said involuntarily.

'Did either of you know about this?' Marlow asked.

'Fifteen years ago ... it was before both our times here, sir,' Timberlake said quickly, although he wasn't too sure about Greening, who prudently said nothing.

'What have you done so far?' The question was aimed at Greening, who deflected it towards Timberlake with a nod, trying to give the impression that he had given him instructions.

'I looked it up in the files, and the story fits with what we've got. I had a word with the clerk of works at the house yesterday and he gave us the name and address of the solicitors who're representing the present owners, whoever they are. Darren Webb's going there later today. I phoned the editor of the paper, and I've arranged to see him and the reporter who wrote the original story in about an hour. I haven't informed AMIP yet; the probability is the body was buried some time ago, so there's no immediate hurry.'

'Yes, I think we can give it another day at least,' Marlow agreed. 'It seems you've been quite busy. Keep me in touch.'

Iain Logan gave a self-satisfied smile when Timberlake walked into his office carrying a copy of *West Thames Times*. With the

11

editor was a woman of anything between thirty-five and fifty-five who at first sight seemed something between a retired madam of a Tiger Bay brothel and a guard in a Russian women's prison. Her intimidating appearance, and the whisky voice which sounded like someone walking over a pebble beach, soon proved to be deceptive; a front to hide a certain basic shyness. She turned out to be pleasant, helpful and shrewd. Logan introduced her as Petra Woodward.

'What did you think of my story?' he asked Timberlake.

'*Yours?*' asked Petra, staring at him ferociously as if he were a punter who was trying to sneak out without paying.

'Sorry, darling,' Logan apologized, with all of a journalist's sincerity. 'Ours.'

'I was more interested in what you left out of it,' Timberlake told him. Logan was taken aback, but Petra gave a sly smile. 'Worried about libel, I suppose,' Timberlake went on. He addressed Petra. 'You were the original reporter. You tell me the whole story.'

She rose. 'Sure. But not in this rat's nest.' Logan started to get up, too. Petra directed a look of incandescent hatred at him and said sharply, 'You needn't come. You weren't here when it all happened.' She picked up an enormous handbag, took an amused Timberlake by the arm and steered him out of the office straight across the road towards the Black Swan – inevitably known as the Mucky Duck – and, to his surprise, on past it to a café further along the road. 'Too early for booze,' she explained as they ordered coffee. 'Besides, I've got five hundred words to write before teatime.'

'Won't you get into trouble, talking to your editor like that?' Timberlake asked.

'Him? That tartan turd isn't my editor. Not any more. I got out a month after he arrived. The man's a first-class journalist but a five-star shit.'

Timberlake kept an instinctive comment to himself. He simply asked, 'So what do you do now?'

'Apart from freelance pieces for local papers, romantic novels. You know: the Rodgers and Lake Library.'

'Somehow I shouldn't have thought it was your sort of thing,' he said automatically, then wished he hadn't.

'Why not? The money's good and it's a highly professional

12

exercise: fifty-five thousand words, give or take a hundred max, with a long list of do's and don'ts.'

'Oh, yes. Chaste kisses, and everyone's a virgin until the wedding night.'

'Not any more. Explicit bonking is in, complete with moans, groans and sweat, as long as they simply can't resist each other and they get married in the end.'

Timberlake suddenly felt uncomfortable at the mention of marriage. He changed the subject. 'Now, the Towers Hall story . . .'

'Quite straightforward, really. Like it says in the paper, the house used to be occupied by Mrs Sophie Pusey – she's French, *very* minor aristocracy when she married, but gave up her title for the Pusey megabucks – and her son Charles Pusey Junior. The grandfather was owner of Pusey Chemicals. The company made a fortune during the war and doubled it when they merged with the Swiss firm to set up a pharmaceutical division, Pusey & Lafôret. Grandad left the business to his son, Charles Pusey Senior, and the firm's still doing very well, thank you very much. When Pusey died he left his widow *millions*. She could afford to play poker with oil sheiks who cheat.'

'What about the house itself?'

'You know when a ship is launched and someone's killed it's always reckoned to be an unlucky ship? Well, that's an unlucky house. It's just plain creepy. I wouldn't be surprised if the grounds are stuffed with bodies.'

'Let's keep to this one.'

'Well, about fifteen years ago young Charles Pusey took up with a local girl, Betty Lock. He was twenty-one, she was seventeen, mature for her age. His mother was French, with very grand ideas, and thought Betty wasn't good enough for him. She tried to put an end to it.'

'But.'

'But then Betty got pregnant.'

'How do you know?'

'Trust me. Actually, it was no great secret. She made a lot of noise about it, became depressed and threatened to make a scandal.'

'Did Charles tell his mother?'

'No, Betty and her father did.'

'What about *her* mother?'

13

'She was dead; she'd died a couple of years before. Anyway Betty and her father called on Charles and his mother. There was an enormous shouting match. Well, not Sophie Pusey: she was too *refained* to raise her voice. She was a cold and supercilious bitch. Charles denied responsibility, and his mother implied that any of half a dozen local lads could have put the bun in her oven.' Timberlake winced. 'Quite untrue, of course. She finally twisted the knife by saying that even if Charles had done Betty the honour of fucking her, she would never allow him to marry her because she was only a little bourgeoise.' She smiled wryly. 'Not in those exact words, though.'

'So what happened in the end?'

'Betty started to become hysterical, shouting she'd cause a local scandal and tell everyone about some of Charles's unpleasant habits. Mrs Pusey was like an iceberg, and Major Lock – he was Regular Army then – and Betty were shown out; but not before he made some dark threats about what he would do to Charles.'

'How do you know all this?'

'My sister Poppy was a maid there. We were a poor family, then.' Petra Woodward was quiet for a long moment. 'Poppy's dead now. I told you it was an unlucky house.'

'I'm sorry.' He let her take her time.

'Three days after the big row when Charles broke the news to his mother, Betty Lock disappeared. She's never been heard from since. And that same week Mrs Pusey – I beg her pardon, *Madame* – Pusey and her son shut up the house and left for France.' She paused for effect. 'Your lot searched for Betty for months, and for five years there were bits on the telly about her on the anniversaries of her disappearance, but she was never found. Until now, perhaps. It is a woman they dug up, isn't it?'

Timberlake glanced down at the heavy black type at the top of the story in the *WTT*. 'Which explains the headline.'

'IS IT BETTY LOCK?'

Chapter 3

After he left Petra Woodward, Harry Timberlake returned to Terrace Vale to make some phone calls. As he walked through the main CID office he met WDC Sarah Lewis on her way out. There was a moment of awkwardness between them.

'Hello, Sarah. How are things?'

'All right, thanks, guv.'

'Good-oh.' It was an expression he hardly ever used.

They both paused, wondering if they should say something else, but neither could think of anything and they moved on.

Ted Greening was standing at the door of his office talking to Detective Inspector Bob Farmer, a man as smooth as a polished mirror, which was one of his favourite household accessories. There was even one on the ceiling of his bedroom.

Farmer had recently been posted to Terrace Vale from Kingsmere-on-Thames, an upmarket area outside the London postal districts, but still part of the Met's bailiwick. Kingsmere had more than its fair share of well-kept parks and commons and was controlled by an enlightened local council; it was reputed that its population had the highest number of university graduates per head outside the university towns. As a result Kingsmere enjoyed a generally better-than-average class of crime. Inevitably in a well-to-do-area there were burglaries, car thefts and white-collar crimes; but little of Terrace Vale's pimping, drug dealing, street prostitution, mugging and general nastiness.

Farmer's appearance reflected his previous background. He was the most elegantly dressed copper at Terrace Vale, and was tall and slim with it. When he took off his jacket in the office he hung it on a clothes-hanger; he always wore a tie. Sergeant Rumsden reckoned he wore one with his pyjamas.

In his early days he was the butt of ribald remarks, but they

15

bounced off him like spit off a hot iron. Many of the sallies were aimed at his lack of hair. He was called Kojak at first, but this was a gross slander; Farmer's hair receded at the temples and was less than luxuriant on the crown, that was all. He was apparently totally unconcerned by it. No one at the station dreamed he had a small cupboard at home full of lotions, creams, ointments, pills and home-made recipes. All useless. And it was quite evident that even if he was on the way to becoming a chrome-dome, it didn't stop him enjoying a rich, satisfying social life with a certain type of young woman – rather dim, impressionable and with big boobs. Which said a great deal about him.

Farmer was a cerebral, odds-playing detective rather than a streetwise copper; he had a long mile to go before he had Harry Timberlake's instinct and street-wisdom. However, he was highly accomplished at internal politicking and subtly brown-nosing his superiors. He was obviously a man with a future.

Greening indicated Timberlake and Sarah. 'See that?' he said to Farmer out of the corner of his mouth like a convict in a 1930s film. 'I think HT's giving the Welsh Rarebit one.'

'Think so, guv?' Farmer felt a sharp pang of jealousy and a more physical pang in his groin at the instant vision of a naked Sarah being vigorously bonked by Harry Timberlake. Since Farmer arrived at Terrace Vale she had steadfastly but politely rebuffed his advances, an attitude which he found totally incomprehensible. Nevertheless, he still believed her resistance would eventually crumble before the combined assault of his senior position, charm and good looks. Farmer's problem was that he couldn't recognize a stone wall when he ran into it.

What was so ironic about the situation was the fact that Harry Timberlake and Sarah had achieved the considerable trick of carrying on a highly charged affair for a year which no one at the station suspected. Now that they had broken up and moved on to new partners, they had begun to look guilty.

'Harry!' Greening called out. Timberlake joined him. 'Professor Mortimer was on the phone about the Towers Hall body. I told him you were handling it and that you'd call him back.' This was basic buck-passing by Greening, who had developed dodging responsibility, decision-making and work to a fine art.

Professor Mortimer answered Harry Timberlake's call with his usual grace. 'Oh, inspector. You were out when I called,' he said accusingly. 'I don't have a great deal of time so I shall be brief.'

That'll be the day, Timberlake thought.

'I shall be required to be at the Central Criminal Court for the Wayne poisoning case for at least two days.' Everybody else called it The Bailey, occasionally the Old Bailey. 'I shall give evidence for the Crown, of course. However, the defence have engaged that simpleton Rossiter to give evidence on behalf of the murderer—'

There was no room in Mortimer's mind for niceties like assuming innocence until guilt was proved, or that 'that simpleton Rossiter' was another professor of forensic pathology whose ability was on a level with Mortimer's own. 'The man has come up with some theory which has the merit of fanciful ingenuity but no scientific value whatsoever. The prosecuting counsel wants me to stay on after I have given my evidence to tell him what questions to put to Rossiter when he's cross-examined.' Prima donnas are models of self-effacement compared with most forensic pathologists. Mortimer paused for breath.

'The Towers Hall body,' Timberlake daringly prodded him.

'Please do not interrupt me. As a result of this commitment, I've been unable to carry out the autopsy, which could prove quite interesting' – Mortimer-speak for 'stomach-churning and grisly' – 'and the body has not yet been X-rayed. It is a most unusual body.'

'In what way?' Harry Timberlake asked.

Professor Mortimer treated the question as if it were no more than static on the line, and pressed on. 'While I am away Dr Smith will carry out a purely preliminary examination at my hospital.' He pronounced the possessive pronoun as if he were the sole proprietor of St Lawrence's Hospital. 'However, I can tell you that at first sight the body is that of a female' . . . Big deal, Timberlake thought . . . 'and the indications are that she was less than twenty years of age at death. That is subject to a more detailed examination.'

'Can you tell me how long she had been dead?'

'Not yet.' And he hung up.

At the reception area of the mortuary at St Lawrence's Hospital Timberlake and Webb were greeted by a small, round woman of about thirty, dressed in a sari and a white coat that was made for someone a good nine inches taller. She had hair the colour and sheen of a wet seal and eyes like expensive dark chocolates. Her skin was unexpectedly light, and its paleness was emphasized by her hair and eyes. Her smile was dazzling.

Timberlake introduced himself and Darren Webb and said, 'We're here to see Dr Smith.'

'I am Dr Smith. Dr Chandra Smith.'

Timberlake blinked, and was silent for a moment. 'I'm sorry,' he said eventually. 'I wasn't expecting—'

'It is perfectly all right,' Dr Smith replied quickly in an accent that could have served as a model for students at the Royal Academy of Dramatic Art. 'I am accustomed to people suffering a certain disconcertment when they meet me for the first time.'

'Well, the name Dr *Smith*—' Timberlake began.

'Indeed. My father is English, my mother Indian, you see. Now, you have come to see the woman from Towers Hall, I believe.' She waved them into the autopsy room with the gesture of a maharanee ushering representatives of the Raj into a palace hall. As they went in Timberlake made a mental note to check that there was such a word as disconcertment. He found it later in his compact, microfilmed version of the twenty-volume Oxford Dictionary.

Over one of the stainless-steel dissection tables was a large studio camera, pointing down at the body of the young woman from Towers Hall. A man of an extravagantly cadaverous build, who looked a likely candidate for a place on one of the slabs at any moment, was operating the camera. He clicked the shutter, changed plates in the camera, fired off the flash, made minute adjustments to the camera focus then repeated the sequence, all with a dizzying speed and dexterity. He was as good as a circus act.

'Will you be much longer, Philip?' Dr Smith asked.

'Last one,' the photographer replied, firing off another flash before packing away all his equipment as quickly as a Formula One team changing tyres. He scurried out of the room in top gear.

The last time the two detectives had seen the body it was muddy and wrapped in some sort of tattered material. Now it was naked, and its appearance had changed so dramatically that it took them aback. The woman seemed smaller than they remembered, but that is not what was so extraordinary.

The corpse looked for all the world, Timberlake thought, as if it had been badly carved from a block of margarine. The face was unrecognizable.

18

'Er, doctor, why is she like—' Timberlake hesitated. He was not sure what he was going to say.

'Adipocere. It is one of the best examples I have seen,' Dr Smith said enthusiastically.

'Ah,' Webb said sagely.

'I'm sure it will get into all the textbooks. I understand that the body was discovered in wet ground.'

Timberlake nodded.

Dr Smith sighed with satisfaction. 'Of course, it was once thought that wet conditions were essential for the formation of adipocere, but now it is realized that is not the case.'

'What else can you tell us about the body, doctor?' Timberlake took good care not to sound sarcastic.

Dr Smith smiled again. 'Professor Mortimer has made it explicitly unambiguous that *he* will perform the full autopsy. I have done only the post mortem examination. However, from the X-ray plates I could ascertain it is, of course, a young woman, most probably Caucasian, and almost certainly of less than twenty years of age.' Which matched up with what Mortimer had said. 'And some seven months pregnant,' the doctor added.

The two detectives regarded each other. Webb spoke first. 'Any idea of the cause of death?'

Dr Smith smiled like switching on a light. 'Goodness me, sergeant, you cannot expect me to venture an opinion on such an important matter before Professor Mortimer has declared his findings and conclusions.' Before Timberlake could speak she added, with another toothpaste-ad smile, 'If I may be permitted a personal observation, I shall be consternated if he decides that death by strangulation is not a possibility.'

'Thank you, doctor. And what do you think the professor's opinion will be as to how long she has been dead?'

'I am sure you know Professor Mortimer does not proffer opinions, but presents facts,' she said, quoting one of his favourite sayings. Dr Smith had a straight face but her eyes were twinkling. Timberlake nodded an acknowledgement. 'To be unreservedly frank with you, inspector, I shall be most interested to listen to his observations on this matter. Dating the age of a body that has undergone the formation of adipocere is an extremely difficult matter. However—'

'The clothes?'

'Indeed. Such as they are. That is very percipient of you. They

19

have been sent to the Metropolitan Police Laboratory for examination. I think they will give us the more accurate assessment. However, there may be another method of determining how long the body has been buried. The nitrogen content of the bones. The longer they have been buried, the less nitrogen.'

'Fancy,' Darren Webb commented sagely.

'Thank you, doctor,' Timberlake said. 'Time we were off.'

As the two men turned to leave, Dr Smith asked, 'Tell me, inspector, do you have any idea of the young woman's identity?'

'Possibly.'

At the door Webb said 'Guv, what's the difference between a post mortem and an autopsy?'

'To be precise, the post mortem is only the external examination of a body, not a full clinical autopsy where they cut open the body and take out the working parts.'

'Yes. Well, I suppose it's all right if you like that sort of thing.' He reflected for a long moment. 'It's going to be a bit rough on the father to ask him to try to identify her looking like that, guv.'

'We'll worry about that when we have to. If. We may be able to get round it. There are other ways.'

'Dental records?'

'And genetic fingerprinting, although that costs' – he was about to say 'an arm and a leg' but stopped in time – 'and there's the possibility of the photographic technique they used in the Ruxton case.'

'What's that, guv?'

'Another time. But you're right. We'll have to avoid getting the father to see her. He was in the army, but he won't have seen any bodies like that. Especially someone close to him. Two to one he'd keel over inside thirty seconds.'

Timberlake wasn't really that unfeeling. He was just hiding his own sensibilities.

Chapter 4

PC Nigel Larkin, a bright-eyed young constable who hummed with energy and could have served for a police recruiting poster, was manning the counter when two women walked in, obviously mother and daughter. The mother was sharp-featured, with greying hair cut fashionably short. Her clothing was neutral: grey suit, pastel-coloured blouse, dark shoes. She wore no make-up. There were two parallel vertical lines on her forehead immediately above her nose, which set her face in a permanent worried frown. The effect was emphasized by lines on either side of her mouth.

The daughter was about the same height as her mother, but fuller-figured. Where the older woman had a general air of apprehensive concern, the daughter looked determined, almost belligerent. Her dark, thick eyebrows and firmly set mouth made the keynote of her appearance one of determination. She wore a jumper and expensive jeans, and was in her mid-twenties.

There was nothing particularly out of the ordinary about them – for visitors to a police station, that is. The mother looked apprehensive, the daughter angry, but many callers have reason to be concerned or angry, or both.

Despite Larkin's youth, from the couple's manner and the way the mother hung back a pace behind her daughter, he immediately could make a fair guess what it was all about. Being a policeman gives you a crash course in the downside of civilized life.

'Sergeant,' he said quietly to Sergeant Rumsden. The sergeant looked up from the sheaves of paperwork he was trying to cope with. He, too, took in the situation at a glance, and advanced to the counter.

'Can I help you, madam?' he asked the older woman.

'I want to see whoever's in charge,' the daughter said firmly before her mother could speak.

This is a request more frequently heard at the counter of a police station than most people would believe. It is the prelude to a complaint that the next door neighbour was trying to poison Pussy or Fido, or that the BBC, CIA, KGB or Martians were beaming radio waves directly into the complainant's head, or a flying saucer or German SS parachutists had been spotted in the churchyard.

This was clearly not such a case. Rumsden didn't press for any details at this point; he merely asked the young woman her name. She replied without hesitation that it was Emma Leyland, and this was her mother, Mrs Rachel Puddefoot.

'That'll be Mrs Leyland, then?' Rumsden said to the daughter.

'No. *Miss* Leyland.' Not even Ms. She didn't elaborate, and gave an address in Railway Cuttings. Rumsden knew it: it was a street of terraced cottages which were occupied by railway workers in the last century but was now full of junior executives, media workers and members of the professions.

Rumsden gave a polite cough and said, 'In view of your request for a senior officer I take it you wish to report a serious matter.' He paused.

'Yes.'

Mrs Puddefoot plucked timidly at her daughter's sleeve. Emma Leyland ignored her and said harshly before her mother could reply. 'I've been—'

'*Attacked*,' Mrs Puddefoot interrupted quickly to prevent her daughter saying the precise word out loud. She pronounced 'attacked' almost like a brief wail, and with an intake of breath. 'You know,' she added.

'I see,' Rumsden said nodded. 'Larkin, nip upstairs and see who's the senior officer in CID, and ask him to come down. And oh, yes; DC Lewis has come in. Tell her I think it'd be a help if she could come down as well.'

Larkin set off as if he were carrying the Olympic torch.

'If you'll be good enough to come with me, ladies,' Rumsden said. He took a key from a rack inside the front office, lifted the flap of the counter and led them to a special room that was totally unlike any other in Terrace Vale nick. It could have been a comfortable sitting-room in a middle-class home, with a table, easy chairs, a settee, carpets, curtains and standard lamps. A second door gave on to the medical examination room.

This small suite was uniquely for interviewing rape victims. The days were long gone of a woman victim being questioned in a stark interview room by male detectives with a barely concealed scepticism, which could seem almost more distressing than the actual rape.

Normally Inspector Bob Farmer was an acquired taste, but Emma Leyland and her mother seemed to be impressed by him. Perhaps it was his immaculate clothing, when they probably expected to see someone like Starsky or Hutch on a bad day, or his sparse hair, which gave him a certain gravitas. With him was Sarah Lewis, who was cursing her luck at being paired with Farmer. WPC Rosie Hall brought in cups of tea for everyone, including herself, in the special interview suite. Despite her air of having come up from the farm yesterday, Rosie was streetwise and could be as fearsome as Attila the Hun's mother-in-law; but now she was in her very comforting Agony Aunt mode. After she had handed round the tea she sat quietly in a corner with her notebook on her knee.

'A few details first,' Farmer said with one of his best encouraging smiles.

Mrs Puddefoot explained she was a widow, formerly married to Gerald Leyland, a tube-train driver, who was the father of their daughter Emma. Three years ago Mrs Leyland moved up socially to become Mrs Puddefoot, wife of a surveyor. It was his first marriage. Mrs Puddefoot, Emma and her stepfather all lived together in an end-of-terrace house. The word 'stepfather' rang silent alarm bells in the minds of the police officers.

Emma began wriggling impatiently in her chair, and Sarah Lewis turned towards her. When it came to questioning Emma about the actual rape Farmer wisely left it to Sarah and joined Rosie, out of Emma's eyeline.

Sarah opened the interview with careful sympathy. She avoided provoking a tart reply from Emma: she didn't say 'I know how you feel,' which would have brought the resentful 'Do you? Have *you* been raped?' Instead she opened with a gentle 'I can only try to imagine how difficult and unpleasant this must be for you. Take your time, as long as you want. Now, where and when did this happen?'

'It was by the tunnel between Churchyard Walk and White Hart Lane.'

'I told you never to go that way at night,' her mother said with crashing insensitivity. Emma Leyland jutted her jaw and ignored her.

Mrs Puddefoot's rebuke was well deserved, even if the timing was wrong. The short cut between the local-line British Rail station and the Railway Cuttings area led down the side of a small common, across the courtyard of a block of flats, along Churchyard Walk, through the narrow tunnel under the railway line and past another patch of waste ground before arriving at White Hart Lane. By taking this route instead of going by residential roads Emma had saved a walk of some six hundred yards. At a very considerable cost. Nobody mentioned this.

Quite calm and self-controlled, Emma Leyland continued her story. Her mother sat hunched up, her hands tightly clasped. Sarah wondered why.

'I'd just come out of the tunnel when this man jumped out from the waste ground and grabbed me from behind with his forearm across my neck. I couldn't shout; I could hardly breathe. He held a big knife up in front of my face and said something like, "Make a noise and I'll cut your fucking throat." ' The bald use of the word seemed to worry Mrs Puddefoot more than the story. 'I was frightened because I could feel him trembling and shaking as he held me. I thought, well, if he's that wound up he could easily kill me, so I didn't resist. He dragged me behind the bushes and raped me.'

'Can you describe him?' Farmer asked.

She shook her head. 'It was dark, and when he wasn't behind me he was too close for me to get a good look at him. Anyway, he had a scarf over the bottom half of his face. It was wool. I felt it against my face.' She shivered slightly.

'What colour?' She shook her head helplessly.

'The man – was he white or black?'

'White, I think.'

'How old, would you say?'

Emma Leyland shrugged. 'Twenty-five to forty.' She paused. 'When it came to it, you know, I kept my eyes closed. I wanted to dissociate myself from everything, as much as possible.'

'Educated voice, or rough?'

She smiled wryly. 'Fairly respectable. London accent.'

'What time was this?' Sarah asked.

24

'About half past eight.'

'This morning, or last night?'

'No; Monday night.'

There was a heavy silence for a moment. 'Three days ago?' Farmer said, unable to keep the surprise from his voice.

Mrs Puddefoot spoke up with a tremulous voice, too loud at first until she managed to get it under control. 'I didn't want her to come. People talk . . . they say things . . . Best to forget it—'

You're not the one who has to forget it, Sarah thought furiously. Farmer, as smooth as a salesman of second-hand Bentleys, explained about confidentiality, and names not being made public. Mrs Puddefoot wasn't convinced. 'Best to keep it quiet,' she mumbled. Emma stared at the wall.

Sarah spoke again. 'How did you manage to be there at that time? Had you come off a train?'

'No. I'm an assistant manageress at the Station Road supermarket, and I'd been on late turn.' This, the detectives realized, widened the spectrum of possible aggressors. The rapist could be someone who knew Emma Leyland personally, someone who had seen her at the supermarket and ambushed her on her way home, or someone lying in wait for any likely victim.

'Did you speak to anyone, or see anyone after the incident on your way home?' Sarah asked Emma. There was a point to this question. Normally only conversations which take place in the presence of the accused can be admitted in evidence. Rape cases are an exception. An alleged victim's demeanour and what she said immediately after the incident are admissible.

Emma Leyland shook her head.

'Do you have a boyfriend?'

'Yes. That is, I did have. It wasn't him. Couldn't be. He wouldn't do anything like that.'

'I'm sure you're right. But you understand we have to check.'

'His name's Trevor Sedgley,' and she added an address. 'But it wasn't him.'

'The clothes you were wearing . . . your underclothes?' Sarah asked.

Mrs Puddefoot answered defiantly, 'I burned them. And the skirt, and tights . . . while Emma was having a bath. I sent her other things to the cleaners.' Sarah suppressed a groan, and then bit her lip to stop herself calling the mother a stupid bitch.

25

'I've still got my knickers. They have his . . . stains on them.'

Mrs Puddefoot looked at her daughter in horror. 'You told me . . . You said—'

Emma Leyland looked away from her. 'I guessed what you'd do. You still want to keep everything quiet, don't you? What the neighbours'll say is more important than catching the bastard who fucking *raped* me!' She turned her head to spit out the word at her mother. 'Why the bloody hell have you come here with me anyway? Stop me saying too much?'

Rachel Puddefoot's lips were compressed into a thin line, but it wasn't to stop her crying. 'I'm your mother. It's my duty to support you.'

Sarah allowed the tension to ease a little before she spoke again. 'Where are they?'

Emma Leyland opened her handbag and took out a pair of knickers in a sealed plastic freezer bag. Her mother couldn't bring herself to look at them. 'You told me—' she muttered again. Inwardly Sarah gave a great shout of joy. If – *when* they caught the rapist, Emma would be a first-class witness.

'This is just a preliminary interview,' Sarah said. 'I'll get a much fuller statement from you later. It may take two or three sessions. With you on your own,' she added quickly. Mrs Puddefoot looked aggrieved.

There was a discreet knock at the door. Farmer opened it a little, blocking the view of the room with his body. 'Doctor's here,' Sergeant Rumsden said quietly.

26

Chapter 5

Martin Stubbs, the bowler-hatted clerk of works at Towers Hall, had given Timberlake the name of the solicitor who was representing the owner of the house. He was Jonathan Mellick, a man who made Fred Astaire seem chubby and looked as if he was dressed by the tailors of undertakers to Transylvanian royal families. He began by being as tight with information as Directory Enquiries.

Eventually Mellick grudgingly admitted that Gerard Lester, an architect, had been responsible for the upkeep of Towers Hall during its fifteen unoccupied years and was now supervising the refurbishment and redecorations. Mellick wrote down Lester's telephone number with a steel-nibbed pen which he dipped into an ornate inkpot.

'And who is the actual owner? Mrs Pusey?' Timberlake asked.

'Yes and no,' Mellick replied after some reflection. Timberlake gave him The Look. It jolted him into explaining.

'Mrs Pusey and her son Charles left England to live in France some fifteen years ago,' Mellick began. 'Five years later she remarried, a Comte Pascal de Gaillmont, a widower with a son by his first marriage – Jean-Louis de Gaillmont. She and Charles Pusey Junior moved into his château near Saint-Rémy-de-Provence.' Now the cork was out of Mellick's bottle, he gushed forth with information. 'Comte Pascal de Gaillmont' – Mellick seemed to relish pronouncing the name, which he did badly – 'died some two or three years ago, which means that Jean-Louis is now the Comte de Gaillmont. I might add that the title is a genuine one, which dates back to Louis XIV.' It was clear that Mellick was tickled several shades of pink to represent an authentic French aristocratic family.

'Who made the arrangements for paying off the servants when the Puseys left Towers Hall?' Timberlake asked unexpectedly.

27

'That, ah, was arranged from this office.'

'Then you will have their names and addresses.'

Mellick was clearly put out. 'I'm not sure that it would be proper for me to . . . ah—' His voice died away like someone walking away into the distance.

'It will save us asking the Press and television to publish a request for former members of the staff to contact us. And I hardly think the present owner would care for the extra publicity.' Timberlake didn't like most solicitors, and it was reflected in his tone.

'I'll see that you get a list,' Mellick said, unhappily.

'By tomorrow.' It was not a question. 'I understand that the family are returning to Towers Hall in the near future.'

'Indeed. Any day now. The countess has decided to re-establish residence in her estate here,' Mellick said, his confidence returning.

'Estate' was a bit strong, Timberlake thought, but said only, 'So she *is* the owner.' Mellick nodded. 'Is Madame de Gaillmont aware that a body has been found in the grounds?'

'I wrote to her, but I have received no acknowledgement as yet,' Mellick replied, slightly ill at ease.

'Has Charles Pusey, or any of the family, been back in the past fifteen years?' Timberlake asked.

'Ah, no,' Mellick said regretting the earlier looseness of his tongue. 'No, certainly not – not to my knowledge. This is all in confidence, of course, to, ah, help you with your enquiries. I shouldn't like the countess to be unnecessarily upset.'

Timberlake rather guessed he wouldn't.

Such of the former servants at Towers Hall who could be traced could give no direct help with the murder enquiries, although they provided some interesting descriptions of the family. Charles Pusey Senior was reckoned to be 'not too bad', 'all right', and 'easy-going'. Apparently he joined the heart attack club early: he smoked several cigars a day, drank port like an eighteenth-century judge, entertained lavishly and dined with the same intensity that he ground down his business rivals and competitors. He wasn't home all that much, and it was generally agreed that this was so he could avoid being with Mrs Pusey.

The son wasn't at all like his father. He kept reasonably fit, liked jazz, the theatre and young women – in particular Betty Lock.

It was when the ex-domestics were asked about the then Mrs Sophie Pusey that the phrases came rolling out: 'icy', 'stuck-up', 'sour', 'very bossy', 'more royal than the Queen', 'she could nag her husband just by looking at him', and, from the ex-gardener, 'she walked around the place as if she'd got an acid-drop in her mouth and a carrot up her bum'.

All very entertaining, but it didn't advance the enquiry one inch.

Detective Inspector Ted Greening was not happy. He was feeling his normal jagged morning self, but now, if he wasn't careful, he would have to be decisive. The prospect was making him particularly peevish. There were two major cases to discuss: the dead body at Towers Hall and the alleged rape. Chief Superintendent Marlow was visiting someone at New Scotland Yard that morning, which meant that Greening was lumbered with taking charge of enquiries. In his office, which smelt of stale tobacco, booze and sweat, Greening was with Inspectors Bob Farmer and Harry Timberlake, Sergeant Darren Webb and WDC Sarah Lewis. All these detectives were clean and neatly dressed – especially Farmer, who, sitting closest to Greening, made a sort of Before and After tableau.

Timberlake spoke first. After he outlined what the clerk of works at Towers Hall and Dr Chandra Smith had told him, he gave a rundown on the former servants' views of the family.

Greening's telephone rang. He picked it up. 'Chief Inspector Greening?' the operator said cheerfully. 'It's Detective Superintendent Harkness at AMIP. He'd like to speak to you about the Towers Hall body.'

Ted Greening's face paled under its alcoholic bloom, and he licked his lips.

These days it's no longer a case of 'calling in the Yard' to help with the investigation of a serious crime like murder. London is divided into eight areas and each has an Area Major Investigation Pool or AMIP commanded by a detective superintendent. He and his team move in to take charge of the investigation of major crimes. The officer in charge of the AMIP group for the Terrace Vale area was Superintendent Charles Harkness. He had met Greening twice, and Greening still had deep psychological scars from the encounters.

'Hang on a sec,' he said to the operator, to give himself time to

29

dodge the call. He had an idea – not a brilliant one, but just about adequate. He held out the phone to Harry Timberlake. 'It's Superintendent Harkness on about the Towers Hall business. You're dealing with it. You can speak to him.'

Everyone in the room realized what Greening was doing – and probably Harkness on the other end of the phone as well. They listened keenly to Timberlake's end of the conversation.

'Good morning, sir. DI Timberlake here. I'm dealing with the case at the moment . . . It's fairly certain that the body's been there for some time, so there's no immediate urgency . . . Of course we'll let you know as soon as we have any information . . . Sergeant Webb and I are going to see the architect at Towers Hall this morning. He's been in charge of the house while it's been empty, and I want to find out who could have had access to go and plant a body . . . Yes . . . Oh, thank you, sir.'

'Right, you two'd better get off, then,' Greening said, cheered that he didn't have to make any decisions about that case. They needed no second invitation.

'Smelt like a five-ale bar in there, guv,' Webb said, wrinkling his nose, as they left Greening's office. Timberlake gave him an icy look. There were times when Timberlake had a positively military attitude towards discipline and respect for senior officers – mostly respect by people other than Timberlake himself.

Greening turned to Bob Farmer and Sarah Lewis. She looked as spry as a model in a mail-order catalogue, and had an air of having passed a very fulfilling night, which she had. It gave Greening the hump again, and he concentrated on Farmer.

Farmer's face was as closely shaved as a marble bust, while Greening's, with the light behind him, looked like a giant bloodshot gooseberry. Farmer had a waistcoat, and a tie that sat with geometric precision in the dead centre of his shirt. Greening's tie – it had to be a tie, it was round his neck – resembled a snake dying of some unpleasant disease. All in all, Farmer's bandbox appearance made Greening feel shabby and sloppy, although in fact he was even shabbier and sloppier than he believed.

'Right,' said Greening. 'Bob?'

Farmer was good at reports, especially ones that put him in a good light, but the best he could do in this case was to make sure he wasn't in a bad light.

Greening thought for a moment. 'Any suspects?'

'There's a boyfriend she dumped, and a stepfather. That's all so far. The only possible lead to an identification is the knife she said the man was carrying. Long curved blade with a sort of wavy engraving, tip broken, bone handle. I'm getting a team to visit the scene to see if they can find anything. But it was four days ago.'

'We'll get the genetic fingerprinting from her knickers,' Sarah said.

'We've got to find him first,' Greening said sourly, 'and there's bugger-all description and no possibility of a photofit picture, from what she says. Well, get the Press and TV on it, just in case someone saw a man wearing a balaclava and waving a bone-handled knife running away from the scene with his dick hanging out.' He lit another cigarette.

'I've already started the ball rolling with the media,' Farmer lied smoothly. Sarah said nothing.

'I suppose she *was* raped,' Greening mused. 'What's the doctor's report say?'

'Haven't got it yet, guv.'

'Sarah? Were you there when she did the examination?' Greening was hoping for a little entertainment in embarrassing her. Like Farmer, he really didn't understand her, despite the time she had been at Terrace Vale.

Sarah looked him straight in the eye. In a firm, level voice she said, 'The doctor said she had a bruised back, consistent with having been forced on the ground. There were further bruises on her left arm and on the side of her neck and the inner surfaces of her thighs. The outer labia of her vagina were contused and had abrasions; there were further abrasions on the inner labia. All of these injuries appeared to be approximately three days old. In the opinion of the doctor Emma Leyland had been subjected to brutal and forced intercourse.'

The silence was long and heavy. Greening was unsure what to say next. When he did speak he exacerbated the situation. 'Stupid bloody cow,' he said. 'She was asking for it, going down the tunnel by Churchyard Walk.'

Sarah took a deep breath before answering. In a controlled, level tone that was worth an Oscar she said, 'No one *asks* to be raped, guv. Is that all?'

He stared out of the window at a blank sky. 'Yeh. You hang on for a minute, Bob.'

Sarah went out, closing the door behind her with an exaggerated care that was far more expressive than banging it shut.

'Cheeky fucking tart!' Greening said furiously. He coughed with a noise like bubbling tar. 'Saying all that in front of us without batting a fucking eyelid!'

'Was a bit much,' Farmer conceded. 'She thinks a lot of herself.'

'Slag,' Greening muttered.

'I'd better get down to the scene, find out if the team's got anything, if that's all right with you, guv,' Farmer said. Greening nodded.

When he left the office Farmer went straight over to Sarah's desk. 'Well done, Sarah,' he said confidentially. 'That had to be said.' He squeezed her shoulder. Sarah managed to stop a flinch before it started.

When Timberlake and Webb turned up at Towers Hall for the meeting with the architect, Gerard Lester, the last workmen at the site were clearing up, preparing to leave. 'The family are coming back tomorrow,' he explained. 'We've got to be finished and out of here before then.'

Lester was a small, wizened man with a head as smooth as a pearl-finish electric light bulb. He looked like a nineteenth-century professional poisoner. Timberlake guessed him to be in his early seventies.

Lester told the detectives his connection with Towers Hall went back to the days of Charles Pusey Sr. When Mrs Pusey, as she then was, left for France with her son he was given the job of ensuring that the property was kept in good repair. His responsibilities included the grounds, the fabric of the house, and cleaning the interior and its furniture from time to time. The house was supposed to be ready for re-occupation at forty-eight hours' notice, 'But no one has been back, not even for a day. I don't know why they didn't sell it.'

'You had the keys to the place, then?'

'No. Mr Mellick, Mrs Pusey's solicitor, kept them. I had to go and get them – and sign for them – each time.'

'What about the times when work had to be done on the house or the estate?'

'I remained here, on site, until the work was finished. I locked up every night, took the keys back to Mellick's office and collected them again next morning.'

32

'Were you always here, every day, all the time?'

'Yes. It was in my contract.' The reply was set in stone.

'So there was no opportunity for anyone to get into the grounds without being seen by you or your workmen?' Webb pressed him.

Lester looked at him coldly. 'None. I want to make this quite clear: it is not possible that anyone got into Towers Hall and buried a body there while work was being done. It's totally out of the question.'

Timberlake and Webb looked at the high walls and gate. Lester knew what they were thinking. 'And they didn't do it when there was no one here. You'd need a hoist to get a body over those walls. What with the walls and the gate and burglar alarms on the house, we haven't even had squatters, not for a single day. You can take it from me that no one unauthorized has been messing around in here.'

They thanked him for his help and turned to leave. As they walked away Timberlake said, 'But that's not really the point.'

'No, guv,' said Darren Webb, who was keen to show that he could think, too. 'Why would anyone bother? There must be easier ways to dispose of a body than breaking into the local Colditz Castle to bury it.'

'Which means—' Timberlake began.

'That it was done by someone while the Pusey family were living here.'

'Yes. I'm rather looking forward to meeting the de Gaillmonts,' Timberlake added sternly.

He would wish he'd never said that.

Chapter 6

Bob Farmer and Sarah Lewis accompanied the squad of uniformed PCs detailed to search the site of Emma Leyland's rape for anything that might be a clue. There was surprisingly little of an advanced civilization's rubbish or anything else to be found: old crisp packets, a stained mattress with a serious case of multiple hernia, plastic packaging and empty cola and beer cans, and an old shoe which had clearly been there for some time as a weed was growing through it. All of the debris was dusty and dull, with one exception. The perky PC Larkin found it.

'It would bleeding well be him,' grumbled one of the squad.

Larkin's find was a two-inch double strand of red wool with a knot at one end. He handed it to Farmer, who took it with little enthusiasm and put it into a small plastic envelope.

'She said he was wearing a scarf, guv,' Sarah said. 'Might be off that. At least it's fresh, compared with the rest of the junk.' Larkin glanced at her gratefully.

'Hmmm,' Farmer replied doubtfully. 'Still, better safe, and all that. Well, I think we've about finished now. I'll tell the squad to go back to the nick while we go and interview the boyfriend who got the elbow.'

The rejected boyfriend was Trevor Sedgley, who lived about ten minutes' walk from Emma Leyland's address. Farmer and Sarah Lewis called on him at his place of work, a garden centre in one of Terrace Vale's more pleasant areas, of which he was the manager. He was about thirty, fresh-faced, blond and cheerful, and was wearing blue denim overalls over a tee-shirt. He appeared quite capable of uprooting a small tree without using a spade, but as dangerous as a pint of pasteurized milk.

When Farmer introduced himself and Sarah, Sedgley was quite untroubled. 'How can I help you?' he said, as if they were going to ask his advice on how to get rid of greenfly.

Farmer smiled comfortingly. 'If you wouldn't mind answering a couple of questions.'

'What's it all about?'

'Just a routine enquiry,' Sarah said. Sedgley studied her and seemed reassured.

'Would you mind telling us where you were on Monday night, say between seven and nine o'clock?' Farmer continued.

The young man paused for a moment. 'Why?'

'If you'll just answer the question, sir,' Farmer said, as pleasantly as he could manage.

Sedgley hesitated. Sarah guessed he was wondering whether or not to make an issue of being told what they were after. He decided it wasn't worth the bother. 'Monday? I was at night school, at the Technical College. I'm taking an art course.' It seemed as incongruous as Toulouse-Lautrec practising the high jump.

His alibi was textbook solid. Sarah was sure it would be confirmed by the art master and several of Sedgley's fellow students.

'While I'm here, would you mind showing me some yucca plants?' she asked innocently. 'You don't mind, guv?'

Farmer nodded.

As they walked away out of Farmer's earshot Sarah said, 'You were friendly with Emma Leyland, weren't you?'

Sedgley stopped abruptly. 'Is this what it's all about? What's happened to her? Is she all right?'

'Oh, yes. It's nothing to worry about, really. It's just that . . . she might be a witness in a case for us, and I'd like to know something about her.'

'She's straight as a die. Dead honest.'

Sarah nodded. 'That was my impression.' She walked on a few yards, and studied a large plant. 'Why did you break up with her?'

'That's a cheese plant. The yuccas are over here. How did you know about us?'

'Her mother mentioned it. Talkative woman.'

'Her *mother*? She's about as talkative as Harpo Marx.'

'Not with another woman. Why did you?'

Sedgley was uncomfortable. 'Emma's bossy.' He paused again. 'And *demanding*. It was getting me down.'

Sarah looked at him with surprise. To her astonishment, Sedgley actually blushed. 'Ah,' she said, guessing the situation. It was more likely that Trevor Sedgley broke off the relationship to keep his strength for lifting yucca plants and sacks of peat. If Emma Leyland was something of a sexual man-eater it could put a very different slant on things.

Madame la Comtesse Douairière Sophie de Gaillmont – a.k.a., in England, the Dowager Countess de Gaillmont – and her stepson Monsieur le Comte Jean-Louis de Gaillmont, accompanied by the comtesse's social secretary Thérèse Chardet, arrived at Towers Hall the next day in a convoy of cars that was less splendid but no less intrinsically regal than Kubla Khan's caravan paying a state visit.

The de Gaillmonts and Thérèse Chardet were in a massive hired Daimler saloon that was a direct descendant of the ancient upright model favoured by the late Queen Mary. Following this at a respectful distance were a couple of Volvo estate cars full of luggage and personal effects. A Harrods van carrying food and drink followed furtively like a stray dog trying to ingratiate itself with passers-by.

They were greeted by the solicitor Jonathan Mellick and architect Gerard Lester. Both were suitably awed: the diminutive Lester gave the impression that if he had a forelock he would pull it, or perhaps twist his cap in his hands.

Mellick had prepared for the arrival of the de Gaillmont family by arranging a series of interviews of applicants, proposed by two of Mayfair's leading agencies, for domestic jobs ranging from butler, chef and housekeeper to undermaids. These interviews would last a minimum of two days, and until the staff were fully operational, the family would stay overnight at Claridges.

Mellick had also warned Sophie de Gaillmont, 'The police wanted to interview you about—' He hurriedly amended this to 'The police would be grateful if Madame la Comtesse would see them at her earliest convenience.'

When Timberlake and Webb arrived for their inter iew the first thing that struck them, apart from the richness of the interior, was that a two-person lift had been installed – discreetly – in the hall. It looked as if it had come from the Hôtel de Paris in Monte

36

Carlo. Thérèse Chardet showed them into a reception room which smelled faintly of paint and furniture polish. Timberlake studied Chardet covertly but carefully.

She was about thirty years old and as neat as a *Vogue* advertisement. Her unfussy chestnut hair framed a pale face which had a minimum of make-up. She wore a severely but stylishly cut dark suit, the sort of outfit a crafty woman barrister would wear when appearing before a stuffy judge. It was an ensemble that should have minimized any natural femininity; in Thérèse Chardet's case it failed totally to hide her sensual figure and inherent sexuality, and paradoxically even emphasized them. She could not breathe without being provocative.

'Madame la Comtesse will be with you in a little minute,' she said with a French accent, translating literally the colloquial French phrase *une petite minute*. The French have a whole spectrum of time definitions, from *un tout petit moment*, through *un petit moment, une toute petite minute* and so on to *un petit quart d'heure*. Timberlake calculated that *une petite minute* would be about three to five minutes GMT.

Webb was slightly intimidated by the atmosphere of Towers Hall and the general formality. He was about to sit down when he caught Timberlake's eye, and remained standing.

After something between *une petite minute* and *une minute* the door opened and Sophie de Gaillmont entered. She was followed by Jonathan Mellick as if he was on wheels being pulled by a string, 'Inspector Timberlake and Sergeant Webb.' Thérèse Chardet introduced them. Timberlake gave a polite nod that was short of a bow. Webb hurriedly followed his example. Sophie de Gaillmont gave a barely perceptible inclination of her head.

'Madame la Comtesse de Gaillmont,' Thérèse Chardet continued.

'Countess,' Timberlake said politely. He was on the point of showing off by speaking to her in French, but resisted the temptation in time. It might be useful if the de Gaillmonts and Thérèse Chardet didn't know he spoke it.

Sophie de Gaillmont was tall and ramrod-backed. With her imperious, strong-nosed face, manner and bearing she could have been the Duke of Wellington's sister. She was not beautiful but she was most certainly handsome, more so than what the French would call *une jolie laide*. Her gown – it deserved better than to be thought of as a dress – was expensively understated, although

Ivana Trump would not have sneezed at her engagement and wedding rings, or her pearls.

She sat upright on a straight-backed chair and studied the two detectives as if she was using a lorgnette. After a long pause, she gave them permission to sit down.

'Yes?' she said.

'We are here about the body that was found in the grounds,' Timberlake said.

Before he could say anything more she interrupted, 'I know nothing of the circumstances which caused it to be there,' she said. 'As you may know, I have not been here for some fifteen years.' She had a French accent like Thérèse Chardet's.

'The body may well have been there longer than that,' Webb said unexpectedly, to make the point that he wasn't a stooge, 'dating from when you were here.'

The door opened and a man of about thirty-five years old entered. He would have been perfect casting for a character in a 1930s play who enters through french windows saying, 'Anyone for tennis?' He had the expensive clothes of a man who can sign the bill without bothering to look at it.

'*Ces individus sont des policiers,*' Sophie de Gaillmont told him quietly. Timberlake was mildly surprised by the use of the word *individus*, which borders on the insulting. 'These gentlemen are two detectives,' she said in English, making 'gentlemen' sound as pejorative in English as *individus* in French. 'Monsieur le Comte de Gaillmont,' she said tersely.

'I know why you're here,' the count said in unaccented English. 'I am afraid I am unable to help you. This is the first time I have been to Towers Hall.'

'You speak excellent English,' Timberlake said.

'An English nanny and then governess,' he replied, with a charming, self-deprecating smile.

Bloody hell he's smooth, Webb thought. Heartened by his own earlier boldness, he addressed a question at the countess. 'Madame, will Mr Pusey, your son, be coming to Towers Hall?'

'He will not be able to help you either,' Sophie de Gaillmont said frostily. 'However, he will arrive in two days.'

'He's bringing my car over,' de Gaillmont said.

'I shall see that he speaks to you then, if you insist,' the countess said. She rose. 'Good day.' It was the aristocratic version of 'Now bugger off.'

'Thank you, countess,' Timberlake said. He nodded to the others. Jonathan Mellick remained mute, probably waiting for someone to switch him on.

Timberlake was thoughtful as he drove himself and Webb back to Terrace Vale nick.

'Anything up, guv?' Webb asked eventually.

'Something doesn't fit,' Timberlake replied slowly. 'Why have they decided to come and establish residence here?'

Webb shrugged. 'Maybe it's a tax dodge.' Timberlake looked dubious. 'Or something to do with inheritance tax. I mean, when people have got that much money, they're up to all the dodges. Or—'

'Yes?'

'Perhaps Charlie-boy Pusey has made a French bird a member of the pudden club and they've all decided to do a runner.'

'Inelegantly, but succinctly put,' Timberlake replied. He shook his head. 'But somehow I don't think so. I expect we'll find out, sooner or later.'

Next on Bob Farmer's and Sarah Lewis's list of people to be interviewed was Lionel Puddefoot, Emma Leyland's stepfather. He had an office in the same block as Gerard Lester's firm of architects, although the two detectives were unaware of the connection.

As soon as they saw Puddefoot they virtually wrote him off as a suspect. He had the physical appearance of a man who could not have raped his stepdaughter if she had been bound, gagged and drugged. At the same time, they both knew how deceptive appearances could be.

'We're making routine enquiries about an incident last Monday, the eleventh,' Farmer began, as smoothly as he could. 'I wonder if you would be good enough to tell us where you were between seven and nine in the evening of that day?'

Puddefoot's manner fitted his physical appearance. He was not the sort of man to be bold enough to ask what incident it was they were enquiring about.

Some of the colour drained from his face. He took a watch from a waistcoat pocket, looked at it intently and tapped the dial as if he expected the watch to answer. His expression lightened. He put the watch back almost with a flourish.

'I was at the cinema. Screen Two in the High Street,' he said.

'Was anyone with you?' Farmer asked.

'No, I went alone,' Puddefoot said.

When interviewees say they were alone at the cinema, detectives' minds suddenly whirr with suspicion. Only one statement is greeted with more incredulity, and that's, 'I bought it from a man in a pub I'd never seen before.'

'What was the film you saw?' Sarah asked politely.

'*The Player*. It was a re-run.'

'That was last week,' Sarah said in a voice of doom. Puddefoot turned the colour of old, uncooked dough. He took out his watch again, tapped it more vigorously and wound it up as if to squeeze the truth out of it. Then, triumphantly, he returned the watch to its pocket again.

'Last Monday, the eleventh,' he said. 'I remember now. I was at a Rotarians meeting at the Embassy Rooms. It was from seven till nine, and then we had dinner. There were about twenty of us there. I'm sure somebody must have seen me.' He was the sort of man very few people would notice in a group of twenty. Or six.

As Farmer and Sarah left, Puddefoot was still plucking up courage to ask what they were enquiring into. He never quite made it.

'We'll check,' Farmer said resignedly, 'but it's a pound to a pinch of snuff he was telling the truth.' He brightened. 'I think we can knock off a bit early and call it a day. We can start on the rest of our list tomorrow. Er . . . fancy some dinner, Sarah?'

Bloody hell, she thought. He *still* doesn't realize he's as transparent as a tart's négligée. 'Thanks very much, guv.' His pulse quickened. 'But I've got a date I simply can't get out of,' she added wickedly with a sigh she managed to make sound almost disappointed. *As if I'd bloody try anyway*, she said to herself. 'See you tomorrow at the nick?'

Farmer made an unintelligible noise.

Chapter 7

It was the first time Harry Timberlake had agreed to stay overnight in Jenny Long's house, despite the fact they had been friends and lovers for more than two years before they parted for a year and took new partners. When they came back together again, he worried at first that the year he had spent with Sarah Lewis might mean starting the relationship with Jenny again from scratch; that he would have to put the little private things between Sarah and himself out of his mind and try to remember how it used to be with Jenny. In fact they took up where they left off as if they had never been apart – almost. To his own surprise he didn't feel the least jealous of Doctor Whatshisname, her lover for the past year – not that he was in any position to be critical. And as far as he could tell, Jenny was unconcerned about Sarah.

Somehow he expected sex with Jenny to be as good as, and probably better than, it had been during the early days of their first relationship because there would be – however briefly – an element of rediscovery. In fact the sex was good, very good, even if the earth was unmoved.

'On a scale of nought to ten, seven point five to eight wouldn't you say?' Jenny said, taking him by surprise, for that's exactly what he'd been thinking.

'Sorry,' he replied, only half-joking. 'I thought I'd done better than that.'

'Darling, it was marvellous. I was expecting about five, after all this time.' Women can be considerate liars, too.

So Timberlake lay satisfied and largely reassured in Jenny's bed as she slept beside him, yet his pleasure was still slightly marred by a vague unease he couldn't quite understand.

He told himself it could simply be that he was in a strange place. Perhaps because she was a surgeon he had expected to find the house clinically clean, neat and tidy. Clean it certainly was, but it was not as tidy as his own home. A telephone clung perilously to the arm of a sofa; there were books on bookshelves, tables and the floor next to an armchair; a pair of binoculars was on the washing machine (*binoculars?*); an unsteady pile of letters and magazines teetered near the edge of a small table beside the front door. The bathroom shelf was crowded in no particular pattern with bottles, pots and tubes, which was rather bewildering because she usually wore little make-up. Although most of her clothes were in the wardrobe and chests of drawers, others had overflowed on to hangers behind doors and over the backs of two chairs in the bedroom; a couple of shirts were hooked over the handles of the wardrobe door.

He began to work out why he didn't like to stay overnight at Jenny's. He supposed it was because he didn't want to put her to the trouble of doing things for him: making a meal and doing the washing-up afterwards, giving him the bathroom first in the morning ... although he thought it all right for him to do those things for her at his flat, so she could have a sort of night off work. Nor did he realize that his explanations – or excuses – for not accepting her invitations to stay overnight were hurtful to her.

His major reason had always been that he didn't want to leave her telephone number with the station if he had to be contacted during the night in an emergency. Jenny said she couldn't care less if the entire Terrace Vale constabulary knew about them. Now he no longer had that excuse, because he had been given a portable phone so the station could get to him wherever he was. And besides, his relationship with Jenny was now about as secret as an advertising poster.

Somewhere deep inside him a tiny voice – tiny, but as insistent as the point of a dentist's probe – nagged at him. He vainly tried to deny his disquiet was because Jenny's getting him to stay with her was the first small step on the long journey to a more formally permanent relationship. He couldn't actually pronounce the word 'marriage' in his own mind.

He could always have found a believable excuse not to spend the night ... or could he? Jenny's invitation this time had been positive to the point of being a command, and Harry Timberlake hadn't managed to say no.

42

'I'm going soft,' he said, not realizing he was speaking out loud.

'Don't worry, darling,' Jenny said, not at all sleepily, 'you'll be all right in a minute.'

She was right, and he laughed. It made him completely forget his worries.

For the time being.

A bright green, long plastic apron, operating theatre 'pyjamas', rubber gloves and twelve-inch brain knife were as naturally fitting to Professor Mortimer as a dress suit and baton to a conductor. The sense of performance was common to them both.

Mortimer's passport declared he was 6 foot 4 inches or 1.93 metres tall. These days, when he was dressed in mufti and his elastic-sided boots, the top of Mortimer's head was barely six feet above the floor. He had a scraggy neck with a prominent adam's apple that gave the impression that a large pickled onion had stuck halfway down his throat. He looked rather like a decayed Gary Cooper. Mortimer should have retired years before, but he had no home life. His wife died, his colleagues said, in self-defence against increasing boredom and in a last desperate attempt to get her husband to take a close look at her at least once.

Despite the relatively small fees paid to forensic pathologists, unless they were appearing for the defence of a well-heeled client, Mortimer was comfortably off, thanks to income from books and lectures. His problem was that he didn't know what he would do if he retired. He had absolutely no outside interests and no children. The only permanent relationships he had were with the pickled contents of sealed jars of formaldehyde in his office. But Peter Mortimer was very good at his job, and he readily admitted it, asked or not.

He had just completed the autopsy on the Towers Hall body. Such liquids which were still present in the body had been drawn off and put into containers, and the vital organs, including the brain, had been removed and similarly potted. In the background was Mortimer's usual mortuary assistant, who would sew up the body when Mortimer had finished addressing the detectives there.

Mortimer cleared his throat with a sound like the rustle of dry leaves in a cemetery. Timberlake, who had been at many of his autopsies, knew that the sound was a short overture to what

43

promised to be a long lecture. Mortimer, with Gertrude Hacker, a respectable one pace behind him on one side and Dr Chandra Smith on the other, faced Harry Timberlake and Darren Webb across the Towers Hall body. Also on the spectators' side of the autopsy table were a couple of junior detective constables who were attending their first autopsy to gain experience. It was clear that they were not enjoying themselves.

The body looked very different from when Timberlake and Webb had seen it earlier. It now had an incision running from under the chin down to the pubic area; the top of the cranium had been sawn off so the brain could be removed.

'Even you can all see that this body has undergone hydrolysis to form adipocere.' The 'even you' reduced the members of his Mortimer's audience to a group of backward, short-sighted children.

'In the initial stages of formation adipocere is greyish-yellow in colour, and is greasy, resembling rancid butter in appearance and smell. The fat burns with a pale blue flame.' Somewhere at the back of his mind Timberlake remembered Mortimer offering this titbit of information at another autopsy. It seemed to fascinate the old man.

'After some years it becomes greyish-white, as in the body here. It also becomes brittle and liable to crumble. By then the disagreeable smell is not nearly as strong.' He bent over the sad little corpse and inhaled noisily. 'There is virtually no odour.' He looked round the group as if challenging them to say they could sniff something. Webb daringly blew his nose vigorously.

'Once the process of formation of adipocere has begun it is irreversible. The fat round the internal organs also changes into adipocere, and it can help preserve them. In this subject the preservation was almost total.

'The determination of age at death was easily arrived at by examination of the teeth. The eruption of the third molars had scarcely begun, which puts the age at approximately seventeen years. Approximately,' he repeated. 'This was confirmed by examination of the degree of fusion of the epiphyses—' Mortimer broke off and fixed Webb with a look like pinning a butterfly to a cork. 'Good heavens, man, don't tell me you don't know what epiphyses are—'

44

'Of course he knows, professor,' Timberlake said calmly. 'The terminal ossification of the long bones.'

'You took the words out of my mouth, guv,' Webb said with a face as straight as an Easter Island statue.

For once Professor Mortimer seemed disconcerted. He gave his dead-leaves cough, and returned to studying the corpse. He missed the wink Timberlake gave Dr Smith, just out of Mortimer's line of sight. She managed to hide any hint of complicity, such as giving Timberlake a pre-autopsy briefing.

'Now, how long it was since death posed certain problems. Mummified bodies are frequently attacked by insects, and in particular the Brown House moth, or false clothes moth. This insect eats furs, skin, hair and internal organs, and the degree of infestation could provide some indication of time. However, there was no significant infestation, because this does not occur with adipocere.'

So why bring it up? Timberlake almost said. Instead he asked, 'Could you establish the cause of death, professor?'

Mortimer treated this with the contempt he thought it deserved by ignoring the question until he was ready.

'The woman was in good health at the time of death and seven months pregnant of a female. The remains of the dress she was clothed in' – *Why can't you say 'was wearing'?* Timberlake thought wearily – 'has been sent to the Home Office Forensic Laboratory for examination. I have also sent bones for testing for chemical analysis.' He waited for questions about this, and was clearly disappointed that there were none. It didn't stop him explaining, though. 'Determination of the nitrogen content, protein, amino-acid and blood pigment status of the bones can help in a general estimate of the date of death.'

Timberlake asked, 'From what you have seen of the body, could it have been there for fifteen years?'

Mortimer regarded him as if were about to trump Timberlake's ace. 'Yes,' he said. 'Or less. Or longer.' Having won that one, Mortimer relaxed a little. 'A cause of death – *a* cause – was strangulation.'

'How strangled?'

'The signs are completely consistent with suicidal hanging.' He took out a pencil and indicated traces on the neck as he spoke. 'If you look closely, you can see the mark left by the noose which lay tightly under the jaw in an upward direction. The noose was drawn up into an apex, leaving a gap, here, where the cord did not cut into the neck.'

'Why the bloody hell didn't he tell us that right at the start?' Darren Webb grumbled, very nearly audibly.

'Could it have been a homicidal hanging?' Timberlake asked.

'These are extremely rare, and difficult to achieve, even if the victim is drunk, drugged or unconscious. The possibility of this being a homicidal hanging is minimal. As I have just said, plainly enough I thought, the signs are completely consistent with suicide. That is what I shall tell the coroner.'

There was a long pause. Suddenly, Timberlake guessed what was going to happen. Mortimer, who had as much sense of humour as a nineteenth-century German civil servant, nevertheless had a strong sense of drama in which he was the protagonist. Not for the first time he had been hiding a fizzing bombshell, waiting until the last moment to throw it. He held out his hand. Gertrude Hacker took a sheet of paper from her voluminous pocket and handed it to him.

'I have received,' Mortimer cleared his throat unnecessarily, 'a report from the Metropolitan Police Laboratory.' He studied the paper. 'The fragments of clothing round the body have been subjected to a number of separate tests. The conclusion to be drawn from these tests—' *Get on with it!* Timberlake shouted silently inside his head ... 'is that the material was, plus or minus fifteen years ... one hundred years old. I am quite confident that the chemical tests on the bones will confirm this approximate date of death.'

There was a long pause of almost audible suppressed fury. Darren Webb was the first to speak.

'But professor,' he said unwisely, 'you told us the body could be less than fifteen years old.'

'Please try to listen to what I say,' said Mortimer with a heavy *Weltschmerz*. 'It could be less than fifteen years from what I could see of the *body*.'

It was all too plain to Timberlake that Mortimer had known about the report on the clothing before everyone had come to hear his little lecture on the autopsy.

And it was also obvious that anyone involved in bringing about the death of the anonymous young woman had long since gone to their own grave.

46

'So that's the end of that,' Timberlake said.

He was wrong. It was barely the beginning.

Madame la Comtesse de Gaillmont had wasted no time in engaging household staff. When Timberlake and Webb rang the doorbell of Towers Hall the door was opened by a maid in uniform. 'Mr Timberlake and Mr Webb,' Timberlake told her. 'We are expected.' The maid showed them into the reception room. As she was English she said 'Her Ladyship will be with you in a moment,' as she left. Not *une petite minute*, or *une minute*.

After what the French would call *une bonne petite minute*, the door was opened by Thérèse Chardet for Sophie de Gaillmont to enter, followed by her stepson, Jean-Louis.

'Yes, inspector?' she said, sounding like Napoleon addressing a Spanish irregular bearing a white flag.

'It has been established that the body of the young woman was some hundred years old. It means that our investigation is finished,' Timberlake said formally, not in the least abashed.

'Then we shall not be seeing you again.' It was difficult to decide whether the 'we' was the royal plural or referred to the group of three. Timberlake would have bet on the royal 'we'; these days even women prime ministers used it. 'I am glad that the matter is closed before the return of my son. He is due any day now. I should not have liked him to be subjected to needless questioning and idle gossip.' Sophie de Gaillmont nodded minimally and went out, followed by Chardet and Jean-Louis de Gaillmont.

'Christ, she makes Maggie Thatcher seem like Mary Poppins. I feel as if I've been for a bollocking at the seventh floor of the Yard,' Webb said as he and Timberlake went to their car. 'I'm glad we won't have to come back here again, guv.'

Fate just loves to hear remarks like that.

Chapter 8

Sarah Lewis lay luxuriating in a bath big enough to stage a model-ship naval engagement. On the wall opposite her was a near-life size photograph of a highly attractive, sensuous-looking young woman, wearing nothing more than a few strategic shadows. She could hardly believe she herself was the subject. She closed her eyes and re-lived the circumstances that had brought her to this situation.

She hadn't mentioned the original incident to Harry at the time. Maybe it was because it wasn't important then, she told herself; later she didn't tell him because it *was* important. Sarah tried to analyse her feelings, measure them, make a balance sheet of for and against, but she couldn't be sure she wasn't deliberately cooking the books.

It started late one night when she was driving home from that funeral, of all things. Her parents had written from Wales to tell her that Aunt Blodwen – of whom she had never heard – had died in darkest East Hertfordshire, and would she go to the funeral and represent her parents. Funerals are normally not a big laugh; Welsh funerals in an alien land like England are definitely less jolly than the average. That none of the mourners seemed to know who the hell she was, or her parents either, for that matter, made Sarah feel depressed to a point barely this side of psychotic. The situation was aggravated by many of the people attending making it plain they believed she was there only to try to grab some of the late Aunt Blodwen's effects. Sarah would have liked to tell them she found all of Aunt Blodwen's effects on view as desirable as the contents of the Dracula Castle basement.

On her way home Sarah was halfway along a cheerless, badly lit road across a common when her car died on her as if it had a massive heart attack. She was in the Metropolitan Police area, just, but it felt as lonely as a country road on Dartmoor. Luckily there was a phone box a dozen yards or so ahead, but much less luckily, when she lifted the receiver it was as dead as Alexander Graham Bell.

Sarah was well aware that she was in a textbook position of maximum vulnerability to attack by men. She decided to see if she could discover why her car had stopped, ignoring the fact that she knew next to nothing about engines.

She raised the bonnet of the car and when she switched on her torch it offered a yellow beam so sickly it almost drooped as it came out of the lens. She could see nothing obviously amiss, and she stared at the inanimate mass of metal hoping for inspiration.

'Having trouble?'

A man's voice beside her made Sarah's heart race, and her mouth went dry. She gripped the torch firmly, ready to use it as a weapon.

A blond man of about thirty-five was standing near her car, not too close to be an immediate threat. Beyond him was a Rolls Royce. She had been so intent on examining her own engine she hadn't heard the whisper-quiet Rolls arrive. Its presence somehow eased her fears a little; she didn't think many muggers drove Rollers, and for that matter, not many rapists either, as far as she could recall. Her relief made her overreact.

'Of course I've got trouble. D'you think I'm knitting a pullover under here?'

The man laughed. 'Of course. Silly question.'

Sarah felt slightly embarrassed. 'Sorry. I was a bit jumpy.'

'Let's see what we can do. For a start, get back in the car and turn off your headlights to save your battery.' That 'get back in the car' was reassuring. Sarah felt her spirits rise. 'I won't ask you if there's any petrol in the tank.'

'You just did,' Sarah said with a smile. 'Yes, there is.'

'How did the engine stop? Did it splutter and cough, or cut out dead?'

'Cut out dead.'

'Uhuh.' He went to his own car and produced a long-handled screwdriver and a lamp which could have served as a stage spot-light. 'When I tell you, switch on the starter.'

Sarah followed his instructions. The starter whirred in vain.

'It's electrical. There's no spark from the plugs.' He did things under the bonnet for a few minutes, then said, 'Now try it.' The started whirred again, and the engine burst into life. The man came round to Sarah's side of the car. 'One of the main ignition leads was corroded. I've cleaned it up and reconnected it, but you should get it seen to as soon as you get home. Where are you going?'

'Terrace Vale.'

'Right. Off you go. I'll follow you just to make sure you get there all right.' Before she could thank him, the man turned back to his own car.

He followed her all the way to her flat. She parked under a street lamp and the man left his own massive, gleaming car to join her. For the first time she had a good look at him. He was attractive with a permanent hint of a smile on his face. He gave the impression that he found life amusing.

'Thank you, you've really been most kind.' She laughed embarrassedly. 'I don't even know your name.

'Julian.' He took out a card and gave it to her. His full name was Julian Tabard, and he had a West End address. The name rang a small, distant bell in Sarah's mind, but she couldn't place him. She read the wrong magazines; if she read some of the others she probably would have dropped the card down the drain.

'Sarah Lewis,' she said. There seemed to be no reason to mention she was a copper and lots of reasons not to mention it. Julian Tabard smiled at her, said, 'Good night, Sarah,' turned and got back in his car before Sarah could make another move.

Later, something prodded Sarah into going round to Tabard's address to thank him properly. The entrance was deceptive: a plain blue door in a mews house within a precious-stone's throw of Bond Street. The door was opened by a perfumed young man wearing black leather trousers, a voluminous chrome yellow shirt, and a mauve silk scarf. Sarah's heart sank. 'Oh, God, I hadn't realized,' she thought, and wondered why she felt disappointed. That didn't last long for she soon learned that Julian's association with the fragrant young fop was only professional: he was Julian's apprentice.

The upstairs part of the house was a revelation. It extended into the next mews house to form an enormous studio room. The far end had a raised dais, and was cluttered with studio lights, props, tripods, backdrops and all the paraphernalia of a major

50

photographer's working environment. The walls of the corridors and other rooms were covered with photographs and reproductions of glossy magazine covers of anorexic-looking women displaying a variety of arrogant, challenging, pouting, belligerent or hooded-eyed expressions. A smile would have torn a ligament. Sarah suddenly felt as if her make-up was running and she had red hands as big as baseball gloves.

At last she remembered that Julian Tabard was one of Britain's leading photographers: a sort of well-dressed and shaved David Bailey who steered clear of television commercials.

From that first meeting at his studio the relationship between Sarah and Julian grew at a speed that sometimes worried her, when it didn't excite her. At first she felt inadequate and gauche compared with the exotic, gaudy, stick-insect women who passed through his studio, but he skilfully cured her of that. He asked her to sit for him just so he could prove that she could look – in her own way – just as attractive and much sexier than the professional clothes-horses.

Julian Tabard was as good as his word; he produced pictures that she could hardly believe were of her. She had an almost narcissistic pleasure in regarding them and occasionally found it difficult to contain her new self-esteem. And all the time she was saying nothing to Harry Timberlake, who sometimes couldn't help wondering what had got into her.

Sarah knew that Harry Timberlake and Julian Tabard had almost nothing in common, except for Sarah herself, although neither man knew of the other. Julian was coercive and persuasive with Sarah as he was with everyone. Timberlake could be subtle and manipulative – even devious – when it was required, but he had a powerful latent air of command just below the surface. He was a strongly masculine man, with none of the gentler, almost feminine traits of Julian Tabard.

There came a time when Sarah wondered what sex with Julian would be like. With Harry Timberlake the physical attraction burst on her, and soon afterwards on him, like a thunderclap. Their sex life had always been passionate and devouring. With Julian it was quite different; their relationship was a slow-growing desire, less immediate, but undeniable. It recalled to her something Dorothy Parker once wrote: the deep, deep peace of the marriage bed after the hurly-burly of the *chaise-longue*.

51

She told Timberlake of her new relationship, quite obliquely, when she went to visit him in hospital, where he was recovering from the injuries he sustained chasing the mass murderer Carl-Heinz Rohmer, alias Charles Henry Newman.*

He asked her whether it was Darren Webb who had given her a lift. 'No, a friend,' she replied. He looked at her sharply. He knew her well enough to understand what she was saying. Unbelievably, yet inevitably, it was over between them.

'Sleeping?' Julian Tabard asked, leaning over the bath. She opened her eyes and mentally returned to the present. 'No, just thinking.' He held out a glass of white wine. She drank some of it, and sighed.

'Anything wrong?'

'Only work. I'm on a rape case. Tomorrow we're interviewing people on our list of sex offenders: convicted and suspected rapists, violent perverts—' She made a sound of disgust.

'Why do you do it?'

She shrugged. 'It's my job.'

Julian looked at her seriously for a long moment, and Sarah guessed he was carefully considering what he was going to say next. All at once she knew what it would be.

'Why don't you quit? Leave the force?'

'It's my job,' she repeated firmly. 'I'm good at it.' She weakened the force of her answer by adding, 'What else would I do?'

'I can offer you a lifetime contract. No worries, no more chasing villains and perverts . . . lots of first-class travel to exotic places—' She stood up in the bath, her skin glistening. Tabard took a large towel and held it wide for her. She stepped out of the bath, turning her back to him. He draped the towel round her, holding her tightly to him.

'I'll think about it,' she said, meaning it.

Panda-car coppers generally agreed that the real disadvantage of night duty was that there were very few cafés, hamburger bars or greasy spoon joints open after midnight where you could put your feet up. Going back to the canteen at the Terrace Vale nick for 'breaks for refreshments', as the quaint official terminology of the police has it, meant running the risk of a Sod's Law operation

*See *Elimination*, the second Harry Timberlake story.

52

which lumbered you with some unexpected unpleasant task just because you caught the duty sergeant's eye. So, PC Dick 'Rambo' Wright and WPC Marie 'Rosie' Hall brought thermos flasks and packets of sandwiches with them when they were on night turn. In fact this turn hardly seemed like night duty. There was a half moon and it was warm enough to be wearing shirtsleeves.

They were both English, and shared with all their compatriots the conviction that hot tea was the best thing for cooling you down, although no one extended this reasoning to believe that cold tea was the best thing for warming you up. Perversely, they believed that hot tea warmed you up as well as cooling you down. There's no arguing with some people.

In the inverse logic of nicknames – like calling a bald man Curly and a short man Lofty – PC Dick Wright was called Rambo because he was small and slight, had fine, gingerish hair and a sharp face with curiously pale eyes. He seemed as menacing as Bambi. Nevertheless, he had a black belt in judo and karate, something he largely kept to himself. His physical self-confidence made him quiet and unaggressive.

WPC Marie Hall was originally nicknamed Rosemarie. The Rosemarie became shortened to Rosie, and most people now thought that was her real name. Although she had spent all her life in a poorer part of London she looked as if she had just come in from milking the cows, and seemed only partly dressed without a straw in her hair. She was probably the only officer at Terrace Vale who thought it was a fairly peaceful area. Her previous posting had been in a part of south-east London where even the cats didn't care to go out at night.

Rosie was doing the driving on this shift. She carefully replaced the stopper and cup of her thermos, closed her sandwich box and prepared to take up the protection of Her Majesty's subjects again. Rambo Wright tidied away his own flask and sandwich wrappers, got out of the panda and carefully brushed the crumbs from his trousers before getting back into the car.

'Shall we have a dekko down The Gut, see what's happening?' Rosie suggested. Without waiting for an answer she pointed the panda car in that direction. Rambo gave a silent inward groan. Rosie's obsession with The Gut was well known to all the officers she shared a duty with.

'The Gut' was the local name for Valletta Street, one of Terrace

Vale's most sordid streets named after towns which were once part of the Empire. The Gut, as every former member of the Royal Navy or Merchant Marine knows, is the main drag of Valletta in Malta, which once boasted more whores per doorway than anywhere west of Bangkok. Terrace Vale's The Gut had fewer tarts and dubious clubs than the Maltese original, but what it lacked in quantity it more than compensated for with bad quality. Which is why Rosie said 'See *what's* happening' and not 'See *if* anything's happening'. There was always something happening in The Gut.

'Let's take a swing round Southington Close first,' Rambo Wright said quietly, but in a tone that brooked no argument. This was the southern limit of Terrace Vale's area, and about as far as one could get from The Gut.

Rosie grumbled and said a rude word, but changed direction to follow Rambo's suggestion. She drove as fast as she dared, but Rambo said nothing. At least she was a good driver.

They were halfway along Southington Close when something to Rambo Wright's left caught his eye. 'Hold it,' he said sharply to Rosie. 'Back up to that turning we just passed.'

'Another cyclist without lights?' she said sourly. Rambo didn't reply.

When the panda was level with the side road they both could see that it was a cul-de-sac, with a large pair of iron gates at the bottom. The massive structures would have been suitable for a Victorian lunatic asylum. In fact they were the main gates to Towers Hall. They stood out clearly because a car, its headlights on, was stopped in front of them. The car's engine was running and the nearside door was open. They couldn't see a driver. It could be that the driver had just nipped out for a quiet pee, but both coppers could feel the hairs beginning to rise on the back of their necks.

Without anything needing to be said, Rosie slowly drove the panda down towards the motionless car. 'Better call the nick, to be on the safe side,' Rambo said quietly. He picked up microphone and reported in.

Some ten yards from the stationary car Rosie stopped the panda. The two police officers got out. Rosie carried a powerful torch, while Rambo kept his hand on his new-style, extensible baton. He crossed in front of Rosie to approach the car from the driver's side.

The first thing he noticed was that it was a French car with a 13 registration. As he got nearer he could make out the form of a driver slumped over the left-hand drive wheel.

'You all right, sir?' Rosie said in her addressing-drunk-drivers voice.

At the same moment Rambo and Rosie saw he was far from all right. The driver had a hole in the back of his head, and the windscreen was splashed with blood.

Chapter 9

When Rosie Hall called in to report a murder, PC Phil Clapton was operating the Terrace Vale radio. The station comic and wag was in one of his rare serious modes and he had asked how she knew it was a murder. In her usual rock-crusher style Rosie pointed out that a man with a gunshot in the back of the head, with no gun in sight, hadn't committed suicide unless he had double-jointed arms as long as an orang-utan's. Furthermore, it was unlikely to be an accident unless some ham-handed prat was sitting in the back seat cleaning his gun.

By the time Harry Timberlake got to the scene, closely followed by Darren Webb, the major-flap circus was in almost full swing. Blue and white tapes had been set up to cordon off the murder scene. There were nearly enough police cars, all with their blue lights flashing, to fill the starting grid at Silverstone. A couple of dog handlers stood by, their German shepherds flopped beside them, looking thoroughly bored and slightly peeved at having been woken up; the dogs, that is. Not for the first time, Timberlake wondered why there had to be so many uniformed coppers in the area. There were a number of policemen he was sure he had never seen before.

Beyond the tapes journalists, photographers and TV people were beginning to congregate. It is illegal for members of the public to listen in to police radio messages, of course, so the media must have found out about the incident from some powerful practitioners in thought transference.

Timberlake and Webb exchanged greetings with Dr Pratt, who was already on the scene, waiting for the SOCOs to arrive and mark out a track for him to approach the car. Pratt had the thoughtful air of a man who was trying to think of a witticism to offer. Timberlake and Webb moved away before he could come up with one.

The senior uniformed officer present was Sergeant Ray Hepburn, who was a front-row forward in the Metropolitan Police rugby team. His nose and ears silently testified to his energetic belligerence on the field. He was not the sort of man whose beer you would drink in a pub.

'Evening, sir,' he greeted Timberlake, and saluted. Like many heavily muscled athletes he had a surprisingly high-pitched voice.

'Hello, Ray.' Timberlake replied. 'Who found him?'

'PCs Wright and Hall.' He beckoned to the couple, who were standing by their panda. As they approached Sergeant Burton Johnson and his team of SOCOs arrived and prepared the ground for Dr Pratt.

Timberlake turned to the two officers. 'Er, WPC Hall and PC Wright, isn't it? Right, tell me all about it.'

Between them Rosie and Rambo gave their brief report.

'What time was this?'

'Oh-one-oh-seven,' Rambo said quietly.

'Thirty minutes ago,' Timberlake noted, looking at his watch. 'Was there anyone about? People? Cars, anything?' They shook their heads. 'Right, you can get back now and write up your reports while everything's clear in your mind. Well done.' They saluted and moved off, disappointed not to see the rest of the show.

Spectators were beginning to congregate on the pavements of the cul-de-sac. They were obviously residents of the large houses in the road because many of them were in dressing-gowns; others were at the windows of their homes.

'Darren, start arranging for our people to take statements – anything they may have heard or seen.'

'I've already organized that, sir,' Sergeant Hepburn said, a touch reproachfully.

'Sorry, Ray.' He smiled. 'Conditioned reflex.' He stayed silent for a moment, then turned to Darren Webb. 'They won't have actually *seen* anything.'

'Guv?'

'Come with me.' He led Webb to the car. 'See? The gates are well set back, with walls on either side of the private roadway. You can't see any of the houses from here. Which means that even if anyone was looking out of their window they still wouldn't have been able to see the car.'

'Bloody hell,' Webb said helpfully.

Timberlake was still thoughtful. 'Odd, that.'

'What is, guv?'

'Look at the house.'

Towers Hall looked black and menacing against the night sky. There was no light, no sign of life. If Norman Bates or Morticia Addams had come walking down the drive towards them Webb wouldn't have been surprised.

'Yeh, I see what you mean. Lights on in most of the houses in the street and people've come out to see what's going on. But up there . . . I've been in livelier morgues.'

'And the car's headlights are shining straight on to the house,' Timberlake said. He paused again. 'Want to bet who the victim is?'

'Too easy, guv. French car, obviously on the point of going up to the house . . . Charles Pusey.'

'Yes, the countess's son. Let's wait till the doc and the SOCOs have finished before we go to see them.'

Dr Pratt came up to the detectives, leaving the SOCOs to begin their work.

'An IC One or Two, about thirty-five to forty years old,' he began without preamble, sounding rather irritable. 'IC' in police-speak meant Identity Code. Number 1 of the six classifications was White Caucasian, 2 was European. 'Killed by a single bullet in the occipital region. Couldn't be sure whether it was a contact wound or intermediate range wound because of the hair. When Professor Mortimer does the autopsy he'll be able to tell you.'

'Interesting,' Timberlake said. 'That it was in the occipital region.' Webb looked at him enquiringly. Timberlake touched the back of his head just above where it merged into the neck.

'A pro killer's shot, guv.'

'Or an execution shot.'

Webb nodded. '*Coup de gras*,' he said knowingly, pronouncing it 'grah'.

'*Coup de grâce*,' Timberlake reproved him. '*Gras* is an adjective meaning fat, or greasy.' He turned to the doctor. 'What about the exit wound?'

'Just above the right eyebrow.'

Timberlake thought for a moment. 'The bullet travelled slightly upwards.' He looked towards the car. 'Can't see from here whether the windscreen has a hole in it.'

'Don't you want the time of death?' Pratt asked, still rather petulant.

'Well, it was some time after eight,' Webb said unexpectedly.

Dr Pratt stared at him as if he were a small dog that had soiled his Persian carpet. 'Really, sergeant. I had no idea you were a doctor, as well. *And* that you could make your diagnosis from this distance.'

'Car lights are on,' Webb said shortly. 'Wasn't dark until after eight.'

Dr Pratt decided not to continue the duel. 'In my opinion, he hasn't been dead for more than a couple of hours at most. There's some degree of rigidity in the muscles of the face, but none in the arms or legs. I expect Professor Mortimer will give you a more accurate estimate after he's taken the anal temperature.' He sniffed and turned away.

Behind Doctor Pratt Sergeant Burt Johnson waved to Timberlake. 'We've done for now with the car,' he called out. 'Come and have a look if you like.'

'Does he have any identification on him?' Timberlake said. Johnson shook his head. 'Nothing. Pockets all empty, turned inside out.'

The engine and the lights had been switched off. Apart from the driver, there was only one object visible in the car: a London A–Z large-scale map. It was open on the right-hand front seat, open at the pages showing the Terrace Vale area.

'Any sign of the bullet?' Webb enquired.

'It's probably in the fascia somewhere, if it hasn't come out of the car,' Sergeant Johnson said. 'When we've got it on the trailer out of the way we'll have a good look at the roadway to make sure it isn't there.'

'Have you opened the boot?' Timberlake asked.

The SOCO nodded. 'Nothing important in there.' Sergeant Johnson, still wearing plastic gloves, took the keys from a small plastic bag, went round to the back of the car and opened the boot. Apart from the toolbox and the folding red triangle sign, compulsory on the Continent, the boot was empty.

Timberlake sighed. 'Well, I suppose we'll have to go up to the house and tell them,' he said heavily. 'Darren, you stay here and see what Professor Mortimer has to say when he gets here.'

'Right, guv,' Webb replied with no enthusiasm whatsoever.

'And don't bother to give him any help with the time of death.'

Despite all the activity in the roadway, inside the gates everything was silent as if Towers Hall was alone on an empty moor. To Timberlake his footsteps sounded loud on the gravel path that led to the front door. The heavy porchway was as black as the gateway to hell.

He remembered that on his last visit he had seen no knocker or doorbell, so he rapped on the heavy wood with his knuckles. He waited, but there was no sound from within the house. He knocked again, harder, hurting his knuckles. This time he thought he could hear movement deep inside the building.

He was taken by surprise when the porch light came on abruptly and the door opened a fraction, juddering to a stop against the safety chain.

He could just see Thérèse Chardet peering round the door.

'Inspector Timberlake?' she said, bemused. She looked past him at the activity on the other side of the gates. 'What is wrong?'

'I'm sorry, but I have to speak to Madame de Gaillmont,' he said.

'At this hour? Madame la Comtesse has been asleep for some time. What can be so important?'

He avoided the question. 'It is a personal matter of some gravity.' He wasn't aware he was speaking like a direct translation from French.

Thérèse Chardet looked at him hard for a long moment. He could not make out her expression, with the hall light behind her. She opened the door, and Timberlake could see that she was wearing a dressing-gown over a plain night-dress suitable for the spinster sister of a nineteenth-century missionary. She was neat, calm and composed, but she exuded a sexuality that could have prompted some men to imprudence in different circumstances.

She led him to the same reception room he had been in before. She walked as decorously as a vestal virgin, but Timberlake was very aware of the body that was somewhere inside the shapeless clothing.

He waited there for ten minutes that felt like an hour, very aware of the ticking of an ormolu clock he hadn't noticed before.

In the distance he heard the low-loader trailer arrive to take away the car and its dead body. Since his last visit a number of expensive ornaments and photographs in heavy silver frames had been added to the decor. He studied the photographs, in all of which Sophie de Gaillmont figured prominently. In many of them she was accompanied by a man who was obviously the late Comte Pascal de Gaillmont. There were photographs of a wedding which rivalled the Prince Rainier–Grace Kelly turnout. Curiously, most of the other photographs were quite old, taken when Sophie Pusey was young, and presumably before she became the Comtesse de Gaillmont. The late Charles Pusey, whose money had made it all possible, did not get a look in.

The lift hummed quietly a few moments before Thérèse Chardet opened the door for Sophie de Gaillmont to make an entrance, followed by her stepson, the count. The countess was wearing a peignoir and night-dress that would not have been out of place at an embassy ball. Without make-up her face looked even stronger than usual.

'You wish to see me, inspector.'

'Yes, countess.' The occasion was too solemn for him to say simply 'Madame de Gaillmont', but somehow he couldn't bring himself to say 'my lady'. 'I have bad news.' She wasn't the sort of woman who needed things wrapped in cotton wool, as her answer demonstrated.

'At this hour, I expected no less.'

'Does your son drive a black Renault Thirty?' He gave her the registration number.

She nodded. 'It is Monsieur le Comte's car. My son is bringing it to England.'

'Then, madame, it is my sad duty to tell you that I fear he has been killed.' He had never sounded as stilted as that in his life.

Sophie de Gaillmont stood ramrod straight, holding on to the back of a chair. The two women crossed themselves.

'A car accident?' Jean-Louis de Gaillmont asked. He moved across to his stepmother and took hold of her arm. It was a gesture, no more. She had no need of his support.

'No. He has been shot.' Before they could put any more questions he added quickly, 'He was in a car, outside the main gates. We're not certain of the circumstances as yet.'

'Was it—' Sophie de Gaillmont began, then checked. 'May I see him?'

'Later, madame. I'm sorry, I have to ask you this: did any of you hear anything, a shot?'

They all shook their heads. 'Our bedrooms are at the back of the house,' Jean-Louis de Gaillmont explained.

'Are there any domestic staff in the house?'

'There are no living-in servants – for the moment, at least,' Thérèse Chardet said. 'There are two maids and a cook who come in daily, and a part-time chauffeur from an agency when we require him.'

'We shall need to speak to you all later,' Timberlake said, 'and the domestic staff. I shall telephone you to make an appointment.'

'You will have to do it through our solicitor,' Sophie de Gaillmont said. 'I have no intention of taking any calls.'

'Madame la Comtesse, please accept my condolences.' Timberlake heard himself with surprise, and wondered why he sounded like a bad actor.

Sophie de Gaillmont gave him a look which could best be described by the French word *insolite*. 'Strange' wasn't strange enough. Timberlake gave more than a nod but less than a bow, and exited. As the front door closed behind him he thought he heard something like a sob.

The Renault had been taken away by the time Timberlake joined Webb, waiting for him in his own car near the gates. Most of the police had gone and even the curious neighbours had almost all drifted back to their homes.

'Has Professor Mortimer been?' Timberlake asked.

'And gone,' Darren Webb said gloomily. 'He said he'd have a proper look at the body in the daylight tomorrow. You can phone him at ten. Until then, bugger all. How did they take it?'

'Like aristos going up the steps to the guillotine. The countess did a marvellous stiff-upper-lip act, but I suspect she was coming apart inside.'

'*Noblesse oblige*,' Webb commented, making no effort to give the phrase a French accent.

'I've had the nasty job of telling a number of people that someone close to them has been killed, but this one was ... it was weird.'

'Foreigners,' Webb said dismissively. 'They're a funny lot. Only joking, guv,' he added quickly.

As they drove back to Terrace Vale nick Webb said, 'Gloomy sort of place, that. I wouldn't want to live there myself. And there was that body buried in the garden ... You had any ideas about that, guv?'

'Pregnant teenager who committed suicide? Probably some poor bloody skivvy who was screwed by the master of the house – a sort of middle-class *droit de seigneur* with no arguments in those days – and got pregnant. She knew she'd be kicked out without a reference or job, so—'

'She did herself in for that? Surely there was something she could have—'

'In those days if a pregnant woman went into a workhouse, when she came out with her child the baby wouldn't have any clothes. The rule was the child didn't come in with any clothes, so it wouldn't leave with any.'

'You're joking!' Timberlake turned a grim face towards him. 'Bloody hell,' Webb said, shaking his head. 'Well, at least we've made progress since then.'

'Not much,' Timberlake said grittily, putting an end to the subject.

'Why?' Detective Superintendent Harkness asked Harry Timberlake. 'Why do you want me to come with you?'

'I'd like you to have a look at Madame de Gaillmont. There's something about her I can't quite make out. Analyse, I mean.'

'What, exactly?'

Timberlake was almost sharp with Harkness. 'If I knew, I shouldn't have to ask you.' Realizing how he sounded, he took the edge off it with a smile. 'Anyway, I shouldn't like to give you any preconceived ideas.'

Harkness shrugged. 'If you think it'll help. But won't it put her on her guard, having me there?'

'She'll think it's a tribute to her rank.'

The room at the morgue for relatives to view bodies had been made as un-funereal as possible, but nothing was going to make it snug. Harkness and Timberlake led Sophie de Gaillmont and

Thérèse Chardet into the viewing room. A glass panel in one of the walls had a closed curtain on the far side. It was easy to guess that the late Charles Pusey was on the other side of the glass.

Sophie de Gaillmont was dressed in unrelieved black, with her wedding and engagement rings her only jewellery. She walked stiffly, holding herself rigidly as if struggling to contain some awful internal pressure. Her face was like a painted skull, the tightly stretched skin almost translucent in its thinness. Thérèse Chardet once offered her arm to help support the older woman, but Sophie de Gaillmont drew her own away without making a dramatic gesture of it.

The two men and two women lined up in front of the glass partition.

'Madame la Comtesse, are you ready?' Timberlake asked. She took two deep breaths before nodding. He pressed a switch near the panel and the curtains on the other side of the glass slowly rolled back.

The morgue attendants always did their best to present the corpses as if they were simply sleeping, although injuries and death pallor sometimes made this something of a problem.

The late Charles Pusey was covered with a white sheet, with only his head showing. He had a crepe bandage round his forehead like a tennis player's sweatband. It successfully concealed the bullet's exit wound above his eye.

Timberlake allowed Sophie de Gaillmont time to recover before asking, 'Madame de Gaillmont, is that your son, Charles Pusey?'

'It is.' Her voice was almost inaudible.

'You are quite sure?' He had to ask it. She remained silent, but after a moment Thérèse Chardet said, 'It is Monsieur Charles Pusey.' Her control of her voice was uncertain and she spoke unnaturally loudly.

'Yes, it is my son,' Sophie de Gaillmont said at last.

Harkness spoke for the first time. 'We deeply regret having to subject you to this. You have our sincere sympathy.'

Sophie de Gaillmont nodded, and turned to the door. This time she did not refuse Thérèse's arm.

When they were alone Timberlake asked, 'Well, what do you think of her, sir?'

'I don't know, Harry,' he answered slowly. 'She's not living in my century.'

As they left the morgue the de Gaillmonts' stately Daimler went past. They caught the briefest glimpse of Sophie de Gaillmont, her head back, and a strange, powerful expression on her face that Timberlake simply could not make out; not grief, not iron stoicism. Thérèse Chardet reached out a hand to touch her, but Sophie de Gaillmont pushed it aside imperiously.

Chapter 10

The collator at Terrace Vale was PC Brian Pegg, who managed to look like a junk bond salesman even in uniform shirt and trousers and had the ready line of chat of a mock auction operator. For all this, he was basically quite a decent chap. He was the station's union representative, and a thorough thorn in the backside of senior officers when he was representing the interests of a colleague on the carpet for some offence. This made him popular with everyone in the two lowest ranks of the police.

As a beat policeman he was about as useful as a canoe in the Kalahari. Somebody once said of Brian Pegg that if he arrested anyone fleeing from an armed robbery, first he'd charge them for having tyres with insufficient tread, and then ask to see their firearms certificate.

He had a prodigious memory for *Moriarty's Police Law* and *Stone's Justices Manual*, which meant he couldn't walk half a mile along a peaceful street without seeing some arcane offence being committed. An early-morning paper boy ringing doorbells as he delivered the papers was 'wilfully and wantonly disturbing any inhabitant by pulling or ringing any doorbell, or knocking on any door', contrary to the Town Police Clauses Act 1847, as amended by several subsequent Acts, all of which Pegg could quote.

Not far from that scene of a crime two yobbos were leaning against a pillar box and kicking it with their heels as they talked, which is expressly forbidden by the Post Office Act 1953, as amended by the Criminal Justice Act 1967, the Criminal Law Act 1977 and the British Telecommunications Act 1981 (although what Telecommunications had to do with pillar boxes was unclear); the Post Office Act states that 'no one shall do or attempt to do anything likely to injure a post office box'.

In Terrace Vale Park a youth flying a large kite which must have weighed more than two kilogrammes was an offence against the Air Navigation Act 1980. But Pegg's *pièce de résistance*, which made him celebrated in Terrace Vale and five surrounding Areas, was when he saw old Mrs Joseph creating a minor disturbance as she tried to stop Mr Potter, the local greengrocer, from serving another customer with potatoes because she, Mrs Joseph, was there before her. Most coppers would have given the old lady a friendly talking to, but PC Pegg saw Mrs Joseph's action against Mr Potter as 'an intent to deter him from buying, selling . . . grain, flour, meal, malt, or *potatoes*', contrary to the Offences against the Person Act 1861.

That same prodigious memory for detail, however, made him an ideal collator, concerned with every form of intelligence about criminals and shady characters. When Bob Farmer and Sarah Lewis asked Peggy – he had long given up trying to stop people calling him that – for names and addresses of local sex offenders, they knew it would be exhaustive.

Theoretically, as the cause of Charles Pusey's death was pretty obvious, Professor Mortimer's verbal report need not have taken long. But Harkness, Timberlake, Webb and Detective Sergeant Braddock, Harkness's bag-carrier, knew better. PC Larkin had yet to learn. The detectives assembled at one side of the body like an audience at a Happening. On the other side was Mortimer in his apron and short rubber boots with Gertrude Hacker, inevitably dressed in her tweed suit, her usual respectful pace behind him. Mortimer studied Larkin carefully through his wire-rimmed glasses, wondering whether he could upset the young debutant.

The late Charles Pusey was lying on his face. He might have been asleep were it not for the facts that the top of his skull was missing and his rather ragged brain was in a dish beside him.

'Cause of death,' Mortimer said without preamble, 'was a bullet wound to the head. The scientific laboratory has the actual bullet, but from the nature of the entry wound, the damage to the brain, and the exit wound, it is almost certain that a large-calibre pistol was used.

'When I shaved the hair in the region of the entry wound I was able to see that the edges of the wound showed signs of burning by the combustion gases and were blackened with soot which was embedded in the skin. In other words, it was what is classed as a hard contact wound where the muzzle of the weapon is pressed hard against the body.

'The exit wound was larger than the entry wound, which is *not invariably* the case. This has sometimes caused confusion in the minds of inexperienced pathologists.' Mortimer gave the impression that *all* other pathologists were fumbling beginners compared with himself. 'If you look closely at the brain—' He waited while the policemen shuffled nearer to the sliced grey mass sitting on a thin pool of blood. Mortimer eyed Larkin, but the young man pressed forward. Webb managed to fix his gaze on the autopsy table a foot from the brain.

'As you can see,' Mortimer droned on, 'the bullet – Pencil,' he said to Gertrude Hacker, his hand behind him. Before he had uttered the order she already had a pencil ready. Mortimer pointed out the track of the bullet as he continued. 'The bullet entered the head in the occipital region, severely lacerating the cerebellum and the brain stem. At that point the bullet began to wobble, intensifying the damage as it passed through the corpus callosum and finally emerging about one centimetre above the right eyebrow. Death was almost certainly instantaneous.'

Everyone sighed silently with relief.

'However,' Mortimer continued, and the silent sighs of relief turned to almost audible groans, 'I recall a case that was reported when I was a student. An elderly man shot himself with a .45 automatic pistol in a garden shelter. The entry wound was under the chin, and the bullet passed into the skull just behind the roof of the left orbit, continued on through the frontal and temporal lobes of the brain, which were lacerated and pulped. Brain matter was propelled through the top of his skull on to the roof of the shelter.'

Webb was getting danger signals from his stomach. He stared at Gertrude Hacker and mentally repeated his thirteen times multiplication table. It was a trick which usually worked when he was having sex and becoming too excited too soon. Although the circumstances now were rather different, the trick worked. His stomach subsided. For his part Sergeant Braddock was patently bored and hard put to stifle a yawn.

'The bullet emerged on the right side of the frontal bone making an exit wound of some 3.5 cm in diameter, approximately one centimetre above the right eye.'

'Aspirin wouldn't do much for that,' Webb muttered to Larkin, trying to sound nonchalant. Larkin looked startled.

'The man then walked from a garden shelter and continued in a circle for about 150 metres. He returned to the shelter and sat down for a while before getting up and returning to the hotel where he lodged. He rang the bell, spoke to the reception clerk, hung up his umbrella, removed his overcoat and walked upstairs to the bathroom. He collapsed and lost consciousness. He lived for three hours after having shot himself.'

This was greeted with the silence it deserved. Detective Sergeant Braddock, who had nothing to lose, asked, 'If that could happen, how can you be certain death was instantaneous in this case, professor?'

Mortimer had the air of a man who was holding the ace of trumps in his hand and a fifth ace up his sleeve. 'When I saw the body in the car it was slumped forward with the head pressed against the lower part of the dashboard. The exit wound on the head was against the hole in the dashboard where the bullet had entered.' He produced the fifth ace. 'And had you been paying attention, sergeant, you would have heard that I said "death was *almost* certainly instantaneous." ' Even the normally imperturbable Braddock looked slightly discomfited.

'I shan't come to the laboratory with you to see the firearms man,' Harkness told Timberlake as they left the morgue. 'You can give me his report when you come back to the station.'

'Will you want me, sir?' Nigel Larkin asked Harkness.

'No. You stay with Inspector Timberlake.' Larkin glowed with pleasure.

'Odd, that,' Timberlake said reflectively. 'The position of the head when he was shot. Looks like the killer took Pusey by surprise – pushed his head forward against the dashboard and then put the gun to his head. Very professional.'

The scientist dealing with the Charles Pusey shooting was Bert Petch, a man with much extra weight but little hair and a nose that looked as if could be used as bradawl. He had a quiet voice and a permanently depressed air, largely due to the fact he was acutely aware that his field of expertise was in instruments that caused death and destruction.

'Interesting case, yours,' he told Timberlake. He went to a cupboard with a number of small drawers and took out a bullet in a labelled plastic bag, which he held up for them all to see. 'This is the bullet that killed him. Hardly deformed at all. According to the SOCOs, it went into the lower part of the dashboard, through the thick sound-proofing material and ended up in the rubber hoses of the air conditioning.'

'What sort of gun was it?' asked Timberlake. Bert Petch ignored the question. Like Professor Mortimer, he was going to give his little lecture first.

'As you can see, it is a metal-cased bullet, and allowing for loss from impact, weighs 265 grains. The base diameter is .457 inches.'

'A forty-five?' Timberlake said, surprised.

'A point four five *five*. This bullet was fired from a gun with rifling that had five lands and a right-hand twist with one turn in 20 inches.'

'It had a 20-inch barrel?' Webb asked in disbelief.

'Of course not,' Petch said testily. 'It was just over six inches long, which means that the twist was about 115 degrees.'

'Ah,' Webb replied.

Nigel Larkin was making a forward spiral movement with his right index finger. 'Sir, what is a land?' he asked politely.

'Rifled firearms have grooves cut into the barrel to make the bullet spin so that it continues in a straight course and doesn't tumble – turn end over end. The raised parts of this rifling are the lands, the spaces between them are the grooves. As I'm sure you know, in addition to marks left by the lands, there are minute irregularities in barrels which leave striations on the bullet which are as individual to each gun as fingerprints. I can tell you that we have not seen a bullet from this gun before.'

'That was quick,' Timberlake said.

Petch was suitably modest. 'Actually, there weren't all that many of this calibre to compare with. Now, given the information on the weight and calibre of the bullet and the rifling of the barrel, the identification of the make of the weapon this came from was simple.' He paused.

Just like bloody Mortimer, Timberlake thought; he wants his moment of drama.

'This was fired from a Webley revolver. In the armed forces it was listed as Pistol, Revolver No. 1 Mark VI, .455 inch.'

'Major Lock,' Timberlake and Webb said in unison.

Chapter 11

In the enquiry into the murder of Charles Pusey the normally mind-numbing, foot-aching routine job of house-to-house interviewing of local residents was not as extensive as usual, for which the uniformed policemen were grateful. Because of the local geography, the non-square Willow Square had only a dozen or so houses, and they had no direct view of Towers Hall or its gates. So asking the neighbours if they had seen or heard anything – any strange people or strange cars – on the night of the murder, or any suspicious people hanging around the exterior of Towers Hall recently, did not take long.

While the uniforms were ringing doorbells, Harry Timberlake and Darren Webb called on the main – the only – potential suspect, Major Gavin Lock.

He was dressed in cavalry twill trousers, leather-patched sports jacket, check shirt and what was clearly a regimental tie. His voice was not loud, but he spoke precisely, articulating his words carefully except for the final 'g' in words ending in 'ing'. Timberlake thought it was a carefully calculated affectation. With a shock he was suddenly aware of what Lock reminded him of: a pike.

The detectives were shown into what Lock called his den, which had dark green walls and heavy voile curtains that combined to give the impression of being under water, an effect which unnervingly emphasized Lock's resemblance to a pike.

The furniture was army officers' mess ante-room style, including a pair of leather armchairs which could have been built by a designer of heavy tanks. Between them the chairs must have cost the slaughter of a small herd of cows. There were some pictures, most of them unremarkable: a couple of group photographs of officers sitting at attention in front of an anonymous building, some engravings of eighteenth-century London, two or three water colours.

One picture, however, stood out. It was a well-executed portrait in oils of a strawberry-blonde girl of sixteen years old or so, sitting by a window. She was pretty, and more than that, for she had an unmistakably sensual upper lip. Her whole being shouted sexual precocity: it was easy to see why Charles Pusey had been attracted to her, and why she had become his lover.

Lock waved to the two men to sit in the armchairs. He remained standing, his legs apart and his hands clasped behind his back in the regulation stand-at-ease position. He appeared poised to shout 'Shun!' at the two detectives and snap to attention himself. He stood motionless, waiting for Timberlake or Webb to speak first, probably hoping it would put them slightly off balance. The ploy failed.

'I take it you have heard of the murder at Towers Hall of a man believed to be Charles Pusey?' Timberlake said firmly.

'Yes. I do not suppose you expect me to say I was angry to hear it. My only regret is that I did not do it.'

Timberlake let this pass. It could be bravado, or a smart bluff: pretending to be frank to conceal a lie. 'Can you tell me where you were between the hours of 8 p.m. last night and 2 a.m. this morning?'

'I was here, at home. I retired at about ten-thirty and woke up at about five-thirty.'

'Was anyone here with you?'

'No.'

'Did you make any telephone calls during that time? Or receive any?'

'No.'

'Did anyone call?'

'No.'

So Lock couldn't prove what he claimed. He didn't have to: there was no way Timberlake could disprove it, either.

Timberlake felt he was attacking a brick wall with tennis balls. He decided to change tack. 'Do you possess a .455 Webley revolver?'

'I own several pistols and revolvers, but not a .455 Webley.'

Timberlake left the question of firearms certificates for the moment. 'Will you show them to us, please?'

Major Lock came to attention and went to a cupboard fitted into a wall. He took a key wallet from his pocket and opened the cupboard. The two detectives could see that the inside of the door had a steel lining.

Hanging on hooks were at least a dozen hand-guns.

Timberlake prised himself out of the armchair, which squeaked loudly as leather rubbed against leather. Webb joined him at the cabinet.

The pistols and revolvers included a Beretta 9mm Parabellum M1951, the best Italian high-powered automatic, which is also used by the Israeli services, and a Steyr 9mm automatic, a famous Austrian weapon. 'One of the most powerful automatics in existence,' Lock explained, 'but it has the disadvantage of a thinnish barrel which is inclined to split at the end.'

There was a Smith & Wesson .32 revolver, a regulation US police weapon, and a 9mm Luger Standard Army automatic with its almost unique design. As Timberlake inspected the weapon Lock said, 'It's not a genuine German-manufactured one: very similar in appearance, but it was one of those made in Spain, probably Guernica or Eibar, for the South American and Chinese markets. If you examine it closely you'll see there's moveable metal plate on the left side used to clean and oil the mechanism. The German version doesn't have it.' For the first time he sounded almost animated.

Webb unhooked a massive revolver which almost could have passed for a small cannon that had lost its wheels.

'Gasser, 11.75mm,' Lock explained. 'Weighs some five pounds. Made in Belgium, designed for the Montenegrin government, but a lot were sold to Balkan and South American countries. Not the biggest revolver, though. Belgium and Germany used to make 15mm cartridges – that's nearly .6 inches – for revolvers that were used on the Argentinian pampas, for some reason. I'm trying to get one.'

These guns, and the others in the cupboard, all had one thing in common. The firing pins had been removed, and the barrels were blocked. They *could* be made to fire, but it would take expert work in a proper arms workshop to modify them. And they were all the wrong calibre.

'Our records show that you have been given a firearms certificate for a Smith & Wesson .22 LR,' Timberlake said. 'I don't see it here.'

Without a word Lock produced a key from his pocket and

73

opened a heavy-duty metal box set in the wall at the back of the cupboard. He took out a long-barrelled revolver, broke it open to check that it was unloaded, and passed it, butt first, to Timberlake. 'As you may know, I am a member of the Carapace Gun and Rifle Club. This is my target-shooting pistol.' He took his firearms certificate from the box. The details on it matched up with the weapon. This could not have been the murder gun either.

'If he could get all those other guns, bunged-up barrels or not, it's a pound to a pinch of snuff he could have got the gun that killed Pusey,' Webb said grumpily as they left. 'That's if he didn't nick the thing when he was in the army. He's certainly got a thing for guns.'

'You know, guns are supposed to be phallic symbols,' Timberlake said.

'Yeah, I read that somewhere, too. Phallic *substitutes*. Big gun, little—'

'Indeed,' Timberlake cut him short. 'Get Nigel Larkin to check with the gun club and our own records to see if anyone is registered as owning a .455 Webley. And have Peggy compile a list of everyone local who's been involved with illegal possession of firearms, convicted or suspected.'

'And he's got no alibi,' Webb went on. He thought for a moment. 'That could be a crafty move. Since that last case with the German,* guv, I believe in the tooth fairy more than I do in alibis.'

Timberlake was also thoughtful. 'Character: that's one of the best indications to behaviour you can get. And I don't believe Lock would have shot Pusey in the back of the head like that.'

'It *was* an execution shot, guv.'

'Yes, but I think he would have shot Pusey face to face. He calls himself "Major". He'd be the officer – even if he is no gentleman – not a Mafia hit man. More than that, if he did it – *if* – I'm sure he would have wanted Pusey to know who it was and why.'

'Well, if he didn't do it, we're up a gum tree without a paddle,' Webb said morosely.

'You're right,' Timberlake conceded. 'In a manner of speaking.'

Farmer and Sarah Lewis knew PC Pegg would come up with a

*See *Elimination*, the second Harry Timberlake story.

comprehensive list of sexual offenders, but his list turned out to be encyclopaedic. It had convicted and suspected rapists, paedophiles, nickers of ladies' knickers from washing lines, gropers, flashers, telephone heavy breathers, senders of very rude letters to well-known women suggesting all sorts of sexual athletics, most of them physically impossible, and enthusiasts of strange and ingenious perversions.

Prominent members of the *Sad Mac** also figured on PC Pegg's list, together with a couple of doctors and one dentist who were strongly suspected of extending their examinations well beyond the area of their patients' disorders.

Bob Farmer looked at the extensive list with disfavour, then passed it to Sarah Lewis. 'Hell's bells,' she said. 'Looking at this you'd think nobody on this patch goes in for straightforward, honest-to-goodness humping.' She regretted it before the last few words were out of her mouth.

'Oh, I shouldn't say that,' Farmer said. He'd never got over seeing Errol Flynn in his youth, and he gave a smile that was meant to be worldly-wise and slightly daring, but came out as nakedly lecherous. Sarah buttoned her lip.

Farmer vainly waited a moment for a reaction, then added rather grumpily, 'Go through it and make out a list of the top ten possibles.' Perhaps she really is a dike, he thought, and she hasn't been having it off with HT after all.

'We'll start on interviews tomorrow,' he concluded.

*See *Vengeance*, the first Harry Timberlake story.

Chapter 12

'Major Lock didn't kill him, sir, I'm sure of that,' Harry Timberlake told Harkness at the next meeting of the murder squad. Also there were Webb, Braddock the bagman, Nigel Larkin, at the meeting principally to learn, and a couple of detective-constable foot soldiers.

'*Really* sure?'

'Sure enough.' Timberlake rubbed his nose reflectively.

'So what now, Harry?'

Timberlake sighed. He hesitated.

'Go on.'

'I hate to suggest it, but more and more I'm beginning to think that the answer isn't here, but in Saint-Rémy-de-Provence, near where the family were living. The murder wasn't a spur of the moment thing, I'm sure. It was premeditated, and for a motive which was born some time ago, which puts it in France.'

'Before we consider that, what are our present options?' Harkness asked rhetorically. 'As we've said, it *could* be a simple opportunist robbery.' He didn't believe it himself; he was just testing the strength of the theory.

'It's asking a lot of coincidence: someone passing Willow Square at the crucial moment and being observant enough to see Pusey's car there. The panda crew nearly missed it, and they were keeping their eyes open,' Timberlake pointed out.

'Well, there's still the revenge scenario,' Webb said.

'Someone saw the paragraph in the local rag about Pusey coming back and waited all day and half the night for him to turn up?'

'Yeh, not very likely, guv,' Webb said, crestfallen.

'And on top of all that you have to believe in fifteen-year-old vengeance, which I don't.'

'What about the Jews and war criminals fifty years on?' said Braddock, who was sitting quietly in a corner.

'That was on a different scale,' Timberlake replied rather tartly. 'What I don't understand is the paradox of the way Pusey was killed. The actual shot, to the back of the skull like that, was like a professional's killing, an execution. But a pro uses a .22, not a thumping great cannon, and fires two or three shots.'

'Perhaps it wasn't meant as an execution,' Harkness suggested. 'The site of the wound could be a coincidence.'

'Don't think so, sir,' Timberlake said. 'It was a hard contact, the muzzle pressed up against the back of the head. The murderer meant it as an execution all right.'

'Then we're back to the opportunist theft,' Braddock said heavily. 'The car was cleared out, remember. And his pockets were rifled.'

'It's still too many coincidences,' Timberlake insisted.

'Not impossible, though,' Braddock said defensively.

Nigel Larkin nervously cleared his throat. 'Could it possibly be drugs related, by any chance?'

There was a heavy silence, and Larkin did a marvellous impersonation of a beetroot.

'Oh, hell. Why didn't I think of it?' Timberlake said wearily. 'Good for you, Nigel.' He kept to himself any thoughts of 'out of the mouths of babes and sucklings'.

'I suppose he might have been a mule,' Timberlake continued, 'bringing in a load of stuff, meeting his customers by appointment in a quiet cul-de-sac, and they killed so they didn't have to pay him. If the forensic laboratory finds traces of drugs anywhere in the car that'll open a lot of cans of worms.'

The prospect of what that scenario would involve filled them with gloom. The ramifications could be enormous.

'I'll check with the Customs and Excise Investigation Division, see if they have anything on Pusey,' Harkness said eventually. 'Darren, you contact the drugs unit at the Yard before they close it down.'

'On second thoughts,' Timberlake said, 'I think the drug angle's a possibility, but not a probability. Pusey certainly didn't need money, and he didn't come from one of the major drugs distribution areas.'

'Nevertheless, it's a line we need to follow,' Harkness said. He looked at Nigel Larkin. 'Well done.' He always tried to encourage officers to put up ideas. Larkin looked as if the Queen had just touched him on the shoulder with a sword.

'If you think it's worthwhile, sir, I'll have another go at the solicitor, Mellick,' Timberlake said. 'He may be able to come up with something. I think he knows more than he's telling us.'

'Exercising his right of silence,' said Webb, trying to be mildly humorous, and failing miserably.

'After you've seen him, why don't you have another go at the family?' Harkness said as if it were a suggestion rather than a directive.

'I've had a pretty fair try there, sir,' Timberlake said. 'They don't seem to know anything.'

'Maybe they *do* know something, but don't know that they know it. See if you can dig it out.'

If it's there, Timberlake thought, keeping the gloomy thought to himself.

'If there are no traces of drugs in the car and if the solicitor and the family don't give us anything new, then we'll consider the Saint-Rémy-de-Provence option. If you go, what will you do there?'

'Get Commissaire Stanghelli* in Marseilles to give me an introduction to the captain of the local gendarmerie. Saint-Rémy-de-Provence is in the same *département* – county – Bouches-du-Rhône as Marseilles. Gendarmes know their own patch and the people in it as well as, if not better than, we do,' Timberlake went on. 'There are precious few secrets in a French rural community. They'll be able to tell me all about Pusey and the de Gaillmonts, and any enemies they had.'

Harkness reflected for a moment. 'Well, we're not getting very far here, I'm afraid, that much is certain. How long would you need?'

'Three or four days, maximum, sir.'

'All right, Harry. *If* you go, I hope we can justify the expense. That's all for today, unless anyone—?'

No one had anything to offer.

Sarah had absolutely detested her day. She and Bob Farmer had

*See *Elimination*, the second Harry Timberlake story.

interviewed three rape suspects during the day; the ones on the top of the list PC Pegg had compiled. The interviews had made her feel grubby.

The first was a thirty-five-year-old victim of a father's weird sense of humour. His name was Ivor Pain, and the jibes he must have suffered as boy and man would have been enough to warp anyone's character. He lived not far from the scene of the rape, in a one-bedroom flat. Any surface of the furniture that didn't have a layer of dust had one of grease, or a mixture of both. When he opened the door to Farmer and Sarah, he was wearing a torn singlet whose original colour was impossible to guess, and pyjama trousers. He had a face like a badly formed boiled potato.

Pain had served one term of imprisonment for indecent assault. Sarah sometimes wondered what a decent assault would consist of. He was now living on social security, and most of the money seemed to be spent on top-shelf magazines. Sarah had a strong unprofessional hope they would have grounds to take him back to the Terrace Vale nick for some intensive questioning. Fortunately for Pain, he had an alibi. When he consulted a cheap calendar with scrawled pencil notes on it he was able to say that he was being visited by his probation officer. 'He told me I ought to clean the place up a bit,' Pain said, a little aggrieved.

'Some people are fussy,' Farmer said in a rare venture into irony.

Next on the list was Perry Wilmot, an attendant of a private car-park on a the site of a demolished factory. Wilmot had served seven years for the rape of a prostitute. He was a forty-year-old crop-haired bully-boy with a sagging belly hanging over the waistband of his trousers. He stank of beer and cigarettes at ten yards, even in the open air. He claimed to have been in a pub with a group of mates, watching a football match on satellite television. He gave the name of the pub, the landlord, and some of the people he was with.

The detectives reluctantly believed him. Sarah was virtually certain he wasn't Emma Leyland's rapist. If he had been, she most probably would have mentioned his size and accent, and very possibly his smell.

Those first two disgusted Sarah. The third suspect, a television repair engineer named Hubert Franklyn, gave her the creeps. They interviewed him at the workshops of the TV rental company who employed him. Franklyn was soft-voiced, soft-handed, and moved

79

like a snake. It was his eyes that rattled Sarah. They were very light-coloured, and dead. Dead as a week-old Moray eel.

He had been charged with the rape of a sixteen-year-old girl, who identified him to the police. At the last moment she refused to give evidence against him, and he was discharged.

'It's not the first time you lot have accused me of something I didn't do. Because of that silly little hysterical bitch, I suppose I've got to expect it. And – don't tell me – you're just doing your job. I suppose it'll affect me for the rest of my life.'

'What you did to the girl will affect her for the rest of her life,' Sarah said fiercely.

Franklyn didn't bluster or protest; he gave a cruel, sly smile. 'You've forgotten I was tried and found innocent,' he said.

'You weren't tried,' Farmer said.

'And you weren't found innocent. You just weren't found guilty,' Sarah added.

Whatever else he may have done, Wilmot wasn't guilty of Emma Leyland's rape. He produced his log-book of calls he had made on the day of the rape, with addresses, times and signatures of the customers whose sets he had repaired.

'I felt as if I'd turned over some enormous great, wet stone,' Sarah told Julian Tabard later that evening. They were having dinner in what would have been a ruinously expensive restaurant for her. She was wearing a model dress that had been sent to his studio for glossy advertising photographs, and he had borrowed it for her. She looked stunning.

'You really should leave the Bill,' he said with a smile. 'I'm going to do a shoot in the West Indies soon. Why don't you hand in your truncheon and come with me? Sea, sunshine, no flat stones to turn over.'

'I'm not really sure why I'm hesitating,' she admitted. 'You know how I feel about you.' She shrugged. 'Maybe because I was brought up in a Welsh Calvinist community where it's a sin not to work.'

'The offer's always open. Being a policewoman's no life for you.'

'I'm a *detective*,' Sarah said quickly. Her instinctive reaction made her think it *was* the life for her. She looked across at Julian, handsome, self-assured, successful . . . and gentle and loving with her. Then she caught a glimpse of her own reflection in one of the restaurant's enormous mirrors: sitting at the rich table in a stunning gown, her hair done by the hairdressers who took care of Julian's models, her eyes bright . . . and she wasn't sure after all.

Perhaps it was an evening for doubts. Harry Timberlake had picked up Jenny Long in a mini-cab and taken her to the Thameside restaurant they'd been to on their very first outing together, in the period before their temporary breakup. He didn't think the choice of that place had any particular significance. The restaurant could boast neither stars nor crossed knives and forks symbols in any reference books, but the food was always excellent, which was reason enough, he told himself.

They argued half-heartedly on the way there, because Jenny said she would pay for the meal this time. Timberlake had many working-class, old-fashioned attitudes that bordered on the Victorian. It was ingrained in him that the man *always* paid. This was a bad mistake, as he realized half a second too late: the words were already echoing on the air.

She pointed out that this wasn't fair or logical, which he had to admit to himself. She was probably earning more than he was – she had a considerable private practice as well as working for the NHS – and they were both unattached, independent persons.

That was *her* mistake. Fifteen-all.

Timberlake said he thought they *were* attached, sentimentally at the very least. His mistake. It conjured up the word 'marriage', which hovered in the air before them like Macbeth's floating dagger. Fifteen-thirty.

This small spat rattled him. He and Jenny had argued over minor things before, but there was, he felt, a new, harder element in this one. Briefly he wondered whether he had gone back to Jenny only because Sarah had found someone else. Was Jenny simply a second-choice replacement?

The meal had a calming effect on them both. The food was uncomplicated, but verging on the superb: grilled sole on the bone, then *noyeaux d'agneau* with artichoke hearts, *petits pois* and new potatoes, and lemon sorbet for pudding. Neither of them found any symbolism in the fact that they both chose exactly the same dishes. Gradually a mild euphoria, tinged with a certain civilized lasciviousness, overcame them. The wines – Pouilly Fuissé and

81

Morgon – and Rémy Martin brandy helped to get them to holding hands across the table.

The evening teetered on the brink of disaster briefly when they had to decide in whose home they would spend the night. Harry Timberlake reckoned he'd won the who-would-pay argument, so he gave in and agreed to go to Jenny's place. This put her in a good mood, and the sex was as good as he'd ever had with her. Intelligent and intuitive as Jenny was, though, she could make mistakes, and she made one right now. Before he had completely recovered from the *post coitus tristus*, she 'casually' wondered whether it wasn't a waste of money for them to keep two homes on the go.

It immediately released Timberlake's private dark genie from its bottle. Why the hell the thought of marriage – because that was what Jenny was aiming at – so panicked him he could never understand, and he couldn't help recalling that Sarah had never suggested anything like that. He conveniently forgot their situation was very different.

Once again, notwithstanding the wine and sexual exercise, it was a long time before he got to sleep. And he wondered again about Sarah.

Timberlake was surprised to find Towers Hall as busy as if a commanding general was due to make an inspection. The cleaning, polishing and general tarting up stopped short only of painting immovable objects white. Thérèse Chardet, who greeted Timberlake, went through the ritual of announcing that Madame la Comtesse would be pleased to receive Inspector Timberlake in a few moments.

Chardet told him the activity in the house was because they were expecting the arrival of Princess Caterina Tozharska, who was Jean-Louis de Gaillmont's fiancée, in the next week or so. Timberlake was pretty sure that Sophie de Gaillmont would explain everything about Caterina Tozharska and her right to be called princess. It was the sort of thing she would be unable to resist. In the meantime, while waiting for the silent fanfare of trumpets that always preceded the entry of Madame la Comtesse he would interview Thérèse Chardet. Maybe she would be less guarded away from the intimidating presence of her employer.

Chardet's attitude towards the late Charles Pusey was curiously ambivalent, Timberlake found. Although on the one hand she appeared to be trying to conceal her feelings towards him – or at least minimize them – she obviously had been warmly disposed towards him, even infatuated, perhaps. On the other hand, any sadness she showed at the thought of his death was a seeming afterthought. As far as providing Timberlake with any sort of lead to a suspect or a motive was concerned, she was as useful to him as a road map of Uttar Pradesh.

Madame la Comtesse de Gaillmont entered peremptorily and surveyed the room like a surgeon looking for a bacillus. She appeared to be satisfied with what she saw.

'I understand that your stepson's fiancée is expected any time now,' Timberlake opened the conversation.

'Monsieur le Comte's fiancée, yes,' Sophie de Gaillmont corrected him. She went on to give the princess's CV and pedigree as if she were being entered for Cruft's.

Of course, Caterina Tozharska was a genuine pre-Russian Revolution princess, Sophie told him. This briefly startled Timberlake, who took 'genuine' to mean that Jean-Louis de Gaillmont's fiancée must be roughly ninety-five years old. He quickly realized that Sophie meant the Tozharska *family* was genuine pre-Revolution nobility. She also made it plain that Monsieur le Comte Jean-Louis de Gaillmont could not marry just anyone, but Caterina's mother was French and Caterina had lived all her life in France, so apparently that was all right. And she was a princess, after all.

'The princess is of a military family. Her father, grandfather and great-grandfather were generals in Russia,' Sophie went on. Timberlake was able to resist the temptation to ask if any of them knew Stalin personally. At last permitting herself the familiarity of using the Christian name, Sophie de Gaillmont went on relentlessly, 'Despite her rank, Caterina decided to take up a career.' She gave an indulgent smile. Timberlake's main two thoughts were that the remark was a laboured, hypocritical meiosis, and Sophie de Gaillmont was the biggest snob he had ever met or heard of. 'She has been away for some time following the family tradition,' Sophie de Gaillmont ended.

This really surprised Timberlake. He wondered what army Caterina Tozharska could be fighting with, and as what.

'She is now a physician of some small reputation, and has been working with the Médecins sans Frontières during the Bosnian and Rwanda conflicts. Medicine is, after all, a profession, and *noblesse oblige*.' She said this with a straight-faced haughty superiority.

Well, at least there would be one non-phoney in the family, Timberlake thought. At last he managed to get a few plebeian words in edgewise, to cover the same ground they had been over before, but there was nothing more to be harvested. He asked to see Monsieur Jean-Louis de Gaillmont.

'Monsieur le Comte is not at home. He is visiting our bankers in town.'

Timberlake was on the point of asking when Jean-Louis would return when a thought struck him with some force, driving the question from his mind. Whenever he mentioned Charles Pusey, his mother showed no more sense of sadness or loss than Thérèse Chardet had done earlier. Sophie de Gaillmont had proved herself to be capable of an iron self-control, concealing almost completely from everyone her emotions. Now her reserve – or indifference? – was too real to be acting.

Was there a dark side to Charles Pusey that had been kept secret within the family? Was the motive for his murder to make sure he was buried with his personal skeleton in the cupboard?

Chapter 13

Sarah Lewis should have known better than to become emotionally involved in a case, but her sense of outrage at Emma Leyland's rape would not go away. It made the lack of success that she and Bob Farmer had experienced all the more galling. Emma had been courageous enough to report the attack on her when a lot of women would feel too ashamed or frightened, Sarah pointed out, and, 'We've let her down. We've done sod-all towards helping her by catching the bastard who raped her,' she fumed.

'Early days,' Farmer said smoothly, as if humouring a fractious child – which only made Sarah angrier. She stamped off to her desk to write up another negative report. 'Sarah,' Farmer called after her. 'We've still got a couple of names on our list.' She was too disgruntled to reply.

'Look,' Farmer said, changing mode. The tone of just that one word was enough to set Sarah's alarm bells ringing. 'If you're feeling a bit down, come and have a drink, cheer yourself up a bit.'

When put to it, Sarah could be as hypocritical as a politician who sold second-hand cars. 'Thanks very much, guv,' she said. 'That's very decent of you.' Farmer was like a parched traveller crossing a desert who at last could see an oasis on the horizon. 'But I'm really not up to it. I'd only make you bloody depressed. No thanks. Really.' Farmer's oasis shimmered gently, and disappeared. It was only a mirage after all.

Sharon couldn't have been more obvious if she had been carrying a banner. She was wearing heels so high that her feet were practically in the ballet dancer's position for dancing on the blocks of her ballet shoes. Her shorts barely deserved the name, for the last third of the cheeks of her bottom were visible below them. She was not wearing tights because they take too long to take off and put on again and can get laddered too easily. Her midriff was bare between the low top of the shorts and the bottom of a strapless bra-like garment which pushed her breasts up and together. A long fur like a hairy boa-constrictor was round the back of her neck and under her armpits, carefully arranged so that all of her trading assets were visible.

She had a full mouth with too much lipglow, and behind her dark glasses she had false eyelashes like Barbara Cartland's, and a bruised eye which had gone from dark purple, through blue to its present nasty shade of green.

Just in case there was someone naive enough not to read the strident signs, she was smoking a cigarette and standing just in front of a well-lit shop doorway.

The man parked his car, carefully locked it and walked the fifty yards to the corner, rounded it and approached her.

She knew him at once. 'Oh, hello, darling,' she said. 'Have you come for business?'

He nodded, and without saying any more they moved along the road to a plain door between two shop fronts. Inside a flight of stairs led up to a landing with three doors. Before they arrived at the top one of the doors opened. A woman who looked as if she lived on a diet of steroid sandwiches appeared in the doorway.

'It's all right, Petal, it's a mate,' Sharon explained. The female Odd-Job gave what was meant to be a friendly smile and withdrew. Sharon took her companion into her place of work. It had a bed, a couple of easy chairs, a bedside cabinet with a drawer, a small flip-top waste bin and a washbasin. Behind another door was a loo. Air freshener had not overcome the smell of stale tobacco, sweat, cheap scent and lust.

Sharon sat on the bed with a sigh of relief, letting her long fur trail on the floor behind her. 'My sodding feet,' she said, kicking off her shoes. She reached round behind her back, unhooked the top half of her skimpy costume and dropped it on the bed. Sharon sighed with greater relief, and rubbed the red lines under her breasts and round her ribs where the garment had dug into the flesh.

'Well, what about it?' she asked. 'What do you want this time?'

Darren Webb said, 'You know me. Guess.' He studied her for a moment.

Sharon laughed. 'I know that look. "What's a girl like me doing being a brass? How did I get on the game?" '

'Not really. How's Eddie?'

'Haven't been to see him for a while. I mean, it takes ages to go to the island.' The island was the slang name for Parkhurst Prison on the Isle of Wight.

'Does he know what you're doing?'

'He doesn't reckon I'm wearing a chastity belt, that's for sure. Anyway, I don't give a toss. Eventually I'm going to pack it in here and go and live with an aunt up in—' She checked. 'Well, never mind where.'

Webb nodded. 'Well, d'you know anyone local with a big shooter?' Sharon laughed dirtily. 'You know what I mean,' Webb said wearily. 'A big gun, like an old army revolver.'

She shook her head. 'Some of the dealers carry, but mostly small stuff, automatics. Easy to hide in a pocket. Leroy the Stick is reckoned to have a couple of shooters at his club. I've seen one. It was about this big.' She held her hands about four or five inches apart.

'Uhuh. Have you heard of any big deliveries recently?'

'Of what?'

He shrugged. 'Anything. Coke, crack or shit probably. Maybe E or speed.'

She laughed derisively. 'What about aspirin?'

Webb remained patient. 'Is there a lot of new stuff suddenly on the street, cheap?'

'No such luck.'

'You ought to stay off it, Sharon.'

'I only smoke a joint or two. I keep off the really hard stuff; no crack or coke.' She paused. 'Want a freebie? I wouldn't mind enjoying it for once.'

Darren Webb shook his head. 'I don't mix business with pleasure.'

She laughed. 'It *is* my business.'

For a long, long moment he hesitated before getting up. Sharon swung her legs up on to the bed, and pulled down the zip on the front of her shorts, but Webb walked straight to the door. 'If you hear anything, give me a ring. It'll be worth something for you.'

'Sure.' She gave him a look which could have been of genuine longing, but he went out.

'Fuck you, Darren Webb,' she said to the closed door, more in hope than anger.

Naomi Webb was born in Streatham, but, as her husband Darren often remarked, it wasn't her fault. She left school at sixteen and somehow got a job selling programmes in a West End theatre. She was obsessed with the stage and volunteered to be an unpaid gofer for The Capitouls, which was probably the highest-standard amateur theatre in London. She swept the stage, sold tickets, repaired costumes, helped the electrician, assisted the ASM, prompted on occasion, and had brief affairs with a sad-looking, bearded playwright and a TV actor who deigned to come and direct the amateurs. She even had a couple of walk-on parts, but never, ever, with a single line to deliver.

It took her a long time to realize that she would never be an actress. It didn't dim her enthusiasm for the theatre, but it gave her more time to live a normal life. She got a better job in the advertising sales department of a TV company. Well, it was show business.

She met Darren Webb at a wedding. He was a friend of the groom, the bride was one of The Capitouls. Darren and Naomi married within three months, and didn't regret a moment of it for five years. When Darren became a detective, and then a sergeant, the marriage came under increasing strain. It would have been remarkable if it hadn't, the detective's professional life being what it is. Once in a while she managed to get Darren to go to the theatre with her, but even when she booked tickets, he frequently had to cry off at the last moment, leaving her to go on her own and sell the spare ticket back to the box office. The few times he did go, he usually fell asleep.

When Darren walked in after his meeting with Sharon she greeted him with 'Your dinner's cold. I'll heat it up in the micro-wave.' They did not kiss. As he walked past her she sniffed. 'Where have you been?'

'Working.'

'You smell of cheap scent.'

'I didn't take the car. I probably got it from a woman in the tube.'

'Hmmm.'

How Naomi managed to get so much meaning into a single

syllable that had no vowel in it was something only jealous women can manage. If she could have done it to order on the stage she would have had Maggie Smith coming round for lessons.

While Darren ate in silence, Naomi carried on reading John Gielgud's autobiography. They didn't speak.

The first of the names left on Farmer's and Sarah's list was Ross Wightman. According to a local report Wightman was arrested seven years previously and charged with attempted rape, alternatively indecent assault, of a young woman in the Norwich area. However, the case had not got as far as a crown court. Wightman had engaged an expensive QC, who cross-examined the woman so effectively at the magistrate's court that it seemed to everyone that she was fabricating the whole incident. Everyone assumed it was a fairly common story of a woman in a fit of alcoholic enthusiasm who had consented to sex with a near stranger, then, racked with guilt, had explained away her lapse by telling her boyfriend she had been raped.

The magistrate threw out the charge without calling on the defence to present a case. He had some hard words to say to the alleged victim, and muttered something about sending the papers to the Director of Public Prosecutions – it was before the establishment of the Crown Prosecution Service – although that came to nothing.

According to the local police the case was weighted against the woman before it started. The magistrate was a well-known local poophead. In the words of the inspector who arrested Wightman, the magistrate was so stupid he wouldn't piss if his trousers were on fire. He was actually heard to say publicly that a man who took a woman to dinner had the right to expect the use of her body. It was such an outrageous opinion that many people couldn't believe he'd actually voiced it.

Wightman's home was in Terrace Vale at the time: he was spending a couple of days in Norfolk on business. It meant that incident went almost unnoticed in Terrace Vale, but it didn't escape Brian Pegg's hoover-like collecting of intelligence.

Sarah rang Wightman's home to find out where he worked. His wife answered and said he always came home for lunch at one o'clock. Sarah, sounding offhand and casual, said she would call on him during his lunch time. When Mrs Wightman asked what it was all about, Sarah used the old formula, worn paper-thin, that it was just routine. She hung up before Mrs Wightman could ask anything more.

At a quarter to one Sarah and Farmer arrived at the Wightmans' three-bedroom semi in Montgomery Crescent, near Alexander Place and Eisenhower Gardens, names which firmly established the age of the small estate. Mrs Anthea Wightman was about thirty-five years old, of medium height, with mid-brown hair cut moderately short in a Louise Brooks style that suited her. She wore a plain shirt and jeans. The general impression she gave was of a woman in a TV commercial for a kitchen cleaner. The table in the neat sitting-room/dining-room was set for two people.

At first Mrs Wightman was apprehensive at being confronted by two detectives, but Sarah's manner swiftly put her at her ease. They deflected her questions by repeating the 'just routine' cliché, and by asking about her husband.

Perhaps without fully comprehending how much she was giving away, Anthea Wightman explained that he worked for a firm of solicitors as a sort of superior debt-collector. Apparently he sent acid-tinged letters that bordered on demanding money with menaces, and visited debtors personally. Almost proudly she said he had the reputation at his firm for getting money from people whom others had written off as bad debtors.

They were on the point of asking her about her husband's movements on the night of Monday the eleventh when Ross Wightman walked in. He looked surprised – who wouldn't, Sarah thought – but not alarmed, even when Farmer introduced himself and Sarah as detectives.

Wightman was about forty years old, solidly built, with thinning dark hair and grey eyes. He wore a grey two-piece suit, white shirt and a club tie, and black shoes. He would have been personable had it not been for his mouth, which looked as if it had been drawn on his face with a thin pencil and ruler. It was the mouth of a man who did not know a great deal about compassion. The poverty of spirit it betrayed was underlined by what used to be called a cad's moustache, except when sported by film actors like David Niven, Errol Flynn and Gilbert Roland. On them it looked good. All it did for Wightman was make him look even more thin-lipped and mean. Whether his job of putting the screws on unfortunates gave him his Scrooge-like aspect, or whether the character revealed by his face made him particularly suited for that sort of work was a matter for speculation.

'How can I help you?' he asked. Before the detectives could say anything he added, 'Do you mind if I eat while we talk? I don't get very long for lunch.'

'It's a routine enquiry,' Farmer began equably, managing to make it sound as if he'd rarely asked the question before. 'Would you mind telling me where you were between seven-thirty and nine-thirty the Monday before last?'

'Why?' There was just the slightest edge in Wightman's question.

'Routine,' Farmer repeated, with an unconvincing smile.

'I'm sorry, inspector, but that's just not good enough,' Wightman said with a politeness that was as unconvincing as Farmer's smile. 'You come to my house while I'm out and then question me as if I was suspected of something. As a matter of courtesy you should tell me what the enquiry is about. Otherwise—' He took a mouthful of food.

Farmer couldn't disguise his irritation. He nodded to Sarah.

'A young woman was raped not far from here and—'

Both Ross and Anthea Wightman spoke at once.

'My husband wouldn't dream—!'

'All right, Anthea. I'll deal with it.'

'Why are you asking Ross? He—'

'Anthea!' He was much sharper this time. 'Why am *I* suspected? Was it someone I know?'

Sarah used a subterfuge that Harry Timberlake had invented, and had become a standard ploy at Terrace Vale. 'A witness saw a car in the vicinity but was able to get only two numbers and two letters of the registration. He wasn't too sure of the order of the numbers, so we're checking on the owners of all locally registered cars that have those letters and numbers.'

'So now will you tell us where you were between seven-thirty and nine-thirty on the night of Monday the eleventh, sir?' Farmer said formally.

Wightman smiled expansively. 'Easy. I was home. I got in just before seven-thirty, actually.' Almost apologetically he added, 'I'm a *Coronation Street* fan, to tell you the truth, and I didn't want to miss it. You can ask Anthea. We watched it together. She didn't see all of it, though. She was in and out of the kitchen doing the meal.'

Farmer was clever, but he wasn't smart. 'Oh, did you?' he said, trying to sound innocent. 'I watch it, too, but I missed that episode. What happened?'

'Oh, Bet Gilroy had a row with old whatshisname in the Rovers, and Curly was in trouble with his girlfriend.'

Farmer and Sarah looked at Mrs Wightman. She nodded. 'Yes, that's right. He was here with me.'

'You're quite sure?'

'Yes.'

'And he didn't go out again?'

'No.'

Farmer paused for a long moment, then smiled. 'Well, that's that, then. I'm sorry we troubled you.'

'It's all right,' Wightman said graciously.

Mrs Wightman saw them out, which wasn't very far to go.

Sarah didn't say a word until she and Farmer were back in their car. 'It's him. He did it,' she said, in a voice like someone walking on broken glass.

'Come off it, Sarah. He's got an alibi, and there's absolutely nothing to connect him with the rape.' Farmer spoke as if he was talking to someone not quite bright.

'He did it. I *know* it.'

'Feminine intuition?'

Farmer's tone made Sarah want to strangle him on the spot. She breathed deeply through her nose a couple of times. 'I prefer to call it gut feeling.' Farmer raised a quizzical eyebrow like Ronald Colman. Unabashed, Sarah repeated. 'I know it. He did it.'

'Bullshit,' Farmer told her.

In Montgomery Crescent Mrs Anthea Wightman turned to her husband: 'You weren't home till after nine. *Where were you?*'

The Terrace Vale nick building had an almost human quality of having its own airs and moods that changed without logic, which affected the life of the inhabitants. On this day it was in a cantankerous, surly frame of mind. In the CID office Sarah had a face like dark storm clouds over Welsh mountains, a couple of detectives were having a stupid argument about nothing in particular and Ted Greening was feeling even more spiteful than usual.

For his part, Harry Timberlake was suffering from a hangover:

not one of your throbbing head, fluttering heart and queasy stomach kind, but a hangover of the spirit. This had been induced by the reaction from the delightful, sexy and stress-free time he had passed with Jenny the previous evening. The reaction was aggravated by Detective Constable Garrison, who was bending the ear of anyone who would listen, and a few who wouldn't, with a loud, whingeing monologue about his ungrateful, nagging bitch of a wife who had just had divorce papers served on him. It soured Timberlake's memory of the previous evening, and evoked more uncertainties he had about the possibilities of his ever enjoying a permanent relationship.

His cup of bitterness had been topped up by the awareness that the investigation into the murder of Charles Pusey so far had produced a big fat zero. All detectives know only too well that the longer a murder investigation continued without any progress, the chances of catching the murderer diminished exponentially. Well, maybe not exponentially, but pretty damn quick.

Timberlake's bitter cup then ran over. Darren Webb came over to his desk with the depressed air of a basset hound with problems. 'Guv, if you go to France, any chance of me coming with you?'

'*My* coming with you,' said Timberlake, covering his surprise with one of his moments of pedantry. 'Trouble at home?' he guessed.

Webb sighed. 'At the moment, if Jesus Christ came back she'd probably give him a bollocking for not being shaved.'

Timberlake smiled sympathetically. 'Sorry. The super would never authorize it. He's not all that madly enthusiastic about me – my – going.'

'Yeh, I reckoned. Still, it was worth a try.'

As Darren Webb moved away, Timberlake wondered if there was some celestial law that said no detective could have a happy marriage.

'Where *were* you?' Anthea Wightman repeated for the dozenth time the following morning.

'You know where I was. I was here. We saw *Coronation Street* together. Otherwise how would I have known about the episode?'

'It was repeated Wednesday lunchtime.'

Wightman pinched his nose between the eyes, and sighed. 'I was with Julia Strang.'

Anthea took off quicker than a dragster. 'That fat cow I saw at the office Christmas party, chasing after you, her tits falling out of her dress? What do they call her? The office bicycle, isn't it? Good God, she's had more laid on her than a railway track! She—'

'Yes, all right! But there never was nothing like that between us. She was crying at her desk when everyone else had gone home. She'd been dumped by her boy friend, and—'

'She could have got herself another one in the train before she got home. Anything that wasn't in an iron lung would do.'

'Yes, well, I took her for a drink, and cheered her up a bit.'

'In front of everyone in the pub? That must have been a marvellous spectacle. Pity you won't be able to go back there again.'

Wightman's patience snapped. 'Look, I made a mistake. I—'

'Why didn't you give her as your alibi?'

'It was a mistake, I told you; a spur of the moment thing. If I'd told the police I was with her you might have got the wrong idea—'

'Or the right one?'

'You see! I swear to you, there's absolutely nothing between us, and there never will be. I don't want to get mixed up with a tart, especially at the office, for Christ's sake.'

'That still doesn't explain why you didn't give her for an alibi.'

Wightman got his voice under control. 'I'll say it again: it was a spur of the moment thing. I knew how you'd react, but that was only secondary. It may sound stupid, but I didn't want to admit to that smarmy detective that I was with another woman. Darling, I didn't want him sniggering about you, making snide remarks to that woman copper about us behind our backs.' He paused, approached her and looked her straight in the eyes. 'I've told you the straight truth. I made a mistake. And nothing – *nothing* – happened.'

Chapter 14

To the complete lack of surprise of everyone at Terrace Vale, the late Charles Pusey was unknown to the Customs and Excise Investigation Department, the Scotland Yard drugs squad, the US Drug Enforcement Agency, Interpol and Uncle Tom Cobley and all.

Detective Superintendent Harkness called Timberlake into the AMIP office. 'It seems you're going to have to make enquiries in Saint-Rémy-de-Provence after all,' he said poker-faced.

'I'll try to bear it bravely, sir,' Timberlake replied.

'Don't be too long,' Harkness warned.

As Timberlake left the office he did something quite rare for him: he whistled cheerfully. It was not only because he would enjoy the trip, but also because he had maintained all along that the key to the mystery of Charles Pusey's murder was not in Terrace Vale, but in Saint-Rémy-de-Provence.

Commissaire Stanghelli* was delighted to hear Timberlake on the phone 'Sacré Timberlake!' he roared. '*Qu'est-ce que je peux faire pour toi?*' 'What can I do for you?'

'I have to make enquiries at Saint-Rémy-de-Provence. Can you give me an introduction to the *capitaine de gendarmerie* there?'

'Of course! I know him well: Capitaine Réné Lapollet. A good man. I'll give him a ring. And when you've seen him, I'll meet you in Marseille and stand you the best dinner you've ever had.'

'*Vendu!*' – 'Done!' Timberlake said.

Sarah Lewis really should have asked Bob Farmer for permission to call on Mrs Wightman again, but she told herself that it was a

*See *Elimination*, the second Harry Timberlake story.

private visit and nothing to do with the rape enquiry. Like hell it wasn't. Anyway, sod what Farmer thought.

When Anthea Wightman saw Sarah at the front door she was suddenly scared. 'My husband's not in,' she said, and her eyes filled with tears.

Sarah smiled reassuringly. 'Please don't worry. It's not an official call.'

Mrs Wightman wiped her eyes on her apron. 'I'm not crying. I was doing onions.'

Sarah laughed. 'That's a relief. Actually, I was just passing on my way to the garage. I thought I'd call in and say sorry we had to bother you both yesterday. I know it upsets a lot of people to have the police coming round asking questions even when they haven't done anything.'

Anthea Wightman nodded. 'That's all right. Look, would you like a coffee? Come through to the kitchen. I always have a pot on the go during the day.'

'Nice kitchen,' Sarah said as they entered.

Anthea served two coffees and gestured to a chair.

Sarah sat, stretched out her legs and sighed. 'I'm glad of the break.'

Mrs Wightman looked at her for a moment, then said, 'Why did—? . . . No, sorry.'

'Why did I join the police? A lot of people ask me that. I don't know. It seemed a good idea at the time.'

'And now?'

'It's still a good idea,' Sarah smiled. 'At least, most of the time.' Her smile faded. 'It can be a bit frustrating when you don't get a result, like on this rape case. The young woman's being pretty brave, but—' She shook her head. 'It'll take her a long time to get over it completely. If she ever does. And she's going to be worried for a long time, wondering if it's made her HIV positive.'

Mrs Wightman looked away. 'I can imagine,' she said in a low voice.

'I don't understand rapists,' Sarah said thoughtfully. 'Well, I suppose I do. I mean, it's well known they don't do it principally for sexual pleasure, except with women they know. In other cases, rape is to do with power, with domination; it's an attack on the woman as a victim, not as a sexual object. It's aimed at *all* women, because basically the rapist hates or despises women.'

Anthea Wightman was shocked. 'Surely not.'

Sarah shrugged. 'That's what the psychiatrists say, and when you reckon what many rapists force women to do . . . God, what a cheerful subject for a coffee break.' She got up. 'I wish I could stay longer – if you'd have me,' she added with a smile. 'But I've got to get on, harassing innocent motorists, while homes are being burgled and old ladies mugged.'

Anthea Wightman was taken aback for a moment, then she smiled.

'Thanks for the coffee,' Sarah said. She left, leaving Anthea Wightman looking pensive.

Saint-Rémy-de-Provence is one of the most pleasant towns in France, with an almost ideal climate. In high summer it can be hot, but the tall, leafy trees of the boulevards provide cooling shade. The town was founded two centuries before Christ by the Greeks, then Romanized a century later. There are important remains of both civilizations at Glanum, on the outskirts, and in the town itself. Many of the modern houses have free natural water supplies from the underground aqueducts built by the Romans.

The Hôtel Mistral de Montdragon, the cloisters of the Saint-Paul-de-Mausole monastery – an asylum where Van Gogh committed himself after having cut off his ear – and other buildings date from the Renaissance. But it is not Saint-Rémy's history that makes it such an agreeable place.

Paradoxically, its attractions made Timberlake grumpy. Marseille can be a fascinating city, with its own pre-Christian history, but that was not why his visit to Marseille on the Roeder case had excited Timberlake. The town was friendly and hostile at the same time, vibrant, rough, tough and dirty with a silent threat of crime and violence that kept the blood racing. Saint-Rémy-de-Provence, on the other hand, was calm, relaxed and cultural. It was a place for leisurely contemplation. He hated being there on business, his visit spoiled by a nasty murder dominating his mind.

Capitaine Réné Lapollet had the most striking head of pure white hair that Timberlake had ever seen. His nose, by contrast, was the size, shape and hue of W. C. Fields's. Like Dr Pratt's hair, it was a feature almost impossible to keep one's eyes away from. At a first meeting, it was only after one had seen Lapollet for a few moments that one noticed that he was tall and slim, and neat as a groom at a cathedral wedding. His eyes had heavy lids, but they failed to hide the man's sharp intelligence.

'So you want to know about the de Gaillmonts and Charles Pusey,' Lapollet said after the usual Provençal greetings and handshakes had been exchanged, and drinks poured out. Timberlake took a cold, dry white wine, Lapollet almost inevitably chose pastis. 'What can I tell you here in Provence that will help you solve a murder in London?' he asked.

'Character,' Timberlake replied. 'I want to know their characters. Understanding character is the first key to the solution of a crime.'

Lapollet nodded. 'You think like a good *flic*.'

Timberlake, who was proud of his own force, didn't think being compared with a French cop was necessarily a compliment, but prudently let it pass. 'And I want to know about their enemies.'

'Oh, enemies,' Lapollet said with an extravagant gesture. 'There were enough of them. But not violent enemies. It is simply that no one liked them, any of them. They were too . . . haughty, arrogant. They kept themselves very much to themselves. It was easy enough: their château is some ten kilometres from here. They entertained very little, and almost exclusively with people from Paris.'

Saint-Rêmy-de-Provence, Timberlake realized at once, suffered from every nation's provincial paranoia and jealousy of the capital city.

'People like themselves?' Timberlake asked.

'There aren't any people quite like the de Gaillmonts,' Lapollet said. He poured himself another pastis. 'They did have some guests at the château. A couple of cardinals, no less, foreign aristocracy – two of your dukes – a Papal Nuncio and' – deprecatingly – 'a cabinet minister or two. Madame la Comtesse was a relentless fisher of titles. In fact it was a perfect modern marriage,' he went on. 'De Gaillmont needed money, she wanted a title. She had masses of it, he had one of France's most respected titles.

'The de Gaillmonts' title is genuine,' he went on. 'In France we have an *Encyclopaedia of the False Nobility*, you know. You see, anyone can add a "de" to his name – even appropriate a name and title belonging to a family that has died out. Or make up a title using the name of a war hero.' Capitaine Lapollet smiled sourly. 'In fact some of our leading citizens have done it. Those ones are the false nobility. But the de Gaillmonts are genuine; they go back to the Crusades.'

'Which explains their haughtiness and arrogance.'

'Actually, the old count wasn't too bad; in fact he was a real hero of the Resistance, which is more than can be said of most of his class. Their attitude to the *Boche* was ... Well, never mind.' He smiled. 'He was a cunning old devil. He had a favourite trick which always worked. When the Gestapo or the Milice were searching for Resistance fighters, he used to wait until they had thoroughly been through a house and found nothing, then slip inside and hide there. The Germans never thought of going back for a second look. He became a local legend.'

'Neat.' Timberlake said. 'What about his relationships with the local people?'

Lapollet chuckled. 'He had lots of those. He was something of an Errol Flynn with the women.' They show a lot of old American films on French television. 'But that second wife ... She hadn't been married five minutes before she learnt the entire family histories of the de Gaillmonts and half the true nobility. She was more royalist than the queen. Staff in uniform ... the whole packet. She raised *snobisme* to an art form. She transformed the way the château was run. The staff didn't know whether to laugh or cry. A real *ribouis*, a *gnaf,*' which were words Timberlake didn't know.

'I think I get the picture,' he said wryly.

'Charles Pusey?'

Lapollet shrugged. 'Ordinary enough. Not like Madame la Comtesse, or Jean-Louis, for that matter. Well, he didn't have a title, did he?'

'What about Pusey's relationships with women?'

'Nothing like his stepfather. He wasn't involved with anyone locally, amateur or professional. He used to go off to Paris from time to time for a few days, though. Maybe he had someone there. To be accurate, there was one *petite histoire* concerning a servant girl but it came to nothing. She left the area, went to live in Marseille.'

'How did he spend his time, apart from going to Paris? Any hobbies – hunting, shooting, fishing ... anything like that?'

'No. As far as I know, he spent most of his time doing things with electronics and computers. I don't know exactly: I'm no expert.'

'Any real enemies?' Lapollet shook his head. 'Did he get on all right with the count, his stepbrother?'

'Surprisingly well. They were more like real brothers – even grew to look like each other, like a dog and his master.'

'Who was which?'

Capitaine Lapollet laughed. 'Just a figure of speech.'

Timberlake looked thunderstruck.

'What is it?' the Frenchman asked.

'God, I'm slow! It's only just occurred to me: de Gaillmont's French registered car outside the de Gaillmont home, at night, dark, and the two men looked like each other—'

'You think someone killed the wrong man?' Lapollet said quietly.

Timberlake nodded. 'Could well be. What can you tell me about Jean-Louis de Gaillmont?'

'Very little. A quiet, rather studious young man. Very interested in French military history, the Foreign Legion and North African campaigns in particular. Bit of an Arabist.'

'He's engaged to a Russian princess.'

'Oh, yes. There's some talk of her trying to reclaim her family estates since the collapse of communism.'

'Where did they meet?'

'An embassy reception in Paris, I believe. I don't know a great deal about her. She's been out of the country a lot: she works for the Médecins sans Frontières.'

'I wonder if she has a former boyfriend somewhere?'

'A jealous lover?' Lapollet shrugged. 'There was no one like that round here. Whether there was anyone in Paris—' He left it hanging.

For another half an hour Harry Timberlake continued putting questions to the *capitaine de gendarmerie*, who was patiently co-operative; but he had little more to tell that was likely to be of any use. There was nothing left for Timberlake but to offer to take him to lunch. Capitaine Réné Lapollet looked sleepy, but his reaction in accepting was as rapid as a mongoose's.

Saint-Rémy-de-Provence is a tourist area, and it was open season on tourists. When Timberlake got the bill for lunch, he managed to read it without wincing too obviously. For all his slim figure, Lapollet had eaten like a python. Timberlake dared not think what Superintendent Harkness would say when he saw it on his expenses sheet.

After the three-hour lunch Timberlake went to see the de Gaillmont château, but it was now closed up, and the local inhabitants had nothing new to tell him of the family.

All the way back to England he pondered the possibility that Charles Pusey was murdered in mistake for Comte Jean-Louis de Gaillmont. It was not opening a can of worms as much as shaking out a sack of snakes.

Chapter 15

Ted Greening's review of the Emma Leyland rape case with the officers concerned was pathetically perfunctory. Unlike Harry Timberlake, who pursued wrong-doers with a zeal born of an Old Testament sense of retribution, more than ever Greening was concerned only with personal problems. The government plan to abolish his rank of Detective Chief Inspector, and the effect this would have on his retirement date and pension, almost totally occupied his thoughts. All he wanted to do was keep his head above water without making waves until he could turn his back on Terrace Vale forever.

Farmer and Sarah Lewis reported only elimination of suspects and no positive progress; the other plain-clothes and uniformed officers could do no better. Greening had no ideas to offer, and no encouragement. His only advice was, 'Well, keep at it.'

'He's as much use as a lead lifebelt,' Sarah breathed to herself as they quit Greening's office and left him to take another dose of his Highland medicine. 'Guv,' she said to Farmer when they were out of Greening's earshot. 'I had a thought last night.' For once Farmer was bright enough not to give his reply a sexual innuendo. Or maybe he was simply too slow.

'Yes, Sarah?'

'When we called on Wightman and his wife. Something he *didn't* say.'

'Yeah?'

'Normally, when you go to see someone who's got form, or been in trouble, they say, something like, "Just because my name's in your book—" or, "I've been straight ever since that business over that whatever—" Well, he didn't say that.'

'So?'

'I don't think his wife knows of the rape charge he got off in Norwich. He was trying to keep it from her.'

Farmer reflected for a moment. 'You may be right,' he said slightly puzzled. 'But does it get us anywhere?'

'That's the problem, guv. I can't decide whether her knowing or not will have any effect on her giving him an alibi.'

'What do you think?'

'I can put up a good argument either way.'

'Then what's the point?' Farmer asked.

'I don't really know. But I think it's something we ought to consider.'

'Look, Sarah,' he said patronizingly, 'Wightman wasn't much of a suspect to start with, and his wife backed him up to the hilt. Forget any funny ideas of feminine instinct, gut feeling or whatever you want to call it.'

Sarah bit her lip and turned away. But Wightman bloody did it! He raped her! she shouted, silently. She briefly fantasized of kebab-ing Farmer's kidneys.

Harry Timberlake hated writing reports and filling in forms. As far as he was concerned, police work wasn't sitting behind a desk: it was getting out and feeling criminal's collars. Most people put disagreeable jobs at the bottom of the list of things to do. Timberlake was one of the sensible majority who get the irksome tasks out of the way first, because once you've mown the lawn and written the cringing letter to the bank manager everything else is downhill, with a following wind. When he tried to persuade people of the logic of this system he succeeded only in getting up their noses. The fact that he was right only exacerbated his offence.

So when he arrived back at Victoria Station, he went straight to the Terrace Vale nick, despite the fact it was late. In the Paris–Calais train and on the ferry he had made notes for his report, emphasizing the theory that Pusey's murder might have been a case of mistaken identity, so typing it up didn't take too long; but it was nearly midnight when he left the nick. He organized himself a lift home in a panda.

As he walked up the stairs to his flat, he was suddenly and acutely aware of the emptiness of his life outside police work. For a moment, before he could stifle the thought, he wondered what his life would be like when he retired from the force. The prospect was so bleak and solitary he forced it from his mind and made himself think of a record to play to raise his spirits.

As he walked in he assumed he must have left a light on in the early morning when he set off for France. He was wrong. Curled up in his favourite large armchair, legs tucked under her, an open book fallen on the floor beside her, was the sleeping Jenny Long. She was wearing his special-occasion dressing gown, and looked as warm, as elegant, as caressable as a pedigree Burmese kitten. At that moment he had a surge of emotion for her stronger than any he had ever felt before. If she had woken up at that moment and asked him to marry her, he would have rushed her out to the nearest parsonage and hammered on the door demanding to be married then and there. Well, nearly.

He could hardly bear to wake her.

In fact he didn't need to. Maybe it was her hospital training that made her sense someone was there. Her blue eyes opened, and she was awake instantly, just as if she were a junior doctor again and had to rush to a ward to deal with a heart attack. She smiled at him; she was one of those rare people who can wake up looking good.

'I rang the nick. They said you'd be back this evening.' She yawned. 'You're late.' He was still so affected by her seductive appearance he remained tongue-tied. She smiled. 'I know, I've caught you out: there's another woman on her way up.' She was joking, but for just one instant she wondered if she had hit on the truth. The thought lasted only a fraction of a second before she almost completely dismissed the thought. 'Can't you say something?' she asked.

A thousand things flashed through his mind, so many that he couldn't decide which one to articulate. A deep down caution – perhaps fear – stopped him saying what eventually became foremost in his mind. He settled for: 'Darling, you look marvellous! You can't imagine what a pleasure it is to see you!'

Which wasn't bad, but wasn't what he really could and should have said, and what she would have liked to hear.

'Are you hungry? I'll get you something while you have a shower, if you like,' she said.

'No, thanks. I ate something on the ferry, and had a cup of tea and a sticky bun at the nick. You can open a bottle of wine, if you like.'

'Fine. Then I'll come and join you in the shower.'

They soaped and rubbed each other with the thoroughness of surgeons preparing to operate and the enthusiasm of a couple of teenagers who had just discovered sex. They deliberately delayed going to bed, using expectation as a sort of mental foreplay. Harry Timberlake played a tape recorded from a Charlie 'Bird' Parker record with Red Rodney on trumpet. It was a collector's piece.

'In the fifties Red Rodney played with the Charlie Parker Quintet in the southern states,' Timberlake said.

'Really,' Jenny replied as if he had just told her a Great Universal Truth, but Timberlake was too involved with the music to notice.

'God, listen to that! Anyway, a lot of redneck bigots didn't like the idea of a white man playing in a black group, so Red said he was an albino.'

'Fancy!' she said, with wildly exaggerated irony. Then, in an apparently casual tone she said something that jolted Timberlake out of his appreciation of the music.

'Are you going to sit there all night boozing and listening to music or are you coming to bed for some serious shagging and screwing?' The unexpected incongruity of her language turned Timberlake's mind off the music and turned his body on.

As Jenny Long drove to the hospital the next morning she sang softly to herself. She was quite confident that it wouldn't be long before Harry gave in and said it was time they got married. After all, even Jericho fell in the end.

'It's a very persuasive theory,' Harkness said next morning after he had read Harry's report. 'In fact it's the only thing of value that's emerged from your trip.'

'I feel annoyed with myself that I didn't think of it before,' Timberlake confessed. 'All I can say in mitigation is that I saw Pusey and de Gaillmont in very different circumstances. In fact I never saw Pusey alive. The only time I saw him in a good light was on the dissection table in the morgue. Besides . . .'

'Yes?'

'There's still the unexplained fact that all the luggage was stolen from the car and his pockets rifled.'

Harkness nodded. 'That is awkward. Perhaps the theft was

purely a crime of opportunity after all, done after Pusey was killed.'

'Well, it means another visit to Towers Hall,' Timberlake said with all the enthusiasm of a small boy faced with a plate of cold semolina. 'I hate the place. It's sinister. It's like the Château d'If: full of ghosts and always cold.' In fact, the Château d'If is these things only to people with sensitive antennae.

Since Timberlake and Webb had been to Towers Hall a flagpole had been erected in the front grounds. A flag with a family crest fluttered from it at half mast. 'Christ!' Timberlake muttered. 'The de Gaillmont Royal Standard.'

The welcome the two detectives were given at the hall was several degrees below warm. Thérèse Chardet looked as if she had been crying, Jean-Louis de Gaillmont had his right arm in a sling and Sophie de Gaillmont was more glacial than ever. She behaved as if she was irritated by Timberlake's efforts to find her son's murderer.

Partly out of politeness Timberlake asked Jean-Louis what was wrong with his arm. Sophie de Gaillmont replied for him. 'I closed the car door on his hand,' she said baldly.

'A rather superior woman surgeon gave me an injection, stitched up the gash, put splints on two broken fingers at West Thames Hospital,' Jean-Louis told them. Timberlake could make a fair guess who that was.

Webb was tactless enough to say that it must have been painful, and offered his sympathy. Sophie de Gaillmont waved it away with the disdainful gesture of a family who complained about nothing less than the guillotine.

'Well, what do you want with us now, inspector?' she said.

'As a result of enquiries I made in Saint-Rémy-de-Provence, I now believe it possible that there could be some confusion over the identities of your son and Monsieur de Gaillmont.' The sense of general shock was almost palpable. It was as if the whole scene was held in a film freeze-frame.

'What exactly do you mean by that?' Sophie eventually said in a belligerent voice.

'I mean, Madame, that the murderer might have intended to murder Monsieur de Gaillmont, and not Mr Pusey.'

'Ridiculous! *Inouï!*'

Timberlake had not seen her this keyed up before. He kept his temper and outlined the reasons for his theory.

'Perhaps, after all—' Sophie de Gaillmont conceded, with an elegant shrug. It was the nearest she would ever get to an apology.

Timberlake and Webb between them put the standard questions to Jean-Louis: did he have any enemies, was there anyone who would want to harm him, had he received any strange telephone calls, had anyone seen any strangers loitering around their home in London or France ... The detectives got exactly what they expected: nothing. Timberlake now prepared to proceed as if he were walking on eggshells.

'Monsieur de Gaillmont, is it possible that you could be the target of a jealous husband, or lover?'

'Preposterous!' Sophie de Gaillmont rapped out before Jean-Louis could say anything. 'And quite insulting, Inspector.' She stood up, and addressed her step-son. *'Il n'est pas très intelligent, ce policier. Je ne sais pas si tu veux rester répondre à ces questions stupides, mais moi, je m'en vais. Fais attention à ce que tu dis.'*

Timberlake concealed his initial annoyance and then interest in her words. He easily understood what she had said: *He's not very intelligent, this policeman. I don't know if you want to stay here and answer these stupid questions, but I am leaving. Watch what you say.* It was not only what she said, it was how she said it that made him think.

'Mademoiselle Chardet—' Sophie de Gaillmont called out imperiously, and sailed out of the room like a four-masted man o' war, with Thérèse Chardet fluttering behind her like a flustered barque.

When the door has closed behind the two women Timberlake turned to Jean-Louis de Gaillmont. 'I apologize if my questions have caused offence, but this is a murder enquiry and they are necessary.' He sounded as apologetic as a Turkish prison warder.

'Of course. I understand. You see, my stepmother had a strict Catholic education, and she is very devout.' With a half-smile he added, 'We have entertained cardinals at our home near Saint-Rémy-de-Provence. The thought of adultery or extra-marital sex is anathema to her.'

'Of course.' Timberlake paused. 'Now that Madame la Comtesse has left, is there anything you would like to tell me in confidence?'

Jean-Louis laughed. 'No, inspector, there are no *aventures* in my life – none that could give rise to a *crime passionel*, that is.'

'That means a "crime of passion" I believe?' Timberlake asked ingenuously, and instantly wondered if he had overdone it.

'Indeed.'

'Is there a former—' He searched for a suitable word. 'A former suitor of your fiancée who might resent you?'

He laughed again. 'Not the faintest possibility.'

Timberlake nodded. 'Very well. Incidentally, has she arrived in England yet?'

'We expect her any day now. I'm looking forward to it. It's been a long time – too long.'

'I'm sure. And you really can't suggest anyone who would want you dead? No jealous—'

'No. Definitely,' he said, still smiling. Then, all at once he was serious. 'No. You must look elsewhere to find the murderer.'

Timberlake sighed. 'Thank you for your patience, monsieur,' he said politely. He gestured to Webb to follow him out. Before they got to the door he stopped before a water colour of a Touareg caravan in the desert on the wall. 'That's very good,' he said admiringly. 'Is it your work?'

'Oh, no. It comes from our home in France.'

'Are they the Blue Men of the Desert?'

'Well done, inspector. Yes, they're Touaregs.'

'Blue Men?' Webb asked, slightly baffled.

Jean-Louis replied. 'The desert Touaregs wear dyed blue robes, and the dye comes off, colouring their skin. The Touaregs were extraordinary people. Unlike Bedouins, for example, it is the men who cover their faces and the women who leave them uncovered. Some years ago, when North Africa was a wilder place, they could be a frighteningly cruel people, yet they had an advanced culture. And a Touareg was always courteous and considerate to his woman.'

'Fascinating,' Timberlake said.

'Well, that didn't get us any much further, guv,' Webb said as he drove them both back to Terrace Vale. Timberlake didn't answer. 'Guv?'

'I'm not sure,' he replied slowly, thinking out loud. 'I'm wondering if it's possible that— *Could* it be possible?'

'*What* be possible?' asked Webb, sounding as exasperated as he dared.

Timberlake hadn't seemed to hear him. 'I've got to look something up. Look up something,' he corrected himself. 'God, if I'm right—'

'D'you mean that Pusey *was* killed in mistake for de Gaillmont?'

'Absolutely not. There was no mistake. The killer got the right man. At the same time, it was the *wrong* man.'

Chapter 16

'The funeral's tomorrow, guv,' Darren Webb said. 'D'you want me to come?' He phrased the question like someone saying, 'Sorry you can't stop for a drink,' as a polite version of 'Get lost'. He added the reason for his lack of enthusiasm. 'It's at 7 a.m.'

Timberlake looked up from the report he was typing. 'Whose funeral?' he asked absently. Rapidly he went through a mental list of desirable candidates, starting with several members of the government down to the mechanic who had dented his car while manoeuvring it in the garage for servicing. The fact that the repaired dent was invisible to the human eye was of no consequence. Timberlake could *feel* it like an old surgical operation every time he got into the Citroën.

'Charles Pusey's. I thought you said you'd go, see if anyone dodgy turned up.'

Occasionally a killer will attend the funeral of his victim, but usually this is when professional criminals are concerned. Still, no one had said that it wasn't one of the criminal classes who had murdered Pusey.

'Where is it?'

'Saint Xavier's Church, 7 a.m.,' he repeated without enthusiasm. 'He's being buried in the churchyard. Very private affair. I suppose they're doing it that early to help keep any crowds away.'

'But that's a Catholic church.' Timberlake reached into a drawer of his desk and pulled out a thick folder of computer hard copies, which he scanned quickly. 'Yes, I thought so. He was baptized at Wallsend Church. That definitely C of E.'

'Where did you get all that, guv?' Webb said, looking at the folder with surprise.

'Petra Woodward got a lot of cuttings from the local rag, for a start. Then I rang Claud Salter.'

'Who?'

'He's the crime reporter on the *Post*. He got me some information on Howard Foulds in the Prendergast case.* He sent me a great sheaf of stories on the Puseys.' Almost apologetically he added, 'I thought there might be something in the family's past which would give us a lead.' He shook his head.

'I suppose Charles Pusey converted to Catholicism some time when he was in France,' Webb said reasonably.

'Living with his mother, that might seem an odds-on-bet. She's more Catholic than the Pope. Well, the last one, anyway.'

'Wonder she married a Protestant, then.'

'I suppose she was prepared to forgive Pusey senior's heresy when she saw his Dun and Bradstreet rating.'

'Yeah. Well, do we gatecrash tomorrow?'

'Might as well.'

'Good,' Webb said, with monumental hypocrisy.

Private was definitely the word to describe the Pusey burial. The only mourners were Pusey's mother, Madame la Comtesse Sophie de Gaillmont, his stepbrother Monsieur le Comte Jean-Louis de Gaillmont and plain Mademoiselle Thérèse Chardet. The priest, a small, shrivelled man of indeterminate age, had spent the past thirty years ministering mainly to the few immigrant Irish and Italian working families in the area. He was clearly ill at ease in the presence of genuine foreign aristocracy, and his apprehension was aggravated by the mourners' lack of any manifest sense of grief. At most of the funerals he conducted it seemed to him that his Irish parishioners were red-eyed and hungover from the wake; the Italians noisily and damply tearful. The trio who were seeing Charles Pusey off to a Better Place made the stone figures on the graves look emotional by comparison. All that, and the presence of hired security guards to keep curious passers-by out of the church and the churchyard during the ceremony gave the priest a bad case of the shakes that made him drop his prayer book twice. Briefly the guards had tried to keep out Timberlake and Webb, but warrant cards easily won the day.

The burial was given its first flavour of low comedy by the appearance of some reporters and journalists from newspaper

*See *Vengeance*, the first Harry Timberlake story.

111

gossip columns, who had mysteriously got to hear of the funeral. One or two of them began spouting about freedom of the press when they were denied entry into Saint Xavier's. The security guards' measured reply of 'Fuck off!' was audible at the graveside.

The two grave-diggers were inside the churchyard because they were there before the security curtain was lowered. Their presence maintained the air of farce. At the thump of the first handfuls of earth on the coffin lid they appeared, one hand holding a hat or cap, the other slightly extended to receive the usual gratuity that was usual from loaded families. Sophie de Gaillmont looked at them with furious incomprehension. The priest, to his credit, plucked up enough courage to explain the custom to her. She gave him a withering look, then levelled a lethal stare at the grave-diggers, who stepped back in alarm. One of them caught his heel in a rail round an adjoining grave, and fell back on to it noisily.

Timberlake couldn't help but wonder what on earth Sophie de Gaillmont was making of all this. Her husband's ancestors had been carried to the family mausoleum with all the pomp, ceremony and gravity of a state funeral. One thing was certain: for all the slapstick quality of this burial, she would find it no laughing matter.

It worked because Sarah was observant and had a good memory. She was also lucky, a talent Napoleon demanded of his generals. When she had visited Anthea Wightman in her kitchen she noticed a couple of supermarket carrier bags in a corner. With them was the printed list of the purchases. In these days of universal credit cards and computers, printouts from tills record each item, unit price, total, method of payment, and, if it is a cash deal, the sum tendered and the change given, and ... the date *and time* of transaction. Sarah had a woman's natural curiosity, intensified by her detective's training. Not that it needed a great deal of sharpening after Sarah had worked in a Welsh sub-post office. She read the list as readily as if it were somebody's postcard. Anthea Wightman had done her shopping on the previous Friday, and had paid by credit card at 13.53hrs.

Most people do their big weekly shopping at much the same time on one particular day of the week. Sarah banked on Mrs Wightman being a creature of habit; she decided to take a chance, and stake out the supermarket the next Friday lunchtime. What she wanted to do was 'accidentally' bump into Mrs Wightman.

The supermarket was sited in a large mall which had shops, public lavatories, a café-restaurant with a sort of indoor terrace of tables, an Underground station entrance and bus station. Sarah, a supermarket trolley beside her, sat on a bench where she could keep the main entrance to the shop under observation. After a couple of hours of inaction she was on the point of admitting to herself that the whole idea was wildly over the top, and that she had as much chance of encountering Mrs Wightman as winning the national lottery and the football pools in the same week. Just as she decided to call it a day she saw her target come out of the supermarket and make for the lifts to the car-park.

She rose to her feet and steered a collision course towards Anthea. Sarah's assumed expression of surprise at meeting her was beautifully judged.

'Oh, hello!' Sarah said, with a rueful smile. 'God, don't you just hate shopping?' It was a remark that practically the entire female adult population from middle-class down would agree with.

'I think it's something to do with the lighting,' Mrs Wightman agreed. 'All those fluorescent tubes and spotlights in that place give me a headache.'

Sarah turned to look at the café's indoor terrace. 'Let's have a cup of tea. Come on.' Without waiting for an answer she swung her trolley round and walked away briskly. She left it by an empty table. 'I'll get them,' she said over her shoulder.

When Sarah returned to the table she gave a deep sigh.

'Anything wrong?'

'Oh, the job. This rape case.' She gave a second sigh. 'People know that rape's a horrible crime, but unless they're involved with the victim – like close friends and relatives, and us, the police – they have no idea *how* awful it is, and the effect it has on the woman.'

'I suppose not,' Mrs Wightman said. 'But do—'

'Very broadly speaking, there are two kinds of rapists,' Sarah pressed on, giving her no time to interrupt. 'There's the man who's known to the victim: he could be a boyfriend who's already had sex with the woman and won't take no for an answer on an occasion when she doesn't feel like it. Or it's at a party when everyone's been drinking and a randy neighbour thinks he's had the come-on from a woman whose husband's away . . . You get the idea.'

Anthea Wightman nodded. 'I suppose every woman who doesn't look like the back of a dustcart knows about that.'

'But then there's the other kind: this last kind – the brutal, wants-to-hurt kind who'll pick on any defenceless woman. We know that if we don't catch him, he'll do it again, and again.' Sarah changed mood, and smiled. 'Sorry I rabbited on like that. Nice way to cheer us up, I must say.' She glanced at the purchases in Anthea's trolley. 'You doing anything special? Oh, you've got noodles. D'you like Chinese food?'

'I've not really tried. The noodles are for chicken soup.' She grinned. 'A little chicken soup won't do you any harm.'

'Oh, you should try Chinese. And don't believe you feel hungry again half an hour after you've eaten. Look, I've got a good Chinese recipe book and a super wok. Next time I'm round your way I'll pop in and lend them to you.'

'Oh, no, I couldn't—'

'I'd like to, honest. To tell you the truth, it'd be a bit of a change to talk to another woman for once. All those hairy-bummed coppers can be a bit of a pain.' Sarah smiled again, and rose. 'Lovely to talk to you.' As she moved away she thought, 'Now where the hell can I get a Chinese cookbook and a wok?'

Sarah Lewis felt she was being something between a spy and a confidence trickster. Normally the present role she was playing wouldn't bother her in the least if it were to nab a miscreant who had done something nefarious against the peace of Her Majesty and her subjects. In fact she would probably have found it mildly exciting. Instead, she felt duplicitous, not to mention plain shitty. The trouble was she was beginning to *like* Anthea Wightman, who clearly trusted her and enjoyed her company. Sarah suspected she didn't have many friends.

Sarah had brought the promised Chinese cookbook and wok. The book was a new paperback she had manhandled for a while to make it look used; the wok was the result of a stroke of good luck: she found it at a local car boot sale. The woman who sold it looked as it she were in the terminal stages of indigestion, which probably put off potential buyers and reduced the price of the wok to a pound. Because she had a rural Welsh upbringing Sarah had a wide streak of superstition in her psyche. She told herself that finding the wok was a good omen. (She mentioned this to

Harry Timberlake on her way from the CID office at Terrace Vale. He was still grumpy and said rather gruffly, 'You can't have a *good* omen. By definition an omen is a portent of something bad.' For once he was wrong, confusing 'omen' with 'ominous'. But even Homer nodded.

He was sorry later for speaking to her like that, but it was too late.)

Once again, Anthea Wightman was genuinely pleased to see Sarah, which deepened her feeling of guilt. She managed to wing her way through a Chinese recipe for the wok she had mugged up.

Eventually the two women sat down for some tea. Sarah's experience of softly-softly interviewing was limited, but she managed the conversation as if she had been doing it for years. She changed the subject any time Anthea Wightman mentioned her husband, and carefully avoided mentioning crime. Only at the end did she do her little act of giving a sad sigh, and Anthea Wightman raised the subject of the rape enquiry for her.

'The frustrating thing about the case – and I'll mention it just this once – is that *somebody* knows, or has a pretty good idea, who did it and out of a misguided sense of loyalty, they're keeping shtumm. Silent,' she added with a perfectly judged wan smile when Anthea looked baffled. 'The trouble is, not just this one rape. Like I told you, if we don't catch him, he'll do it again, and again. And next time, or the time after that, it won't just be rape.' She paused and looked Anthea Wightman straight in the eye. 'Sooner or later he'll *kill* some poor bloody woman.'

Reaction to her ambivalent feelings about Anthea Wightman didn't really hit Sarah until the end of the day. Writing up her pocketbook and then her reports kept her busy and relatively calm. There was one abrasive moment when Bob Farmer was sarcastic on the subject of her spending her 'breaks for refreshments' with Anthea Wightman. After that he changed mood to being friendly and chatting up Sarah. It was a transparently calculated performance that wouldn't have taken in an apprentice villain.

Eventually he returned to a previous theory that Sarah was really a lesbian after all. It was the only possible explanation for her repulsing his subtle, almost irresistible advances, he thought.

There was a fleeting moment when he wondered whether she had something against bald men – not that he was *bald:* he just had thin hair. He dismissed the thought; he had too much else going for him to be rejected for his *hair*. Besides, the expensive Chinese ointment he had recently discovered seemed to be working.

Sarah made no secret of her visits to Anthea Wightman, for a number of reasons. First, she was a good copper, who went by the book as far as procedure was concerned. Well, most of the time. Second, she genuinely believed that Ross Wightman, alibi or no alibi, was the man who raped Emma Leyland. And finally, a motive that had nothing to do with justice and right: when Wightman was nicked, Sarah was determined to get full credit for her part in the case.

By the time she had finished Sarah felt as knackered as a Portsmouth whore on Nelson's birthday. On impulse, she picked up the phone and started to dial a number. With a shock she realized whose number it was, and stopped. Timberlake's. She dialled another number quickly.

'It's me,' she said, her Welsh accent stronger than usual. 'I'm absolutely shattered. If I come round, will you give me a drink and a kind word?'

'Where are you? Terrace Vale? I'll come and pick you up, right now.'

'No, it's all right. I'll get a cab. I'm too tired to drive. Put the kettle on the hob, bach,' she said, keeping up her Welsh bit.

An hour later, after a long soak in the jacuzzi while enjoying *foie gras* sandwiches and half a bottle of Bollinger, followed by an all-over massage with a ludicrously expensive *après-bain* lotion, she felt like the Queen of Sheba.

Julian Tabard bent over her naked body and gently kissed her, starting with her lips and working his way slowly down her body. Sarah decided she felt more like Cleopatra after all, or maybe Madame Recamier, whoever the hell she was.

He gently lay beside her and continued to caress and kiss her. He saw beautiful young women in all states of undress every day of his working life, but they were always posing, pouting and simulating sexual provocation. Sarah's sheer unstudied naturalness bowled him over. He caressed and kissed her with more purpose.

'Oh, darling, you're so marvellous to me,' she said, meaning every syllable, and vulnerable as no one at the nick had ever seen her.

'Give it all up. You deserve better than mixing with no-goods and criminals. Life's short, Sarah darling: leave the police and enjoy life. Let me take care of you. Marriage, if you like,' he said.

'That's not fair, taking advantage of me when I'm defenceless and not feeling like arguing.'

'All's fair, and all that.'

'Anyway,' Sarah said with a wicked witch's chuckle, 'I'm not prone to argue.'

As he began to excite her, Sarah's last non-sexual thought was that maybe it would be a good idea to resign from the Met after all.

Chapter 17

Timberlake was strangely ill at ease. Uncertainty and self-doubt were not normally part of his make-up. However, the theory he had formulated about the murder of Charles Pusey was so extreme, he had to admit to himself, that he hesitated to put it to Superintendent Harkness. He admired the man, and valued his good opinion. He didn't want to destroy it with a half-baked idea that Harkness would demolish politely but comprehensively.

But it *wasn't* a half-baked theory, Timberlake told himself sternly. It was his *duty* to explain it.

At the door to the office allocated to the AMIP murder squad Timberlake hesitated. Darren Webb was coming along the corridor. 'Darren, I'm just going to see the guv'nor. Come in with me, will you?'

Webb looked surprised, and Timberlake mentally took a free kick at himself. What the hell was he doing, thinking that Webb's presence would give him moral support? All it would do was include a witness to his making a fool of himself.

Harkness was with Sergeant Braddock in the office, going through reports. He was wearing rimless spectacles, the first time Timberlake had seen him wearing them. Harkness took them off with a hint of embarrassment. It made Timberlake feel a little better, but not for long.

'Can I have a word, sir?'

'Of course. Come in Harry – and sergeant. Oh, ask someone to bring us in some coffee, please.' Darren Webb stuck his head round the door and made a vigorous pantomime of the order to PC Brian Pegg, who thought himself rather above that and resented being asked to do what he considered a WPC's job.

The four men sat almost silent until Pegg brought in the coffees. He tried to make a production of putting them on the desk in the hope that they would start talking while he was still in the room and might pick up some tittle-tattle. He finally withdrew, thwarted.

'Well, Harry?' Harkness said at last.

Now he had to tell Harkness his theory, it seemed as unsubstantial as smoke. He could feel cold sweat beginning to trickle down his back.

Mentally he quickly retraced his carefully thought out thesis. His certainty persisted even though he had to admit to himself that others might say it came somewhere between incredible and preposterous. He had worked it out by applying the principle of Occam's Razor. William of Occam, the learned and contentious fourteenth century schoolman wrote – in Latin – 'Entities should not be multiplied except out of necessity'. A reasonable paraphrase would be 'Don't complicate things unnecessarily'.

Timberlake felt that Sherlock Holmes had stated the principle more directly. 'When you have eliminated the impossible, whatever remains, *however improbable*, must be the truth.' Unfortunately, although he was sure his theory *was* the truth, there was one fact he would like to dismiss as an impossibility, but could not. Which meant that William of Occam and Sherlock Holmes were no use to him at all.

He spoke in a firm, assured voice that was far from how he felt.

'I think that the man who claims to be Comte Jean-Louis de Gaillmont is, in fact, Charles Pusey. The man who was killed in the car outside Towers Hall was the real Comte de Gaillmont.'

Timberlake had never known such silence. Then Braddock sucked his teeth, sounding like a half-blocked wastepipe. Darren Webb moved in his chair, making it creak like a roll of thunder. His left leg was beginning to go to sleep, but he didn't dare move it in case it created yet more uproar.

Harkness had enormous confidence in Harry Timberlake's abilities, but this starkly outrageous statement strained his admiration for the younger man a matter of millimetres short of breaking point. There was one big, one enormous, instant objection to the theory and Harkness put it to Timberlake at once.

'But that would mean that the countess herself is involved in the ... masquerade ... and murder,' he said quietly and undramatically.

Timberlake nodded. He wasn't sure he could still keep his voice

119

under control. At last he said, 'Yes, sir. It does. And she is; to the hilt.'

Normally Darren Webb would back up Timberlake in public, even if he might argue with him in private. But he was so shocked that he unthinkingly said, 'But she identified the murdered man as her son.'

'And Mademoiselle Wotsername Chardet confirmed it,' Braddock pointed out.

'True enough. And the key to that is Sophie de Gaillmont's character.'

'What actual proof do you have?' Harkness asked.

'Nothing – to take to court. Yet,' he added. 'It's a number of small things – inconsistencies, actions, words – and behaviour out of character. No, *in* character if you accept my premise of the substitution.'

'Well, let's hear your reasons,' Harkness said. There was an implicit warning in the fact that he didn't add 'Harry'.

'I didn't fully appreciate the . . . oddities in their chronological order, but that's how I'll explain them, more or less, if you'll bear with me.

'First, in the car where the man everyone said was Charles Pusey was murdered, there was an A–Z London street guide on the passenger's seat, open at the page with Towers Hall. But Charles Pusey had lived there for nearly eighteen years! He wouldn't need a map to find his way home, even though he had been away a long time. And the reason there were no bags in the car is obvious now. They would have given away the fact that the driver was not Charles Pusey, but Jean-Louis de Gaillmont.' He looked directly at Harkness, who stared back impassively.

'Next, when I went up to the house, it was dark. Thérèse Chardet opened the door and said they all slept at the back of the house, and they all said they hadn't heard a shot. Nor, apparently, did they hear the thousand and three sirens on our cars and vans, although they woke most of the neighbours. *But they heard my knock, with my knuckles, on the front door*. There isn't a knocker or a bell push. They were expecting a call.'

Harkness's face was beginning to unfreeze.

'The first hint that really hit me was in a conversation I had with Jean-Louis de Gaillmont – the man who calls himself that – when I said I wondered if *he* might have been the target of the

120

murderer, and that the man we took to be Charles Pusey was killed by mistake. I got some very odd reactions to the suggestion, from him and Madame de Gaillmont.'

Harkness shrugged. 'Surely that was natural enough.'

'Yes. But that's not what started me thinking back to one or two things. I mentioned a water colour of an Arab caravan in the house. Darren was with me.'

'I remember, guv.'

'I asked' – he smiled wryly – 'the *alleged* Jean-Louis if Arabs were Blue Men of the Desert.' Timberlake took out his pocket book. 'I noted down what he said as soon as we got to the car. Remember?' he asked Webb, who nodded. 'Jean-Louis said, "Yes, they're Touaregs." He went on to say, "Touaregs are extraordinary people. Unlike Bedouins, for example," and the rest about not covering their faces.'

For once Harkness looked puzzled.

'Jean-Louis, they told me at Saint-Rémy-de-Provence, was an expert on French military history in North Africa, and Arab affairs; an Arabist. But *no-one* who had studied the North African campaigns, no Arabist, would say "Bedouins", or "Touaregs". It would be like saying "childrens", or "mices". Bedouin is plural. One man of a group of Bedouin is a Bedou. It's one Tarqui, several Touareg.'

Harkness nodded. 'Indicative, perhaps, even strongly so, but hardly conclusive.'

'Agreed. But there's more. Everyone who has come into contact with Sophie de Gaillmont has emphasized how hyper-aristocratic she is – or at least, has become since she became the Comtesse. When I was last at Towers Hall, she said something to ... "Jean-Louis". It was something like "*Je ne sais pas si tu comptes rester répondre à ces questions idiotes, mais moi, je m'en vais. Fais attention à ce que tu dis.*" '

Harkness himself translated. ' "I don't know whether you reckon on staying to answer these stupid questions, but I'm going. Be careful of what you say." ' He thought for a moment. 'Was it that she told him to be careful of what he said that worries you?'

'Only partly. But she *tu-toyed* him: used the second-person singular, called him "tu". It's the form most people use for speaking to children, relations, close friends, lovers ... The grand Comtesse de Gaillmont would never have done that to the comte in

121

front of a third person, even if it was one she believed didn't speak French. She wouldn't even do it in private.'

'Oh, really,' Harkness said, apparently sceptical again.

Timberlake was unruffled. He could see that the superintendent was beginning to wonder. 'Sir, did you ever see *La Grande Illusion?* It was on late-night TV recently.'

'I saw it when it first came out,' Harkness said wryly.

'You remember that Pierre Fresnay played an aristocratic French officer who was a POW in the 1914 war. Jean Gabin was a private soldier. In adversity, they become sort of friends. There comes a point when Gabin says *"Si on se tu-toyait?"* Suppose we call each other "tu"? And Fresnay, the aristocratic officer, says *"Je ne tu-toye même pas ma mère."* I don't even say "tu" to my mother.'

'It was only a film,' Braddock said with a tinge of scorn.

'But that was absolutely authentic. Believe me, sir. Sophie de Gaillmont would never say "tu" to the real comte.'

'But why—?' Harkness began, but Timberlake cut across.

'There's more,' he said quickly. 'What would be Charles Pusey's biggest problem of passing himself off to his bankers and lawyers, for example?'

'His signature! But he can't sign because he's injured his hand.' Webb said unexpectedly. The other three men had quite forgotten him.

'Absolutely right!' said Timberlake. 'Convenient, to say the least.'

'But his hand'll get better,' Braddock said doggedly. 'He'll have to sign eventually.'

'In the meantime, he'll have all the time he needs to practise and perfect Jean-Louis' signature.' In the corridor outside, someone dropped a pin, which they all heard clearly. 'And how did he injure it?' Timberlake went on.

'The Comtesse shut a car door on it,' Webb said, encouraged by his success.

Timberlake smiled like someone saying 'Checkmate' in a national championship. He said slowly, with emphasis, 'Sophie de Gaillmont never opened or shut a door in her life; at least, not after she married Pusey senior with all his money and servants. People open and close doors for her: she sails through without lifting a finger. She didn't shut a car door; she would have just got out when somebody opened it for her and moved on.'

Darren Webb looked at Timberlake as if he were seeing him for the first time. Even Braddock was looking less sceptical.

'Yes, but—' Webb shook his head. 'It's all a bit above me, guv, but it sounds right, somehow.'

Timberlake pressed on. 'The identification of the body at the mortuary. It was supposed to be her only son, for God's sake! Did you see how she behaved? What's the cliché? "Admirable self-control? Heroic self-control?" And you must have seen her in the car.' He looked at each of the other men in turn. 'What was her expression?' There was another heavy silence. 'It took me a long time to realize, and then I got it. It was *triumph!* She'd got away with it!'

'That really is going a little far,' Harkness interposed mildly. 'It's a completely subjective assumption.'

The significance of the criticism wasn't lost on Timberlake: it meant that Harkness was going along with most of the rest of what he had said so far. 'With respect, sir, I've had more chances of seeing her close up than you have. And on its own, perhaps that assumption would be biased, because I don't like her.' Almost as an aside he added, 'She said in French I wasn't very intelligent.' Harkness's lips twitched. 'But in the context of the whole situation, it's not that extreme.' Before Harkness could say anything more, Timberlake hurried on. 'Then there was that weird funeral. Charles Pusey was baptized Church of England. In the newspaper cuttings they had the names of his godparents. I rang two of them. Neither had ever heard of him converting to Catholicism. But the real Jean-Louis de Gaillmont . . . he *was* Catholic, and the Comtesse Sophie de Gaillmont, friend of cardinals, bearer of a name of an ancient Catholic family, couldn't bring herself to give him, a Catholic, a Church of England service, and bury him in a Protestant churchyard.'

'But she could kill him,' Harkness said sharply. 'Is that what you're saying?'

Timberlake did not flinch. 'Yes.' He took his time. 'The one was a physical crime, which could be absolved and forgiven by confession and penitence. The other would have been a spiritual one, which could not – at least, not by Sophie de Gaillmont herself. She is an extraordinary woman – a *sui generis*.'

'I'm sure you haven't overlooked a possible motive,' Harkness said, in a tone that Timberlake had never heard before. It made him quail for a moment.

'It's Madame de Gaillmont's one weakness.' He gave another pause, but Harkness's face was still unreadable. 'She is obsessed with titles, the concept of nobility and aristocracy. Everyone who has been in contact with her has mentioned it. Petra Woodward, the local journalist whose sister was a maid at Towers Hall when Sophie was Mrs Pusey; the people at Saint-Rémy-de-Provence . . . She even brought herself a title, by marrying Comte Pascal de Gaillmont.'

'What?'

'He had an ancient title, a château and estate, but no money. It was a classic situation. Now she's even put up a flagpole and a flag with what I suppose is the family crest at Towers Hall.'

'I wonder if they've got planning permission?' Darren Webb mused out loud, and wished he hadn't, as Timberlake and Harkness crushed him in a pincer movement of icy stares.

Timberlake went on. 'Why else would she suddenly uproot the family from the bloody great château and grounds where everything ran on oiled wheels, and come to live in a tatty London suburb? Oh, yes,' he said quickly, 'Towers Hall is one of London's biggest houses, on the scale of Kenwood House and Sion House, but it's not up to the French place.' He looked Harkness directly in the eye. 'Sophie de Gaillmont came here because she could never get away with passing off Charles Pusey as Jean-Louis de Gaillmont in France . . . let alone killing him. But here . . . just she, Pusey and Thérèse Chardet need to be involved in the plan. They were the only ones actually to identify the body as Pusey's.'

'Why Chardet?' asked Harkness.

Timberlake gave a silent cheer. His chief was beginning to accept his theory. 'Sophie de Gaillmont dominates her. There could be all sorts of reasons: money; a daring intrigue which sounded thrilling until the actual execution, but by then it was too late and now she's in it up to her neck; she might even have feelings for Pusey.'

'Assuming – just for the sake of argument – that you're right, why would Jean-Louis de Gaillmont come to live in England? His roots are in France.'

'Maybe he didn't realize the move was meant to be permanent; he thought he was coming for a few days, or weeks.'

'There's something I don't like about your scenario, Harry,' Harkness said at last.

Harry, thought Timberlake. He's on my side again. 'Yes, sir?'

'It's too damned plausible.'

'Yes, sir. But there's a "but".'

He had carefully built a fragile-seeming structure that nevertheless held together. Now, he topped his own creation and sent it crashing. 'The whole thing fits together neatly like a giant jigsaw puzzle . . . Except for one last piece, which is the wrong shape and the wrong size. It means that the whole theory collapses. It's wrong. All wrong. But I can't see *why* it's wrong. I still believe—' He stopped dead. An expression of something like horror spread over his face. 'Oh, my God! I've just realized . . . How could I have missed it? Because I was too bloody full of my own cleverness! I just hope it's not too late!'

Chapter 18

The Emma Leyland rape enquiry was still under way, but it was quite clearly slowing down, and the guiding hand – nominally Bob Farmer's – seemed uncertain of which course to take. The squad of detectives working on the case had been reduced, while most of those remaining were privately admitting to themselves, if not to each other, that the chances of catching the rapist were disappearing quicker than summer snowflakes. The exception, of course, was Sarah Lewis, who was certain she knew who was guilty, and was determined to prove it.

The trouble was it was costing her much more than she expected – too much. At first all she wanted was to break down Anthea Wightman and make her admit that she was giving her husband a false alibi. Anyone who was doing something like that deserved no consideration whatsoever, Sarah thought. The end justified any means. She was so sure of herself and so tunnel-visioned that she hadn't asked herself *why* Anthea Wightman was supporting her husband's claim he was home when Emma Leyland was raped.

Sarah had seen Anthea Wightman twice since she had taken her the wok and the cookbook. The relationship had progressed beyond small talk and exchange of recipes and household tips that could have come from *Reader's Digest*. More than ever she suspected that Anthea had few other friends, which exacerbated her sense of guilt and self-disgust at what she was doing.

But it had to be done.

Sarah unthinkingly addressed PC Brian Pegg with what would normally be an inoffensive cliché. 'Peggy, will you do me a favour?'

He rolled his eyes and leered in a way that Groucho Marx

would have found excessive. Sarah ignored the performance. 'Ross Wightman, one of your names on the list of possibles in the Leyland rape case—'

'The one whose rape charge was thrown out at the magistrate's court in Norfolk? What about him?'

'Can you find out whether he was married at the time? If he was, whether it was to his present wife?'

Pegg's memory was as sharp as ever. 'He was single, I'm pretty sure. But I'd better check. Tomorrow do?'

'Brilliant,' Sarah told him.

Harry Timberlake sat at his desk, staring intently out of the window at a cloud which seemed to be trying to make up its mind whether or not to start raining. He was not making any meteorological speculations: he was trying to work out how he could avert a tragedy he feared.

The phone rang. He was too late.

'Inspector Timberlake?' the caller asked. The instant Timberlake heard the voice, he was gripped by an icy foreboding. 'This is Monsieur de Gaillmont speaking. There has been a disquieting development here. Can you come to see us, please?'

There was the sound of another telephone being picked up. 'It is a matter of the utmost importance. Be good enough to come at once.' However they were phrased, Sophie de Gaillmont did not make requests: she gave orders.

Harry Timberlake knew with an awful certainty what they were going to tell him, but he dare not let them know he had guessed – deduced – what the trio at Towers Hall had planned. He had to act as if he took everything they told him at face value: he did not want them on their guard, but confident they had got away with everything. Briefly he considered telling Darren Webb what he thought, but decided against it. He couldn't be sure that Webb wouldn't subconsciously give them one small hint.

'There's trouble at mill,' Timberlake called out with an excruciating Yorkshire accent, trying to sound unconcerned. 'We've got a royal command to Towers Hall.'

Sophie and Jean-Louis de Gaillmont and Thérèse Chardet were seated in a semi-circle in the same room where Timberlake and Webb had always been received. The family looked like a group who had just heard that they weren't mentioned in a will after all.

127

Inevitably, the formidable Comtesse Sophie de Gaillmont was the first one to speak. She was economic with her words.

'The Princess Tozharska has disappeared.'

At that moment Timberlake's fears were confirmed. The last piece of his jigsaw fitted at last. Timberlake silently counted to ten before replying in a steady voice. His first – almost overwhelming impulse – was to charge at them all head on, but he managed to repress it. He had to go along with their charade, he reminded himself, pretend to be surprised, pretend to accept their apprehension as genuine.

'Indeed,' Timberlake said levelly. He thought he'd done rather well. After a pause: 'Where and when was she seen last?'

Sophie de Gaillmont regarded him as if he had antennae and eight small furry legs. 'Here.' She appeared suddenly bored – no . . . *unconcerned* was the word, Timberlake thought. She made a small gesture towards Jean-Louis de Gaillmont, who took up the story.

'My fiancée arrived here at roughly nine o'clock last night. I was out, but I arrived home about an hour later. She appeared perfectly normal, happy to see me again. We stayed up until quite late, about midnight, talking – all of us. Then Caterina said she was tired, and decided to go to bed. After we had been in bed about an hour, I guess it was—'

Sophie caught Darren Webb's expression. 'Each of us in our separate rooms,' she said in a voice that could have frozen ice cubes. He nearly blushed. Timberlake was glad he hadn't marked Webb's card before they arrived at Towers Hall.

Jean-Louis de Gaillmont continued, 'After an hour or two, I thought I heard the telephone in my room give a brief ring, as if someone had picked up one of the other extensions.'

'Did anyone else hear it?' Timberlake asked. The two women shook their heads.

'When one of the maids took Caterina's morning coffee to her room she found the bed had not been slept in and her bags were not there.'

Sophie de Gaillmont delivered the punchline. 'She was nowhere in the house, and her car had gone.'

Normally this situation would not have made the detectives concerned for Caterina Tozharska's safety. It was not unusual for a young woman suddenly to run away from a boyfriend, fiancé

128

or a husband because she had cold feet about him or hot pants for someone else. Webb didn't envy Timberlake for having to put this suggestion to Sophie de Gaillmont.

'This situation is not unusual in itself,' Timberlake began, sounding much calmer than he felt. He went through the usual list of questions in a routine fashion. He turned to Jean-Louis. 'I must put it to you: is it possible that she had changed her mind about the marriage? Another man—?'

Sophie replied, slashing the air with words like sabres. 'Totally impossible. *Inoui*! Preposterous.'

'We talked about our wedding at some length last night,' Jean-Louis said. 'She was anxious that we should marry quite soon.'

'Not *anxious*,' Sophie de Gaillmont said firmly. 'Eager. Earnestly so.'

'Mademoiselle Chardet?' Timberlake said.

Thérèse Chardet was startled. Perhaps she thought everyone had forgotten her.

'Certainly,' she answered hurriedly.

'Thinking back to last night, could she have been concealing something from you?'

'Not from me,' Sophie said. Timberlake believed her. She would have got the Order of Lenin as an interrogator in the Stalinist KGB.

'We'd better have a word with the servants,' Timberlake said.

'There's no point,' Jean-Louis told him. 'We still don't have any live-in staff yet, and Mademoiselle Tozharska arrived after they had all gone home.'

'What about friends? Does she have any here in England she could have gone to stay with?'

'None. She is like me: she has spent very little time in England,' Jean-Louis said.

'Well, if you'll give me details of her car, we'll set enquiries under way.'

There was an awkward silence. 'I'm afraid we don't know them. She said she hired a car at Heathrow. I didn't see the make or the number.'

Timberlake rose. 'Never mind. We can find that out. Take care of that, will you, Sergeant Webb?' Timberlake looked at the countess. 'If you hear from her before we do, you'll let us know, of course?'

Sophie gave a minimal nod, and started to leave the room. Question Time, it was evident, was over.

'What did you think, Darren?' Timberlake asked on the way back to Terrace Vale. Webb was driving his own car with Timberlake as his passenger.

'Weird, guv. Iffy. I can't make them out. What about you?'

'I hate that place. It's got a very nasty aura. As for the family . . . They remind me of people from *The Twilight Zone* and *Beyond Reality*. Everything and everybody's fifteen degrees off normal.'

'Yeah. I can't say I blame Princess Whatshername for doing a runner.' He thought for a moment. 'But she can't have run off because of another man. There wouldn't be any point in turning up in the first case. She could have simply sent him a Dear John letter.' He paused again. 'Perhaps when she saw the countess she suddenly realized what a dragon she was going to get for a mother-in-law.'

'You haven't got it yet, have you?'

'Got what? You mean the phone call?'

Timberlake took a deep breath. 'They've fucking murdered her.' Webb nearly drove into the back of a bus. Timberlake hardly ever used the word.

'She was the only other one who would know that Jean-Louis de Gaillmont is really Charles Pusey,' Timberlake went on. 'She'd never go along with the substitution. She had to be got rid of. Now let's get back and tell Harkness.'

Computers have their uses. Darren Webb began telephoning the major car rental companies with desks at Heathrow to enquire whether Caterina Tozharska had hired one of their cars the day before. An operator at the third firm – 'Iris speaking, can I help you?' – rattled a few computer keys, said she would call Webb back to check that it was a genuine police enquiry. Satisfied of Webb's bona fides, Iris could help him: she said Caterina had rented a Ford Orion, and had paid the deposit with a gold Amex card. She passed on the registration of the car and Caterina Tozharska's credit card number.

Five minutes later the car's details were on the list of vehicles to be looked out for. If anyone used her credit card, including Caterina herself, the police would be automatically informed.

130

'I'm afraid you're probably right about Tozharska having been killed, Harry,' Superintendent Harkness said heavily. 'Our only hope is that we find the car and it gives us something.'

'There's one more thing on our side, sir. They don't suspect we know the truth.' Bitterly he added, 'They think we're just a load of thick PC Plods.'

In fact Brian Pegg took longer than a day to get the information Sarah had asked for. She was debating whether she should prod, plead or complain when he stopped her on her way out of the Terrace Vale nick. 'Your man Wightman – he wasn't married when he was up before the Norfolk magistrate.'

'Great!' Sarah said. 'You're a real jewel, Peggy.' She had a second thought. 'I don't suppose you—'

Brian Pegg was one move ahead. 'He was married five years ago – two years afterwards.' He adopted a mock official tone. 'To Anthea Gazzard, spinster of St Austell.' In his normal voice he added, 'That's in Cornwall.'

Which means, Sarah said to herself triumphantly, almost certainly Anthea has no idea of his little adventure in Norfolk. It's hardly the sort of thing he'd be likely to tell her. 'You're a mind-reader, Peggy,' she said out loud. 'I'm really very grateful.'

'How grateful?' he said, out-mugging Groucho Marx once more.

'*Very* grateful. But not *that* grateful. I can read your mind, too.' If it's not bloody Bob Farmer it's sodding Brian Pegg, Sarah said to herself rattily. What the hell is it with men?

She quickly dismissed Farmer and Pegg from her mind as she set off for home. Her initial feeling was one of elation at the thought she was a step nearer to nailing Ross Wightman; then, as she drove, the moral and ethical implications of what she would have to do to stitch him up so firmly he couldn't wriggle a little finger began to trouble her. She opened the window of her car as if to let some air blow the mists of doubt from her mind. 'I'll sleep on it,' she said out loud while she was stopped at a traffic light. A motorcyclist beside her looked at her, startled, and stalled his engine when the lights turned green.

Chapter 19

Because no real progress was being made in the Towers Hall murder investigation, the daily AMIP-led morning conferences were becoming shorter, even though there was the disappearance of Caterina Tozharska to be considered. The conference was on the point of breaking up when Sergeant Rumsden appeared in the doorway with a sheet of telex paper in his hand. He walked over to Superintendent Harkness and gave him the message. 'Thank you, Sergeant Rumsden,' he said. Harkness made a point of remembering names. Rumsden nodded and went out, giving Timberlake a cheerful wink on the way. Everyone – Timberlake, Webb, Sergeant Braddock, Nigel Larkin (who had managed to get himself absorbed into the murder squad by a process something like osmosis) and a couple of detective constables – all waited to hear what Harkness was going to say.

'Caterina Tozharska's car has been found. Burnt out.'

One of the detective constables asked politely, 'Any sign of the woman, sir?'

Timberlake glared at him. The man should have known better: if there had been a body it would have been the first thing Harkness would have said. 'Where, sir?' Timberlake asked, more cogently.

'Waste ground by the river at Woolwich. It's been taken off to the laboratory for examination. Because the enquiry about the car originated here, we'll be dealing with it, of course.' A few minutes later the meeting broke up.

As Timberlake and Webb gathered up their gear Nigel Larkin said wryly, 'Pity it's not true that they have blue blood, guv – members of the aristocracy, I mean. Then all we'd have to do to know if the comte really is the Comte de Gaillmont or Charles

Pusey would be to give him a whack on the nose and see what colour blood came out.'

Timberlake, who was feeling spiky, was about to tell him not to be facetious, and not to make suggestions about whacking people, when he stopped dead as if the Gorgon had given him the eye. Larkin stepped back in alarm, expecting a regal bollocking for his presumption. 'Oh, you clever bugger,' he said. And meant it. 'Find out if Charles Pusey Senior died in hospital,' he told Darren Webb. 'If he didn't, who his GP was.'

'Maybe that woman journalist knows, guv. The one on the local rag. It might save some time.'

'Petra Woodward. Yes. What is it – sunspots or something? The reason everyone's so bright this morning?' He left his question unanswered and got his contacts book from his desk to find Petra Woodward's telephone number. He was lucky: she was in, but sounded grumpy.

'Inspector Timberlake? What the hell you doing ringing me at the crack of bloody dawn?'

'It's a quarter to nine.'

'God Almighty! *That* early? Mind you, if you're ringing to tell me someone's murdered Iain Logan, I'll forgive you. I didn't do it myself, but I wish I had.'

It took a moment for Timberlake to remember he was Petra's former editor on the *West Thames Times*. 'I wonder if you can tell me something about Charles Pusey Senior. Can you remember how he died? Was it in hospital? At home?'

'Couldn't you have sodding looked it up at St Catherine's House? He died in hospital.'

'What of? Which hospital?'

'I'm going to send you a bill for this.' In an aside to someone at her end of the line. 'Where you going? Get back into bed.' Then to Timberlake again, 'He died after some big abdominal operation at, er, South-West Thames General. Hey, inspector, is there a story in this?'

'Could be. If there is, you'll get something exclusive.'

'God, you know how to talk to a woman!' Then as an another aside, 'Not you, you useless lump.' She gave a tiny pleasurable squeak and hung up.

Sometimes the good guys have a stroke of luck. Jenny Long

was a consultant surgeon at South-West Thames General. All he had to do was ask her.

He rang her home, but the answering machine was on. He decided to go to the hospital.

Sarah's main worry was that Anthea Wightman might be becoming suspicious of the number of visits she was making. But, one way or another, there wouldn't be many more 'casual', friendly calls. Any time now they would be nasty encounters. In for a penny . . . Sarah picked up the phone. She had an excuse, albeit a feeble one: she needed her wok and cookbook back.

When Sarah got to the Wightman home she and Anthea talked about food and a film on TV the previous evening. Sarah had kept away almost completely from the subject of her work. The only occasion she referred to it was when she mentioned there was a very high proportion of broken marriages with CID officers. Anthea asked whether it was because the long, uncertain hours and strain meant detectives were poor performers or got home too tired to care. 'This *woman* detective definitely isn't,' Sarah laughed. From then on they talked about men and sex.

Sarah said she'd had an affair with another detective.

'Not the one who came with you—?'

'Him? Not bloody likely. I can't imagine going to bed with him.' She shuddered as if she had trodden in something nasty.

'How was it?'

'Full of good sex. Best I'd had until then. And we were good friends with it.'

'But it's over now? What happened?'

Sarah shrugged. 'He went back to his previous woman friend, and I met someone else. Totally different: you know, chalk and cheese. No, cheese and chocolate.' She smiled, and Anthea didn't ask her which was which.

They both talked some more of previous lovers: a few who provoked nostalgic smiles, a few who provoked giggles, a few who provoked grimaces. Eventually Anthea got round to the subject Sarah half-hoped for, half-dreaded: her husband.

'He's all right, really, I suppose,' Anthea said, the 'really, I suppose' damning in its implications. She paused for a long moment, and said something Sarah guessed she'd wanted to tell someone for a long time. 'It's just . . . he's not all that considerate.

134

You know, pumping away like it's a competition, or a *battle* – you know . . . And it's getting worse. On top of that, he likes to talk dirty.' The corners of her mouth turned down briefly. 'I have to fake orgasms half the time.'

'Half the time isn't bad. Some women don't even know *how* to fake it.'

She was still uncertain whether or not Anthea Wightman knew about her husband being charged with rape in Norfolk. But Sarah was dead certain that he *had* raped Emma Leyland.

South-West Thames General Hospital was a jewel in the crown of the National Health Service when it was opened some fifteen years previously. True, its architecture owed much to the shoebox school of design. It dominated the local skyline with the menacing massiveness of the Lubyanka. However, its no-costs-barred installations and equipment spurred medical staff to pull strings, call in favours, lie and fight with gritted teeth to be appointed to the new hospital.

Within a few years some of the departments had earned an international reputation for being leaders in their field – heart surgery, paediatrics and neuro-surgery among them. Now the inside of the building was showing signs of premature wear and care, as were most of the medical staff. The only people who were in good spirits and financial health were the managers. One of the recent improvements the managers had instituted was that in-patients in the seventeenth-floor eye clinic were taken down to the fifteenth-floor at night to sleep, then shuttled back to the seventeenth in the morning. Honestly.

The latest planned development in the search for increased efficiency, economy and medical care was the closure of the hospital as surplus to requirements for London. The millions of pounds-worth of equipment would be removed from the South-West Thames General and re-installed in another hospital five miles away, at unimaginable cost. This particular piece of Alice in Wonderland economic logic failed to impress staff and relations of patients who were left on stretchers in corridors because of a shortage of beds.

Harry Timberlake didn't bother to look for a space in the hospital car-park. There would be a better chance of finding a four-leaf

135

clover growing in Piccadilly Circus. He drove on two streets past the hospital and found ample room to leave his car outside an undertaker's shop. The space was often unoccupied: maybe people thought it was unlucky to park there.

He walked through the thronged ground floor reception area to the lifts at the back, which were notoriously as infrequent as the number 9 bus at rush hour. When a lift did arrive people piled in like lemmings on an upward course. Practically every floor up to the twenty-first was selected, except the thirteenth floor. There was no number 13 button, for this was the floor with the operating theatres. Presumably surgeons weren't superstitious, and sedated patients didn't realize where they were going anyway. The floor was reached by special non-public lifts.

Timberlake got out at the fifteenth floor and went to a small reception area where Eloise Cholmondeley – pronounced 'Chol-mon-de-ley' and not 'Chumley', she always explained – was at the desk. She recognized him immediately and her flashing smile was like the sun breaking through thunderclouds. Eloise was from Nigeria, and would have graced any fashion house's catwalk.

'You want Mrs Long?' she asked. Surgical consultants are not called 'Doctor', but 'Mister'. Jenny Long was a consultant surgeon and insisted on being called 'Mrs', even though she wasn't married. 'She's just up from operating. I saw her going towards the senior doctors' common room.'

He thanked her and walked along the corridor with an arrow and a cryptic 'SDCR'. He was about to knock on the door when it was opened from inside by a man in a less than perfectly clean white coat with a slightly tatty stethoscope hanging out of his pocket like an aged snake trying to make a break for freedom. The man had a moonscape skin which was inadequately hidden by a beard, and a deeply ingrained dyspeptic expression. Timberlake recognized him immediately; he had met him briefly when he was working on the Prendergast case,* and remembered he had bad breath. He stepped back a pace without making it too obvious. It was a wise move.

'Hello, Dr Jones.'

Jones looked at him unenthusiastically. Timberlake smiled. 'We met when you were at St Bill's.' The hospital's name was St William's, but only insiders called it that.

*See *Vengeance*, the first Harry Timberlake story.

136

Jenny Long called out from inside the room. 'Harry! Come on in.' He entered and shut the door on a puzzled Dr Jones.

Jenny was in an armchair, a cup of tea on a small table beside her. She was wearing shapeless operating theatre greens; she didn't have a scrap of make-up, and her attractive blonde hair was hidden beneath her theatre cap. Timberlake thought she was one of the most beautiful creatures he had ever seen. She read his thoughts perfectly, and smiled.

There was only one other occupant in the room: a man of about fifty-five in an armchair with the *Journal of Neuro-Surgery* open on his knees. Behind his glasses his eyes were closed, and he was making a light bubbling noise.

'Good heavens, Harry, what are you doing here?'

'I wanted to have a word; I've been doing a lot of thinking, and there's something I want to ask you.'

She looked at him with astonished eyes, and managed a nod. She waited for him to go on, but just before he could speak the door was flung open and a group of five or six doctors entered, laughing and joking and talking about golf. The other man in the room sat up straight with a start, allowing the *Journal of Neuro-Surgery* to fall to the floor. Timberlake swore under his breath.

'Yes?' Jenny Long prompted.

'It's, er, private, actually,' he said. He nodded towards the others.

'Look, I'm off at six.' She lowered her voice. 'I'll meet you at your place.'

'I won't be home until about eight myself. Paperwork.'

'Never mind. I'll pick up something on my way round and get a meal ready.'

'Marvellous.' He considered kissing her, but changed his mind and made a puckered-lips gesture instead. He moved off, failing to see her expression as she watched him go.

Jenny bought a bottle of Morgon to go with the meal. It was more expensive than their normal wine, but this was going to be a special occasion. She decided to do nothing complicated or that took a long time to cook. Avocado pears with prawn filling, fillet steak with new potatoes (scrubbed, not peeled), ready topped-and-tailed Kenya string beans, Charentais melon, Boursin cheese and biscuits would make a more appetizing meal than Timberlake usually bothered to make for himself.

She spent as much care in putting on her make-up and deciding what she should wear. Timberlake's reaction to how she looked when he called at the hospital governed her choice: she went for simplicity, and when she regarded herself in the full-length bedroom mirror she was well satisfied. She looked not only highly desirable, but also almost as if she could be married in white without blushing.

The table was laid and all the preparations for the dinner made half an hour before Timberlake was due home. With time to spare Jenny was able to study the flat – Timberlake had moved a year earlier from Clapham, where he was living when they first met. This new flat was more modern and the district more upmarket, yet there was a curious sort of detachment about it. It had the impersonality of a hotel room, or a private room in an expensive clinic. She went over to the extensive bookshelves. There were a number of dictionaries: the microfilmed version of the full Oxford Dictionary, a two-volume French–English dictionary, a 1950- and a 1978-edition Fowler, two different Thesauruses, some technical books on forensic science and pathology, half a dozen books on jazz, Lytton Strachey's *Eminent Victorians*, two copies of *Candide* – a French version next to an English, *The Odyssey* and *The Iliad* in translation... She smiled when she saw *Crime and Punishment*... Among the fiction she was surprised to see Anita Brookner, less so to notice Proust, Graham Greene, Dickens, Le Carré, Jane Austen, Melville, Hardy...

Jenny left the books – they told her nothing about Harry Timberlake she didn't already know – and went over to the hi-fi system. There were few compact discs, but lots of vinyl records and stacks of tapes, which, she half-remembered, were recordings of some of the rare records. She selected one without looking and put it on the machine. It was one of a pianist, accompanied by a rhythm section. The music was familiar, but for a moment she couldn't make out the name before recognizing it as 'Over the Rainbow'. To her astonishment, and some chagrin, she realized she actually liked it.

'George Shearing,' came Timberlake's voice from behind her. 'Born in London, 1919. He started recording in 1937, then worked with Claude Bampton's Blind Band. He's an American citizen now.'

'He's quite goo—... marvellous,' Jenny corrected. 'I shouldn't be surprised if he'd have made a good classical pianist.'

Timberlake kissed her, and grinned. 'He was taught to read music from Braille, and he can play all Bach's *Well-Tempered Clavier*, plus God knows how many other classical pieces from memory. Which he has done, all over America, in concerts with symphony orchestras.' Jenny had the grace to look contrite. 'Listen to him for a moment,' he said, 'and see if you can tell what's special about his playing.'

She listened, but although she found the music increasingly attractive, she didn't have enough technical appreciation of the playing.

'It's called "locked-hands" technique. The chords are played with the hands moving in parallel, or similar movement. Just listen to the harmonies . . . and the counterpoint. Bloody brilliant.'

Well, if we're going to be married, I suppose I'll get used to it in time, Jenny thought. I might even actually *enjoy* it.

It was a perfect evening, Jenny Long was a model of patience in not reminding Timberlake the whole reason for her being there was because he wanted to ask the question he couldn't ask in public. The meal was great, the sex was almost registered on nearby seismographs. At the height of afterglow, and before *post coitus tristus* set in, Jenny said, 'Darling, this afternoon you said there was an important question you wanted to ask me.'

He asked it, and Jenny nearly fell out of bed.

Chapter 20

Harry Timberlake's face was registering 'I'm on another planet' as he sat at his desk. He was still baffled by Jenny Long's incomprehensible behaviour the previous evening. It couldn't have been PMT: she had strong views on mental attitudes overcoming the physical syndrome. And if she hadn't had a positive intellectual approach to that particular problem she had easy access to any medication she might need.

He had simply asked her to have someone dig into her hospital archives to find out the late Charles Pusey Senior's blood group, and to look into Jean-Louis de Gaillmont's records for the same information. After all, she herself had treated him for the damaged hand.

It was as if a door to a deep freeze had suddenly swung open.

'That's what you were talking about at the hospital this afternoon?'

'What else?' Which didn't thaw the atmosphere one degree. 'What did you think I wanted?' Timberlake asked.

When a predator in the wild like a panther or a jaguar picks one particular animal in a herd to hunt, it 'locks on to' that individual target, and will even run past another possible prey as it chases its selected victim. Timberlake the hunter had 'locked on to' the Towers Hall murderer and was oblivious to everything else. Jenny had been almost mortally wounded by a sharp sword of disappointment, but the tunnel-visioned Timberlake was unaware of it: he had only one thing in his sights.

The afterglow of sex had changed to cold ashes. Jenny acidly asked him whether he was aware he was asking her to do something unethical and—

'*Unethical*? Pusey's been dead for years! You can't even *libel* the dead!'

'—and Jean-Louis de Gaillmont is my patient. You're asking me to break a professional confidence. I've always known you can be selfish and unprincipled, but I didn't realize your lack of consideration extended to me.'

Once Timberlake had recovered from this uncharacteristic blast from Jenny he said in a voice like breaking glass, 'I *am* trying to catch a murderer. I'm sorry your principles prevent you from helping. Never mind,' Timberlake went on. 'I'm sure I can find someone at the hospital to help me – if only for money if not for public duty.'

Jenny didn't get out of bed and go home, but simply turned her shapely naked back to him, and switched off her bedside lamp and all conversation. Somehow it was a more telling gesture, one which reinforced the following morning when she got up, showered and left without uttering a syllable. In the words of the old ballad, as far as she was concerned Timberlake was less than the dust beneath her chariot wheels.

Now, in his office, Timberlake was trying to remember whether he had told Jenny in a moment of stupid alcoholic facetiousness that she had a big bum or tiny tits.

In the meantime, he decided to put into action part of Plan B, although with his luck he had little enough hope for it. He picked up the phone and called Capitaine Lapollet in Saint-Rémy-de-Provence. After a polite exchange about the weather in the two countries – cold and raining in Saint-Rémy, sunny and warm in Terrace Vale – the Frenchman asked, 'How goes the investigation?'

'Badly. I need a favour. Do you think you could find out for me the blood group of Comte Jean-Louis de Gaillmont?' he asked.

After a pause, Lapollet said, 'Can't you get it from his English doctor?'

'He hasn't seen one yet, as far as I know.'

'It could be a considerable problem here. Doctors here have a very strong sense of confidentiality. If the patient is alive, rich and with influence.'

With a flash of minor inspiration Timberlake asked, 'What about his father, Count Pascale?'

'Ah,' Lapollet said with satisfaction. 'In France, everything about everybody is recorded on a piece of paper somewhere. The dead can have few secrets. I shall find out and let you know. I owe you that much for that memorable lunch.'

Too true you do, Timberlake thought. 'A fax will do for the answer.' He gave Lapollet his number and rang off quickly before the Frenchman could ask what the hell it was all about.

He was relapsing into dark introspection when it was punctured by Nigel Larkin, who entered as if he had just arrived at Aix from Ghent.

'Guv! They've collared the two perps who nicked Caterina Whatnot's car and torched it!'

From which Timberlake deduced without difficulty that Larkin had been watching a lot of American TV police series. Without difficulty he managed to resist any urge to reply 'Tell me about it! Make my day!'

'They're in one of the Woolwich nicks. The DI is on the phone. Shall I tell him we're on our way? I've got the address.'

Timberlake had noted the 'we', but decided to let it pass and gave Nigel Larkin an A for effort. 'Okay. Leave word for Darren Webb where we're going.'

The DI at Woolwich was a David Bushman. He was a little older than Timberlake, and had a bullet head, beetling brows and a wonky nose. His smile – a rare grimace which disconcerted rather than pleased – revealed a set of teeth that were broader than they were long and looked strong enough to crack beef bones. He had the body of a chucker-out in a dockside pub. All in all, he looked a proper bastard. Which he was.

'What's your interest in this, Harry?' he asked.

'I'm enquiring into the murder of a Charles Pusey.' Timberlake didn't feel inclined to go into the question of the victim's identity at the moment. 'The woman who hired the car, Caterina Tozharska, is missing. She could be an important witness who's been murdered herself to stop her providing vital evidence. I just want to confirm the movements of the car, and to eliminate your two bodies from the enquiry.'

'Fair enough. Although I don't think my two little tearaways have got the bottle to top anyone.'

'Yeah, I doubt if they're involved, but I want to cover everything.'

'The two faces have got form: burglary, taking away without consent – for joyriding, actually – assault, blagging, Christ knows what . . . you name it.' He handed over two files. 'Jason Hyde and Wayne Stubbs. Right little bleeders.'

'Have they made statements?'

Bushman gave Timberlake a knowing, cynical smile. 'Oh, yes. I persuaded them to cough the lot – to nicking the car and then burning it. Nice new wagon like that—'

'How did you collar them?'

'No prints on the car, of course, but they left an empty petrol can nearby. Stupid little shits. They had Hyde's dabs on it. He and Stubbs are known associates so we pulled them both in. We managed to find the petrol station where they bought it and the assistant identified them.'

'Well done. Any preliminary report on the car?' Bushman handed him a sheet of paper. 'Interesting,' Timberlake observed, and passed it on to Larkin. 'Anything strike you?'

'No traces of any suitcases in the car or the boot, guv?'

'Right, Nigel.' He turned back to DI Bushman. 'Do the couple know what I'm working on?'

'Nah. I thought I'd let them stew a bit. I'm not just a pretty face.'

Both Timberlake and Larkin couldn't resist a chuckle.

'Which one should I see first?'

'Hyde. He's all fucking mouth and trousers, puts on the tough act, but he's the one most likely to crumble. Though I doubt if he's got much more to tell you than's in his statement.'

Timberlake nodded. 'I expect you're right,' he said mildly.

Bushman winked. 'His mate Stubbs is a chutney ferret, which tells you something about Hyde. The macho front is just over-compensation.'

'Right,' Timberlake said. Bushman looked all physical, but he obviously was perceptive as well. Maybe he wasn't the sort of person Timberlake would invite to dinner at the Savoy, but he'd be great to have beside you going down a dark alley at night, he thought. 'I'm grateful for your help. Any chance of seeing their statements?'

'Sure. I xeroxed a couple of copies in case you asked.' Timberlake's respect for the primitive-looking Bushman increased.

'Could we borrow an interview room?'

'Sure.'

'You want to sit in?'

'Might as well. By the way, you the Timberlake who nicked that German ponce* who did all them women?' Timberlake nodded.

*See *Elimination*, the second Harry Timberlake story.

'When I saw you I thought you might be,' Bushman said cryptically.

'What's a chutney ferret, guv?' Larkin asked quietly as they went to the interview room.

'An active homosexual,' Timberlake said tersely. Larkin looked thoughtful and coughed.

Jason Hyde was a pimply youth with the complexion of porridge. His hair was close-cropped to the top of his skull where he had a sort of Velcro strip which burgeoned into an Elvis Presley greasy quiff overhanging his forehead. He was wearing a black, armless singlet and jeans which were a public health hazard.

'Who're these geezers?' he said in a belligerent whine. 'And what about giving me back my fucking jacket?'

'It's got more chains on it than Houdini,' Bushman explained to Timberlake. 'That's why we took it off him.' He glared at Hyde. 'And watch your fucking language.'

Hyde was sitting on one side of a plain table, a uniformed policeman beside him. At Bushman's nod, the PC exited. Slowly, keeping his eyes firmly fixed on the youth, Timberlake sat opposite him. Nigel Larkin took the chair next to his guvnor, while Bushman leaned against the door.

Timberlake switched on the double-cassette recorder. He announced the date and time, and went on. 'This is an interview of Jason Hyde at Market Lane police station, Woolwich. I am Detective Inspector Harry Timberlake of Terrace Vale. Also present are CID aide Nigel Larkin of Terrace Vale, and Detective Inspector David Bushman.' Hyde began to shift uneasily in his chair. 'Mr Hyde,' – the polite address paradoxically increased Hyde's uneasiness – 'I remind you that you are not obliged to say anything unless you wish to do so, but anything you do say may be used in evidence. Do you understand?'

Jason Hyde, in a misplaced fit of bravado, parroted the last few words of the caution with Timberlake. 'Yeah, yeah,' he said.

'Do you want a solicitor present?'

'Whaffor? I've already made a statement. So I torched the car. I'm very sorry. I just don't know what come over me. I must've been upset because of all the trouble at home and lost me head.' He grinned and winked towards the cassette recorder. 'I come from a broken home.'

'I'm not interested in the criminal damage to the car,' Timberlake said in a deceptively quiet voice. He paused for effect. 'I am conducting a murder enquiry.'

Hyde made a noise like the alarm on an electronic watch. '*Murder*?' he squawked. 'I ain't done nobody!'

'We shall see,' Timberlake said. Behind him Bushman gave his version of a smile. It didn't reassure Hyde.

'According to the statement you made to Detective Inspector Bushman, you took the Ford Orion from a car-park, after you had seen it there for two days, on the third day.'

'That's right. Asking for it, it was.'

'You saw it first on . . . Monday the second, and it was still there on Tuesday the third and Wednesday the fourth.'

'Bleedin' 'ell, you lot are slow. I've already *said* all this.'

'I understand that Detective Inspector Bushman and his team are still trying to find a witness who actually saw the car in the car-park when you say it was.'

'Yeah. Bet they're busting a gut, trying. What's the difference, anyway?'

'The difference, Jason,' Timberlake said confidentially, 'is whether you picked it up in the car-park after it had been there for two days,' his voice hardened, 'or whether you acquired it while the owner was still in it.'

Hyde thought about this for a moment, then squawked again. 'It was abandoned! Been there two days! We never saw no owner!'

'So you say. Anyway, your story is that it was on the third day that you and your accomplice decided to steal it.'

'Not *steal* it. Borrow it.'

'I see. How did you manage to steal – borrow – it?'

'Easy. We got all the gear from a mate of – from a man in a pub. Said his job was getting back cars from geezers who hadn't kept up with the instalments.'

'Equipment for breaking into cars was found at their flat – Hyde's and Stubbs's – that is,' Bushman interjected.

'Ah,' Timberlake said. 'Then how did you get the car out of the car-park without a ticket?'

'Free car-park,' Hyde said triumphantly. Timberlake nodded as if he hadn't known that already.

'So you decided to borrow it to do some joy-riding.'

'Yeah. Do a bit of a tear-up round the estate in front of me mates, you know what I mean?'

'Before you gave the car back.'

'Yeah.'

'*Burnt out*?' Timberlake fixed him with an incandescent stare. 'Why did you burn it? You burnt it to destroy any evidence that you'd killed the owner, didn't you?'

'Nah! We never killed nobody! There wasn't nobody in it! Honest! You're not fitting me up for some murder!'

'*Why did you burn it*?'

'For a bit of fun, you know what I mean.'

'No, I don't.' After shouting at Hyde and doing his man-eater act Timberlake now went into the nice-guy mode. 'Look, Jason, I know how these things happen. I can understand. You just meant to frighten her, didn't you, and maybe she started screaming. Then it got out of hand. But you didn't *mean* to hurt her, did you?'

'I never touched her! I never saw her! She wasn't there!'

'Oh, very likely! Why didn't you steal the suitcases out of the boot? Because you were afraid the contents might be traced back to you?'

Hyde looked at him wide-eyed. 'We didn't know there was nothing in the boot.'

'Talk about fucking amateur toe-rags,' Bushman said later. 'Didn't even look to see what they could nick before they burnt the car. Kids like that'll give villains a bad name.'

'Well, they didn't have anything to do with the woman's disappearance, that's for sure,' Timberlake said.

'So it's been a waste of time.'

'Not altogether. I'm pretty sure that Caterina Tozharska was killed the same night she arrived in England, which fits in with the rest of my theory. Hyde's story confirms the timing.'

'Good luck, then, mate,' said Bushman. It wasn't the happiest of best wishes. The words were hardly out of his mouth when Timberlake's portable phone buzzed. It was Detective Superintendent Harkness calling.

'I've finished here, sir,' Timberlake said.

'Right. Go straight to Towers Hall when you leave. There's been another suspicious death.' He rang off before Timberlake could ask who the hell it was this time.

Chapter 21

The police presence at Towers Hall was relatively minor for a suspicious death: one car and a van at the front gate, keeping back a pack of Press, radio and TV journalists and amateur rubbernecks; a couple of pandas and a jam butty car – so called because of its white, yellow, red, yellow, white marking on its side – the SOCOs' van plus Dr Pratt's Audi, and Professor Mortimer's aged upright vehicle.

Darren Webb met Timberlake in the hallway. 'It's Thérèse Chardet. She's hung herself.'

'Hanged herself,' Timberlake replied automatically.

'That, too,' Webb replied, making sure Timberlake didn't hear him.

Whether the de Gaillmonts liked it or not – and they made it clear they didn't – the heavy-handed, heavy-footed, nosey officers of the law were allowed upstairs, beyond the one reception room they had seen before.

As Timberlake entered Chardet's room two undertaker's men were putting her body into a temporary coffin. She was wearing a night-dress which was totally different from the one she had on when she opened the door to Timberlake the night of the shooting: this one was sheer and revealing. Her face was carefully made-up.

Funny how so many suicides want to look their best when they kill themselves, was his first thought. Immediately afterwards, as he glanced at her again, he felt sad for the awful waste.

In addition to the corpse there were now Timberlake, Webb, Larkin – still managing to cling on like a burr – Dr Pratt, Professor Mortimer, Gertrude Hacker and a couple of SOCOs.

'If I'm called out to any more bodies here I'll consider doing a group rate,' Dr Pratt said, determinedly waggish as ever.

Mortimer looked at him as if he had spoken Chinese. Turning

147

to Timberlake he said, 'Death by hanging, almost certainly suicidal. No signs of violence, apart from the ligature. Time of death, probably midnight, plus or minus an hour. Post mortem tomorrow nine-thirty.' Without glancing left or right he went out, followed by Gertrude Hacker.

'How did she do it?' Timberlake asked Webb.

'Curtain rope over that,' he replied, glancing upwards to a large oak beam which ran the full width of the room. 'Very convenient, these old houses, for people who want to top themselves. Climbed on a chair and kicked it over. Probably half-pissed.' He indicated an empty half-bottle of brandy and a glass on the bedside table. 'When she didn't come down to breakfast one of the maids came up. There was no answer and the the door was bolted. They broke in – it's a Mickey Mouse bolt – and found her hanging. Someone called us.'

'Any note?'

'Yeah. Odd, that. It was in the bed. *In* it, not on it.' He handed over a single sheet of paper in a plastic envelope. 'Only one set of prints.'

'She didn't want anyone to nick it before we got here,' Nigel Larkin said unexpectedly.

'Quite possibly,' Timberlake said. He looked at the note. It had three words: '*Vous savez pourquoi.*' 'You know why.'

'What the hell does that mean?' Timberlake mused.

'I'm sorry, I have no idea what it could possibly mean,' the man calling himself Jean-Louis de Gaillmont – because that is how Timberlake thought of him – said politely. 'From her handwriting it seems she was under considerable strain, or emotion at the time.' Quickly he added, 'That is a stupid remark. Of course she was, if she was on the point of committing suicide.' He handed back the note in its plastic envelope marked 'Evidence'. He was seated on the edge of a chair in the reception room where all previous meetings with the de Gaillmont family had taken place.

'Had you noticed a change in her manner recently?' De Gaillmont shook his head. 'Had she received any unusual letters? Or phone calls? Visits?'

'None of those. In any case, she received very little correspondence.'

'Can you think of any reason why Mademoiselle Chardet would want to kill herself?'

148

'None. I find this whole situation ... grotesque, nightmarish. First Charles's murder, then Caterina's disappearance – pray God she is still alive' – he crossed himself – 'but it must have been something enormous to drive Thérèse to suicide – enormous in her own mind, that is – for she was a practising Catholic, and suicide is a mortal sin. Perhaps, in some way that we do not understand, she felt responsible for Charles's death.'

Timberlake's pulse quickened. 'Why should she feel that?'

'I don't know. I'm just' – he made a helpless gesture – 'trying to find some reason – no, not reason, but *cause* for the dreadful act. We must pray for her soul.' He appeared badly distressed, and needed some time to recover.

'I'm sure her priest will declare that she was not in full possession of her senses at the time, and so no sin was intended,' Timberlake said, rapidly improvising on the theme of 'while the balance of her mind was disturbed'.

Jean-Louis looked relieved. 'I pray you are right, inspector. Are you a Catholic?'

'No, but this situation is not new to me.' He paused. 'Did Mademoiselle Chardet have a lover? Any sort of affair?'

'Absolutely not! And in any case, we have been in England only a matter of days.'

'What about in France?'

'If she did, I am totally unaware of it.'

'She was a mature young woman ... attractive—'

'Really, inspector, I knew nothing of Thérèse's private life.'

Well, he could always ask Madame la Comtesse Sophie de Gaillmont, although that was not going to be much fun, Timberlake thought grimly.

Jean-Louis smiled sadly. 'Thérèse hardly had time for anyone outside our home. She was very devoted to the family. She will be sadly missed.'

Which seemed to be that, Timberlake thought. He had learned little enough of Thérèse Chardet, but he had learned quite a lot about the alleged Jean-Louis: he had put on a first-class performance and behaved as he would have expected a genuine French Catholic aristocrat to behave. For a moment he felt a cold finger of doubt touching his heart before he willed it away. 'Of *course* he's really Pusey,' he told himself sternly.

For all that Sophie de Gaillmont looked as unshakeable as a Mount Rushmore sculpture, Timberlake perceived that she was

149

uneasy. Her hands were in their usual position, motionless as marble, with fingers interlaced, in her lap, but now her knuckles were white. Her French accent was more marked, and her syntax was occasionally uncertain.

She answered the same initial questions he had asked Jean-Louis with the same flat denials.

He held up Thérèse Chardet's last note. 'Have you any idea what she meant by this, madame?' he asked politely.

'Not any,' she replied, looking straight past it and him. Timberlake did not lower it until she at last glanced at it.

'No,' she conceded at last. 'In any case, one would hardly expect someone about to commit the melodramatic act of a *petite bourgeoise* to make a particularly intelligent statement.'

And the greatest of these is charity, ran through Timberlake's mind. 'On the other hand, madame, it might be the one moment of her life when she was at her most lucid,' Timberlake said softly. Sophie de Gaillmont stared at him with something like shock. 'How long had she been in your employment?' he asked.

'Since eight years.'

'Did Mademoiselle Chardet have any romantic associations?' he asked, choosing his words carefully.

'She had none. I should have known if there was any involvements. She spent most, if not all, of her time with this family.'

'She was not engaged, or had a regular man friend?'

'I have answered that question. I consider it an impertinence that you repeat it.'

'Then I may take it that she had no close men friends?'

'You may take what you like.'

'What about her own family? Did she have any, do you know?' She shrugged. 'She never mentioned any.'

'In all the eight years?'

'In all the eight years.'

'And there were no ... entanglements ... when she was in France?'

'For the last time, monsieur, *no!*' she said. She seemed on the point of saying something else, but remained silent. She rose, signalling that the interview was over.

Timberlake had one more question, to which he already knew the answer. 'And you have still heard nothing from Princess Tozharska?'

'Not yet.' She caught Timberlake's look. 'I am quite certain that we shall, and that she had good reason for her absence,' she said, with enormous conviction. She left the room, leaving that extraordinary statement hanging on the air behind her.

While Timberlake had been doing the above-stairs interviews, Webb had been questioning the servants. He had dug out one nugget. 'Most of them said that Chardet suddenly went very broody three or four days ago. Normally she was fairly cheerful – for someone working for a dragon, that is. Then, for no reason that any of them could guess, she became very quiet and down in the dumps.'

'That's interesting,' Timberlake observed, as they drove back to Terrace Vale. 'The de Gaillmonts said there was no change in her. That was a mistake... They didn't admit it because they knew why. Anything else?'

'Nothing much really, guv,' Webb confessed. 'There's still only day staff in the place; no one stays overnight. Last one goes home at nine, after dinner. There's a roster. One funny thing, though. There was absolutely no gossip. People like the de Gaillmonts normally treat servants like non-persons, right? They talk as if they weren't there. Well, Madame, Jean-Louis and Thérèse What-shername were always tight-mouthed when any of the servants were about.'

'I'm not surprised. They had a lot to hide. What bothers me is that Chardet must have known from the outset the plan to substitute Pusey for Jean-Louis, and went along with it. Why *suddenly* would she have an attack of conscience? If that's what it was?'

'And *if* there was a plan,' Webb said daringly.

'Don't you start,' Timberlake said sharply.

'Oh, one thing,' Webb said, quickly changing the subject. 'The chauffeur – did you see him?'

'The poor woman's John Travolta?'

'Yeah. Name's Nobby Clarke, although according to a couple of the maids it should be "Knobby" with a K. Woman chaser, thinks a lot of himself. He reckons Thérèse was frigid. He made a pass at her and she froze him out.'

'Him? So would I!'

'I should hope so, guv,' Webb said, grinning. 'By the way, where's the Eager Beaver?'

151

'Nigel Larkin? I didn't think he was up to doing interviews at Towers Hall.' Darren Webb looked pleased. 'I left him at the nick, going through my cuttings file, see if a fresh pair of eyes might see something I've missed.'

'Shouldn't think so, guv.'

But Darren Webb was being unfair to the Eager Beaver. He *had* spotted something.

It was quite late by the time Timberlake and Webb got back to the Terrace Vale nick, but Detective Superintendent Harkness was still there. After the two detectives had given him a brief summary of their interviews, Timberlake said, 'I didn't learn anything to make me change my mind about the substitution. I still believe "Jean-Louis" is really Pusey, although I must admit he put up a convincing performance.'

'What about the countess?'

'Stainless steel and concrete. As regal as the last Empress of China. Frankly, sir, I've never met anyone like her.'

'There isn't anyone like her,' Webb grumbled.

'The one thing we got out of all the interviews was that something badly upset Thérèse Chardet two or three days ago. Her whole attitude changed,' Timberlake said. 'What it was—' he shrugged. 'The de Gaillmonts denied it, but I'm sure the servants are right. As I said to Darren, Chardet must have known from day one – and that was a long time ago, in France, before they all came here – she must have been part of the plan to substitute Pusey for Jean-Louis, and went along with it. So why should she suddenly start moping about the place and have a change of heart? If that's what it was,' he repeated.

'Perhaps she found out she was pregnant,' Harkness suggested.

'She was not pregnant, and there had been no parturition,' Professor Mortimer told his audience at Thérèse Chardet's post mortem.

'She hadn't had children.' Timberlake said quietly to Webb.

'Live, stillborn or aborted,' Mortimer added, who had good hearing for a man of his age. Too good sometimes, Timberlake thought. 'However, she had been sexually active,' Mortimer added.

'Well, she was nearly thirty,' Sergeant Braddock mumbled.

Gertrude Hacker's hearing was as good as her chief's. Her glare at Braddock said more about her than it did about him.

'In fact, apart from the cause of death, strangulation from self-inflicted hanging, the subject has little or nothing of any interest to a pathologist,' Mortimer said finally.

What an epitaph. Timberlake said to himself. 'When will the histological report be available, professor?' he asked.

'Tomorrow.'

'Will you arrange for a copy to be faxed to us at Terrace Vale, please?'

'If you think it will mean anything to you', Mortimer said cuttingly. He treated all laymen as if they would require expert help to decipher H_2O. He inclined his head towards Gertrude Hacker, who nodded to Timberlake. Mortimer had given his agreement by proxy.

'Give the de Gaillmonts' solicitor – Mellick – a ring,' Timberlake said to Darren Webb as they left one of Mortimer's assistants stitching up the gaping remains of the once-attractive Thérèse Chardet. 'Tell him to let the de Gaillmonts know we're on our way to see them right now.'

'Supposing they're not in, guv?'

'They will be. They're keeping their heads down.'

While he waited for Webb outside in the street Timberlake took a deep breath of what passed for fresh air in London. He preferred the odour of the oxides of carbon, tinged with sulphur, soot and diesel-engine fumes, to the uniquely unpleasant smell of the morgue. Timberlake smiled at the prospect of giving the de Gaillmonts a shock. He could hardly have guessed that he himself was the one who was due to be flabbergasted.

The two detectives were shown into the usual reception room by a frightened-looking maid, uncomfortable in a 1930s domestic servant's outfit, where they had to wait, like supplicants collecting for charity, until one or both of the de Gaillmonts deigned to appear.

Jean-Louis de Gaillmont was the first to arrive. Rather coldly he said, 'Good day, gentlemen. You demanded to see us, I understand.'

Timberlake gave no reaction to the 'demanded'. Just as coldly he said, 'As a result of today's post mortem examination of Mademoiselle Chardet there are questions I must put to you. I thought it better to see you at once, privately, rather than have the coroner raise them when you were unprepared.'

De Gaillmont's expression softened. Before he could speak the door was flung open by the maid, looking even more frightened, and Sophie de Gaillmont entered like a sudden Mediterranean thunderstorm.

'I intend to make the strongest possible representations to the authorities about this . . .' she hunted for the word ' . . . *harassment*. What is your pretext for forcing yourself on to us once more?'

'At our last meeting, madame, you said that Mademoiselle Chardet had no . . . romantic entanglements, I think was the expression I used. After examining her, the pathologist states unequivocally that she had been sexually active.'

'Then the man is a charlatan or incompetent, probably both!'

The vehemence of her reply surprised even Timberlake. He dearly wished Professor Mortimer could have been with him. Their confrontation would have been worth buying tickets to watch. Webb was trying to be invisible.

'He has an international reputation, madame. I must ask you to think again: can you think of any man with whom she might have been intimate?'

Sophie de Gaillmont turned to Jean-Louis. 'Get the solicitor Mellick on the telephone at once. He is to speak to the inspector here.'

Jean-Louis hesitated, then shrugged. He went to the telephone and dialled while Sophie stared directly at Timberlake. It took all his will power not to look away. 'Engaged.' Jean-Louis' voice broke the spell.

'No matter. I shall inform him that if the police have anything further to ask Monsieur le Comte or myself, they must make arrangements through him, and I shall require him to be present at the interview.'

'That is your right, madame,' Timberlake said, sounding much more composed than he felt. By now he actively hated the pair of them for the crimes he was sure they had committed.

The telephone rang. Jean-Louis answered it.

'*Caterina*, darling! he said excitedly. 'Where are you? Are you all right? What happened? Why did—'

Sophie de Gaillmont moved as quickly as dignity would allow her and took the telephone from him.

Timberlake felt as if his guts had just dropped into his shoes. He listened intently to Sophie's end of the conversation.

'Caterina! Are you well, my dear? . . . Where are you . . .? Why didn't you tell us . . . I see. How long will it take? . . . Are you sure? . . . Well, please keep in touch . . . Yes, of course I'll tell him.' She hung up. To Jean-Louis she said, 'She sends her love.' She turned and fixed Timberlake with one of her imperious stares.

'The Princess Tozharska is well. She has had to go abroad for urgent business concerned with the application for restoration of her family estate.'

'But why did she—?' Timberlake began.

'That is all I have to tell you. Be good enough to leave. I wish to speak privately to Monsieur le Comte.' She turned her back, leaving Timberlake no choice but to leave. Webb skipped out thankfully behind him.

As soon as they were out of earshot, Webb said, 'Well, the fertilizer has hit the fan good and proper, guv. That blows your theory about swapping identities clear out of the water.'

Timberlake was so shaken he didn't even rebuke Webb for a gross mixing of metaphors. He was too busy wondering where the hell he could go from here.

Chapter 22

By the time Timberlake returned to the Terrace Vale nick, his initial dejection at learning that Caterina Tozharska was alive – a development which exploded all his carefully reasoned theories – was giving way to a healthy scepticism.

'It's rather too convenient that Princess Tozharska should telephone right at the moment that Darren and I happen to be there,' he said to Superintendent Harkness

'Then what was the call?' Harkness asked reasonably. 'If they arranged for someone to telephone at that moment, it suggests the existence of another accomplice. Things are complicated enough without bringing another player into the game.'

'Darren, get on to British Telecom, see if there's any way of knowing where the call could have come from,' Timberlake said.

'Maybe there's another line in the house, and the call came from inside,' Sergeant Braddock said.

'That still leaves the problem of who the accomplice was,' Harkness objected. 'Darren, you interviewed the servants: was there anyone who could have been bribed to do it?'

'I doubt if the de Gaillmonts would risk involving one of them,' Timberlake said before Webb could answer. He nodded agreement. 'So have a go at British Telecom, Darren.'

'Right, guv,' Webb said. He made a mental note to pass the chore on to the Eager Beaver, alias Nigel Larkin.

'The more I think about it, the more unlikely it sounds,' Timberlake said. 'Why was Tozharska's car at Woolwich? Why weren't her suitcases still in the boot? If they ever were. What could have happened to make her shoot off in the middle of the night to go abroad?'

'Yeah! Why didn't she leave a note, or wake somebody?' Webb contributed. 'And why didn't she contact the family earlier?'

'Busy travelling, perhaps?' Harkness was playing the devil's advocate again to test the strength of the theories.

'She couldn't have been *that* busy,' Timberlake said. 'And from what I heard of our end of the conversation, she told the de Gaillmonts practically nothing.'

'Guv, I must say that they both sounded very convincing, though,' Webb said apologetically.

'Sure they did. They've been preparing this whole situation for God knows how long,' Timberlake said. 'Working on it, planning. Look at the lengths they've gone to. And so far they've not left a single tangible clue, not a scintilla of evidence. They've got us stymied.' Webb decided to leave asking Timberlake what a scintilla was until later.

'Frankly, I'd be a little easier in my mind if we knew where that phone call came from,' Harkness said. 'If we could explain that, it would go a long way towards persuading me the whole thing was a set-up, and not one of those awful coincidences that can derail an investigation.'

Timberlake shook his head. 'There was something wrong with that call. Something they didn't get quite right.'

'Timing, perhaps? You need to be a good actor to make a one-sided phone conversation sound realistic,' Webb said surprisingly. 'My wife told me that.'

'No, it wasn't that. My bet is they rehearsed it anyway. They've been so thorough with everything else. But there was a false note, somewhere. I just can't put my finger on it.'

'You really are convinced of your conspiracy theory of a substitution, Harry.'

'It's cast iron, sir.'

'Cast iron's inflexibility can also be its weakness. It shatters before it bends.'

A smile spread over Timberlake's face. He began to chuckle.

'What is it?' Harkness asked.

'Oh, it was phoney. I'm sure of it now.' The other two men waited for him to go on. 'A silly mistake that nearly slipped past me. *Why did they all speak in English?* The natural language of Sophie, "Jean-Louis" and Caterina Tozharska is French. The de Gaillmonts had to speak in English so I could understand what was supposed to be going on!'

'Bingo!' said Webb.

'So what's next?' Harkness demanded.

'Square One,' Timberlake said with a wry smile. 'I'm going back through all the statements and the newspaper cuttings file I've got on the Puseys.'

In fact, he didn't need to. At the door to his own office he was intercepted by Nigel Larkin, the Eager Beaver. 'Did you see my note, guv?' Timberlake stared at him. 'The note on that file you asked me to go through.'

'God, I'm sorry, Nigel; I haven't had time to look at it yet. Come on in.'

The fat cuttings file had a note clipped to the cover: LUCINDA PUSEY? Inside there were a few cuttings with yellow Post-it labels attached. A number of newspaper stories about Charles Pusey Senior had references to his 'beautiful sister, Miss Lucinda Pusey'. The last one was dated some two years after he married Sophie de Collonet. For a moment Timberlake wondered whether the de Collonet family appeared in the *Encyclopaedia of the False Nobility*. After that, nothing. No reference to her getting married, divorced, attending her brother's funeral, of her dying.

'It's weird,' Timberlake agreed. 'I wonder what happened to her? Although I don't see what that could have to do with this case. Still, it's a loose end, and I hate loose ends. Well done, Nigel.'

Larkin was on the point of leaving when Sergeant Rumsden appeared at the door. 'That's handy,' he said. 'I wanted to have a word with you, Harry: young Nigel here.' Larkin looked apprehensive. 'D'you still need him as a CID aide? We're not all that flush with bodies in uniform.' Larkin looked at Timberlake with the soulful eyes of a spaniel who was bursting to be taken out for a walk.

'I'd be grateful if you could spare him, Anthony,' Timberlake said, flattering the sergeant by calling him by the full version of his Christian name. 'He's been very helpful.'

'Fancy that,' Rumsden replied, his answer having more layers of meaning than an onion. 'Well, fair enough ... for the time being,' he added warningly over his shoulder as he went out.

'Thanks, guv,' Larkin said.

'See you tomorrow,' Timberlake said. He looked at his watch. Probably too late for solicitors to be in their offices, but worth a try. He dialled Jonathan Mellick's number, but got only a scratchy recording from an answering machine. Timberlake decided not to leave a message to say he would be calling tomorrow.

More than ever his flat seemed like a room in an institution. He didn't feel hungry, and he couldn't think of any music he wanted to play. Turning on the television would mean getting up from his armchair. He wondered if he should call Jenny Long and try to make his peace with her. That would present problems, he told himself, because he still didn't know what he had done wrong, which would make it difficult for him to make any apology sound sincere.

Timberlake stared at the telephone, and when it rang it made him jump.

'It's me. Sarah,' she added unnecessarily. 'It isn't a bad time to call?'

'No, it's fine. I'm alone.'

'Can I come over and see you? Old Pals' Act. There's something I want to talk to you about.'

His mind raced. He was on the point of saying, 'What is it?' but checked in case she told him over the phone. 'Sure. As soon as you like.'

'Have you eaten? Shall I get something?

'No, and yes. Chinese'll do.'

'Right.'

While he waited for her he looked round to see if the flat needed tidying, then took a shower, which normally he wouldn't have done until just before going to bed. What the hell—? he kept asking himself.

Sarah Lewis arrived in her usual working clothes of a two-piece in what the French unreasonably call *caca d'oie* – goose shit – which nevertheless looked junior-executive smart. Provocative it wasn't. He didn't know how he felt about that.

They spread the Chinese takeaway on plates on a low coffee table and ate using forks and fingers. He opened a bottle of his favourite wine – which used to be hers when they were together – which went down without a struggle. He opened a second bottle when they got to the coffee.

'I've got a problem,' Sarah said at last. 'This rape case—'

So she had come to see him to talk shop. For the second time

159

that evening Timberlake couldn't unscramble his feelings.

'I know who did it, but I can't prove it. His wife's giving him an alibi. Loyalty, I suppose. Misplaced.'

'Shouldn't you be discussing this with Bob Farmer?'

Her expression answered that question. 'He thinks I've got it wrong. But I *know* I've got the right man.'

'Despite the alibi?'

'I told you: misplaced loyalty.' She took a large mouthful of the wine. 'Look, chummy was done for rape in Norfolk. The local police were absolutely certain of it. He virtually admitted it after he got off, thanks to a smart brief and a stupid bloody magistrate. His wife doesn't know; she thinks he's cleaner than Snow White.'

'And you're wondering whether you ought to tell her.'

'He raped Emma Leyland, I'm positive. Harry, you of all people know about gut feelings.'

He took his time. 'Then if you've got what the French call an *intime conviction* that he's guilty—'

'He was guilty and got away with it, and if we're not careful, he'll get away with this one, too,' she said hotly. 'But suppose I do tell her about the other case and she still sticks by him?'

'You could be in very deep shit, because he could make an official complaint that you had ruined his marriage.'

'What should I do, Harry?'

'I don't know. But *you* know what you're going to do. You'd made up your mind before you came here.'

Sarah took another large mouthful of wine. 'Bastard,' she muttered. She said it meaninglessly, the way footballers do when they miss a good scoring chance.

'Sod you. You're right, of course.' She stood up, and swayed. 'Oh, bloody hell, I can't drive like this.'

'I'm not fit, either. I'll ring for a taxi.'

'How will I get my car back home?'

They both knew how this little *pas de deux* would end, but they went through all the steps before agreeing that Sarah would stay the night. Part Two of the performance was concerned with where she would sleep. To the surprise of both and the disappointment of at least one of them, the arrangement was that Sarah would sleep in his bed, and Timberlake would sleep on the divan.

He woke more than once during the night, thinking he could hear Sarah moving around, and there were times when he hoped she would come and ask him whether he wasn't uncomfortable on the divan and wouldn't he be better . . . and the rest. The next morning when she had some breakfast wearing only one of his shirts he was on the point of making an unequivocal proposition. What stopped him was beyond him . . . and her. It made him very gritchy for a few hours.

Jonathan Mellick greeted Harry Timberlake and Darren Webb with the minimum of enthusiasm that politeness demanded. When Timberlake explained the reason for his visit even that lukewarm civility chilled.

'Is Lucinda Pusey still alive?' Mellick could not deny that she was. 'Where is she living?'

The solicitor prevaricated with all his professional skill, but Timberlake was adamant. Mellick pleaded lawyer–client confidentiality, which didn't wash because he wavered when he was asked in what respect Lucinda Pusey was his client.

Timberlake did his own spot of prevarication. He reminded Mellick that he was engaged on an enquiry into the murder of Lucinda Pusey's nephew, and not following up a parking offence or failure to be in possession of a TV licence. He failed to mention that he believed Charles Pusey was in good health and was a major suspect in the murder.

Timberlake further pointed out that if he had to he could eventually find Lucinda Pusey's address through the Department of Social Security, Inland Revenue and various other official bodies. He hoped that Mr Mellick would have sufficient social conscience to save the time of the Metropolitan Police in general and Timberlake in particular in this most serious affair.

Mellick was unaccustomed to policemen treating him with such persistence, but Harry Timberlake was something special. Eventually, mustering as much dignity as he could in face of the onslaught, Mellick capitulated.

He wrote an address on a piece of paper, using his usual steel-nibbed pen and inkwell. 'When Miss Pusey's brother died, he left a trust fund for her to provide her with an income. He also bequeathed her the freehold of an apartment with a further trust fund to pay for its maintenance.'

Timberlake guessed how Mellick was squaring revealing this information with himself. It was all in Pusey's will, which one of the investigating team would eventually have thought of digging out from public records. And Mellick was looking after the trust funds for the late Charles Pusey: Lucinda was not his client.

'She is something of a recluse,' Mellick warned Timberlake. This was on a par with saying that Hitler was not very nice. 'I think it advisable that I telephone her and arrange for her to receive you.'

Chapter 23

Lucinda Pusey's apartment was a penthouse in Eaton Square. Lady Bracknell would have been gratified to note that it was on the fashionable side. Timberlake decided to take WPC Rosie Hall with him when he called. If Lucinda Pusey was the recluse Mellick had said she was, perhaps Rosie Hall's deceptively country-fresh, mild appearance might make Lucinda feel more at ease.

Mellick had warned Timberlake that there was no name or number for the penthouse on the Entryphone to the house. There was only one anonymous button, which Timberlake pressed. An electronically distorted voice said 'Yes?', and Timberlake announced himself as plain Harry Timberlake. The doorlock buzzed.

The lift was equally secretive. Floors 1 to 4 were marked, but there was nothing to indicate that there was a fifth-floor penthouse. He deduced without strain that he and Rosie Hall would have to walk up from the fourth floor.

Lucinda Pusey's front door would not have been out of place on the entrance to a Pharaoh's tomb. It was bronze, with massive bosses and bars. There were three keyholes: two for Bramah locks and one that looked as if it took a key for a strong-room door. From the inside he would discover that it did a better job of defence than the Maginot Line. There was a spyhole at the height of Timberlake's chest.

Timberlake knocked on the door with his knuckles, and held up his warrant card at the level of his face. After a moment there were the sounds of locks being turned.

He had seen photographs of Lucinda Pusey when she was young, forty or more years earlier, and he wondered how she looked now. He had seen Roman ruins in France and North Africa, and they were sufficient basis for his imagination to be able to reconstruct their former nobility. He supposed that despite the possibly cruel depredations of the decades there would be some hint of her youthful beauty to recall how she had once looked.

When she opened the door, it took all of Timberlake's self-control not to gasp.

Standing in the doorway, lit from behind in *contre-jour* from the windows on to a terrace was a heap of shapeless black clothes with a heavily made-up chalk-white face peering out of the folds. It made her dark eyes look like coals.

'Well, come in,' the spectre said in a surprisingly firm voice with a genuine Eaton Square–Cheltenham Ladies' College accent.

'Miss Pusey,' he said, 'this is Woman Police Constable Hall. I am Detective Inspector Timberlake.' A skeletal white hand emerged from the black clothes. To his dying day Harry Timberlake would never know what possessed him to do it, but he gently took the hand and kissed it. It was clean, dry and slightly perfumed. After they left Timberlake told Rosie that if she ever told another living soul what he had done he would personally arrange for her to be transferred to Scotland Yard's post-room for the rest of her police career.

'Don't worry, guv,' she said. 'I was on the point of curtseying myself.'

The apartment must be worth well more than a million now, Timberlake calculated, and it was furnished to that standard. It was neat and clean. Through the french doors on to the terrace he could see well-kept flowers and bushes in large pots and troughs. He wondered who looked after the place. The only odd elements in the apartment – apart from its occupant – were neat piles of old magazines, many of them having long ceased publication, and three or four leather-bound scrapbooks carefully placed on small tables.

Lucinda Pusey waved to them to sit down and offered coffee from an ornate ceramic thermos jug. Rosie served it.

'I take it that Mr Mellick has told you I'm enquiring into the death of your nephew. Miss Pusey, do you know of anyone who would want to kill him?'

It was as if he had thrown a lighted match into a box of fireworks.

'Yes! That fucking awful woman! That fucking awful French whore! There's nothing she's not fucking capable of!' Lucinda Pusey's eyes were staring, wild.

The outburst was so ferocious and the language so shocking coming from a seemingly frail and cultured woman, for all her weird appearance, that for a few seconds Timberlake was lost for words. Lucinda Pusey, he thought, was seriously unbalanced. Keeping his voice under control he said reasonably, 'But she was his mother.'

'You mean you've never heard of parents killing their children? God Almighty, it began in Roman times – before, in ancient Egypt – and has carried on ever since.'

Perhaps Lucinda's wild allegation was less outrageous than she knew, if the murdered man was Jean-Louis de Gaillmont and not Charles Pusey. 'True,' he conceded, 'but what motive could she have?'

'Who could tell? She's mad, you know. Oh, not screaming, strait-jacket loony; she was obsessed. She killed my brother. A gentler, kinder, more lovable man never existed, and she killed him.' From what Timberlake had read in his cuttings file about Pusey Senior's business methods, 'gentle' and 'kind' were not adjectives that sprang immediately to mind.

'I thought he died in hospital during a heart operation.'

'Who caused him to have a heart attack? She did, of course – and deliberately. She was always bullying him into being more *gentlemanly*, in cultivating the *right* people, making donations to the *right* organizations and *right* party so he'd get a title. She was aristocracy-mad; spread her legs for anyone who had a decent title. It's all here, in black and white. She never let up . . . never gave Charles any peace . . . And after she killed him she bought her fucking title from some decadent French frog with Charles's money. She gives me the *shits*!'

Lucinda Pusey paused for breath and wiped spittle from the corners of her mouth with the sleeve of her unidentifiable garment. Her voice became softer, more plaintive, and she seemed to be unaware that she was thinking out loud. 'Why did you have to marry her? Why did you have to marry her? You didn't need her, Charles; we had each other.' Thin tears filled her eyes and began to run down her cheeks, leaving tracks in her make-up to reveal grey, wrinkled skin beneath. She looked unimaginably old, and yet she could not have been much more than seventy. 'Well, we'll be together again soon enough, and I know God will forgive us,' she said.

'Miss Pusey,' Timberlake said gently. 'About your nephew—'

165

She looked at him, and her eyes cleared. In a normal voice she said, 'No, I can't think of anyone who would want to kill young Charlie. Except that awful bitch. I always liked him, you know.'

'Major Lock, Betty Lock's father?'

'That silly little man, and his silly little tart of a daughter?' She made a sound that was the nearest to 'Pish tush!' that Timberlake had ever heard. 'I'm sure you have a great deal to do, so I shan't keep you any longer.' Her eyes became vague again. 'It was good of you to call.' She rose.

As the massive front door closed behind Timberlake and Rosie Hall they could hear the heavy locks being turned.

'Talk about off her trolley, guv!' Rosie said when they were back in the street. 'And what was all that about God'll forgive us? What d'you reckon she meant by that?'

'What did Tutankhamun have for breakfast on his fourteenth birthday?'

Rosie stared at him. 'Sorry, guv?' He repeated the question. 'I don't know.'

'Exactly. And what the hell will that matter two thousand years from now?'

Harry Timberlake gave a full verbal report on the interview with Lucinda Pusey to Detective Superintendent Harkness with Darren Webb and the AMIP foot-soldier detectives in attendance. No one thought it got them any further forward in another investigation that was badly running out of steam.

'There's a fax from Professor Mortimer,' Harkness said, handing it to Timberlake. 'I think you'll find one item quite interesting.'

Timberlake read the sheet, with Webb looking over his shoulder. 'A hundred and forty milligrams of alcohol per hundred millilitres of blood—'

'Well bevvied,' Webb commented, 'but we knew that anyway.'

'These are the ones.' Timberlake indicated items on the report. 'Ethinyloestradiol and Norethisterone.'

'What the hell are they?'

'They mean she was on the pill.'

'Maybe she thought she might strike lucky and score,' Webb suggested, not believing it himself.

'Much more likely she was having an affair with someone. If

she was looking for a one-off she'd be more likely to be carrying a condom.'

'Then either Sophie and Jean-Louis de Gaillmont were lying, or they didn't know,' Webb said. 'My bet is they were lying.'

'Mine, too. So who was her mystery lover?'

'D'you know, guv, you sound just like Barbara Cartland.'

Timberlake looked annoyed at first, but then couldn't help grinning.

At the end of a day's play top chess players, their coaches and advisers study the position of the pieces and try to work out the possible permutations and combinations of the next handful of moves open to their principal and his opponent. Sarah Lewis had no coaches or advisers to help her with all the possible permutations and combinations of the dialogue she would have with Anthea Wightman, after she had 'innocently' revealed that her husband had been charged with rape in Norfolk.

For one mad moment she contemplated mentioning that Wightman was dead lucky to get away with it, but she quickly dropped this hot coal of an idea. Eventually she accepted the inevitable and decided to play it by ear.

Where to meet was the next thing to consider, which didn't take long. Some neutral ground might be a good idea, Sarah thought, somewhere public where Anthea couldn't shout and scream at her. Then she changed her mind. Anthea's home would be best because the impact of the news would be sharper in her own environment. And her surroundings would constantly remind her of what Sarah had told her; there would be no safe shell to retreat into, no way to shut it out of her mind.

'She's better free of him. Who wants to be married to a rapist?' Sarah said out loud. She was really doing the woman a favour, she told herself.

Sarah was no hypocrite. It took only a few seconds for her to realize that she was being anything but altruistic: she was prepared to tell Anthea something that might well devastate her life – all for Sarah's own obsessive desire to catch a criminal.

And further her own career, she had to admit to herself.

Sarah's main problem was how to make a call on Anthea Wightman appear casual and unplanned. Fate, or whatever you want to call it, solved the problem. Or maybe subconsciously Anthea was

167

sending a signal. That's probably what Freud would have said. In the wok cookbook she had borrowed from Sarah she had left a letter from her mother. Sarah said she'd take it back. 'No trouble, Anthea.'

Nigel Larkin, looking even more eager beaverish than usual, appeared in the door of Timberlake's office. 'Got a minute, guv?'

'Sure.'

'Which phone is your direct line? There's somebody I think you'll want to speak to.'

Timberlake decided to play along. He indicated the phone.

Larkin placed himself between Timberlake and the telephone and pressed the buttons. 'Engaged,' he said. 'I'll have another go in a minute.' He replaced the receiver, went to the window, looked out and whistled tunelessly. Timberlake was beginning to become bored with Larkin's little game but the younger man forestalled him.

'I've got a feeling the Assistant Commissioner, Crime, is going to give you a ring, guv,' he said nonchalantly. The telephone rang. Larkin beat Timberlake to it.

'DI Timberlake's office,' he said. 'The Assistant Commissioner, Crime's secretary? Tell your guvnor Inspector Timberlake's too busy to talk now . . . Yes, the grotty old Assistant Commissioner can write in for an interview if he wants to speak to him . . . Drop dead!'

Timberlake snatched the phone from him. A woman's recorded voice repeated, 'Earth A . . . Earth A . . . Start test.'

'What the hell is that?' Timberlake asked.

Larkin beamed. 'It's the engineers' callback system for testing a line. Every exchange has a three-figure number that puts you through to the system.' He picked up the phone and dialled three digits. 'That's the code for this exchange,' he said, and handed the phone to Timberlake.

The same recorded voice said, 'You are connected to . . . 0171 . . . 723—' and then Timberlake's number. 'Start test.' The recording went on repeating the same message while Timberlake listened fascinated.

'Hang up, guv. This time it's going to be Caterina Tozharska.'

A matter of some twenty-five seconds later the phone rang, but

168

it seemed much longer. 'Earth A . . . Earth A . . . Start test.'

'I don't know why it is, but practically every phone I tried had something wrong with Earth A. Whatever that is,' Larkin said, trying to subdue his enormous pleasure.

'So that's how they got "Princess Tozharska" to ring just at that moment—' Timberlake said slowly. 'That's bloody marvellous, Nigel. Bloody marvellous. How did you find out?'

Larkin looked surprised. 'Sergeant Webb told me to get on to British Telecom and ask how it might have been worked.'

'Well, good for Darren,' Timberlake said, thinking of a few things he might say to his sergeant about passing bucks. 'I'll go and see Superintendent Harkness and tell him what you came up with.'

Eager Beaver Nigel Larkin was metamorphosed into Cat that Has Eaten the Cream.

'You look a bit tired,' Anthea said.

'That's a man's remark. It means "You look old." Or, "God, you look awful." ' She smiled. 'No, not tired. Just a bit stressed.'

'Mmm. D'you ever wonder if the job's worth it?'

'All the time. Particularly when you see marriages breaking up, people drinking too much . . . Still, there is job satisfaction. When you catch a criminal, at least you're helping other people, doing a public service; stopping him – or her – doing it to someone else. For a while, at least.'

Come off it, Sarah told herself. You're like stag-hunters and pheasant-shooters who say they're doing it for the good of the animals. You bloody well enjoy it, the you-against-them, the *hunt*.

'Don't you ever feel a bit . . . I don't know . . . upset at being responsible for someone going to prison for years, at what it might do to his family?'

Sarah checked her instant reaction and managed to speak calmly. 'In the first place, I'm not responsible: he is, for committing the crime. And all my sympathies are with the victims. People sometimes seem to forget them. When you've had to pick up the pieces after muggings, armed robberies, GBH, drunken driving . . . when you've seen what it does to people when their houses are robbed and vandalized, *they're* the people you feel sorry for.'

'Yes, I never thought of it like that. I suppose you have to have been a victim yourself to understand.'

Sarah felt as if she'd been punched in the stomach. She pulled herself together and said, 'Anthea, I'm sorry we had to come and question your husband like that. It was routine. When there's been an indecent assault, or a rape – anything like that – automatically we see everyone on our list.'

'What list?' Anthea asked sharply. 'You said you were checking on car registrations.'

'Oh, yes, we always say that. I shouldn't have told you about the list.'

'What list? What are you talking about?'

Sarah pretended not to notice Anthea's tone, and tried to keep her own voice nonchalant. 'Oh, you know: a list of people with a record of involvement in sexual offences.' She added quickly, 'Not just people who've been convicted – everyone, including those who've had the charge dropped, like your husband – or just suspected and not even charged.'

'What d'you mean, "like my husband"?' Her voice was harsh, almost unrecognizable.

Sarah's own distress was all too real. She had gone way beyond the point of no return and could be heading for personal disaster. Then, too, she was feeling deeply sympathetic for Anthea Wightman. 'Oh, my God! You didn't know?'

'Know *what*? What has he done?'

'Nothing! Nothing, really.' She kept the "really" ambiguous. 'Anthea, please, you mustn't let him guess I've told you. I thought you'd know already. It's nothing really. About five years ago, some silly girl in Norfolk said he'd raped her. It didn't get very far: it was thrown out in the magistrates' court. Ross didn't even have to give evidence. The trouble is, like I said, even if you're innocent, you're on the list.'

'Why didn't he tell me?' Anthea asked, mostly to herself.

'He was probably too embarrassed to tell you.' Anthea Wightman didn't reply. 'Anyway, you've been married for—' She checked just in time. '—How long is it? You must know what sort of man he is.'

'Yes,' she said tonelessly.

Oh, yes, you know all right, Sarah thought. She could recall Anthea's actual words. *It's just . . . he's not all that considerate. You*

170

know, pumping away, like it's a competition, or a battle – *you know . . . And he's getting worse. On top of that he likes to talk dirty. I have to fake it half the time.*

'Anthea, please, whatever you do, don't tell him I told you about Norfolk. I could lose my job. *Please.*'

'Yes, your job. Of course.' Her voice was strained, brittle. 'Well, I must think about getting dinner. Thank you for coming.' Her face was like a death mask.

At the door Sarah said, in all honesty, 'I don't know what to say.'

The reply 'I think you've already said enough' was forming in Anthea's mouth, but she bit her lip and stayed silent.

There are black days and black days: black like thunderclouds and black like the inside of a tomb. There are some black days when you wish you hadn't got out of bed, some when you wish you hadn't been born.

Timberlake's day was at the bottom end of a black hole.

It began when a handwritten note from Jenny Long was delivered. It said:

Charles Pusey Senior: Blood group O.

Jean-Louis de Gaillmont: Blood group AB.

Timberlake was so exercised by these data that he hardly noticed the final words, which had nothing to do with the previous information.

Sorry, darling. Love, J.

He found a piece of card he had prepared from a text book.

He compared the note with the table on the card . . . and compared it again. And again. However hard he willed it to be otherwise, the answer was the same each time.

A man with a blood group O could not be the father of a child with the group AB.

Charles Pusey Senior could not possibly be the father of Jean-Louis de Gaillmont.

Jean-Louis was genuine. The murdered man *was* Charles Pusey Junior.

That was final enough in itself, but within minutes a fax arrived from Capitaine Lapollet. If such a thing was possible, it made things worse by rubbing salt into Timberlake's near-mortal wounds. It said the late Comte de Gaillmont's group was

171

A, which meant that he *could* be Jean-Louis's father. It didn't mean he *was* his father, but this last blow was piling Pelion upon Ossa.

All Harry Timberlake's carefully constructed theories crashed in ruins under the weight of this incontrovertible evidence. And with them, his reputation.

Chapter 24

Harry Timberlake could not remember ever having been so comprehensively baffled. In his career there had been investigations that had gone wrong: patently guilty men who had gone free on a technicality or at the collective whim of a stupid jury; cases which came less to a dead end than died of atrophy; even cases that had failed to get off the ground.

Never had he been so utterly wrong; worse, he could not see why or how he was wrong.

Everything fitted his theory that Sophie Pusey de Gaillmont had conspired to replace the Comte Jean-Louis de Gaillmont with her son Charles Pusey – everything except the inconvenient, irrefutable facts of the blood groups, which proved that Jean-Louis de Gaillmont could not be Charles Pusey. Timberlake tried to convince himself there were loopholes in the data he had been given. Perhaps the hospital records were wrong or Jenny Long had misread them was his first hope, but the chances were so slim as to be discounted. Then he remembered that a person's blood group could change after death. He had read of a well-documented case when a headless body was found; later, when the head turned up the blood groups of the two parts of the same person were different. The blood group in at least one of the parts had changed post mortem. This possible explanation had to be dismissed as soon as it surfaced, because Charles Pusey Senior's and Jean-Louis de Gaillmont's blood samples were taken in life.

Timberlake got up from his armchair to put on some music, but when he got to the racks of cassette recordings of his classic jazz discs he couldn't think of anything he wanted to hear. He became aware that it was late evening and it was quite dark in his flat. He didn't bother to turn on a light.

The doorbell rang. He decided to ignore it. When it rang again he was prompted to unhook the telephone, and switch off his mobile phone. The doorbell rang once more, insistently. After a moment he heard a key in the lock and the front door open. Jenny Long – it had to be her with a key – entered.

She took in the scene at a glance, but gave Timberlake an escape hatch. 'Hello, darling. I did ring. Were you in the loo?' Casually she switched on a couple of lights.

Timberlake never lied to Jenny. In the first place he hadn't had any reason to . . . and he had an uncomfortable feeling that she'd know anyway if he was lying. The nearest he got to it now was an indeterminate grunt and a shrug.

'I rang the nick and Darren Webb told me you'd gone home. He said you were feeling rather fed up, so I thought I'd come round and cheer you up.'

'Thanks,' he said without enthusiasm. He forced himself to add, 'And thanks for the note.' He couldn't bring himself to mention blood groups.

'I'm sorry I was rather bitchy when you asked me. Bad day, I suppose.'

'I'm sorry, too. I did bang on a bit. And all for—' He paused. 'Talking about having a bad day—' Timberlake took a deep breath and launched into an explanation how the information she had given him had smashed his case to pieces.

She didn't make the mistake of offering platitudes and fatuous remarks like 'I *know* it'll come out right, darling—' or 'I know how you feel'. Instead, while he was explaining his theory and how it had disintegrated, she made coffee.

She sat close beside him. 'What you need is a break. You've been working too hard and you've got too close to things. Look, one of my colleagues has dropped out and I've had a last-minute invitation to go to Rome for a three-day conference on micro-surgery. A pharmaceutical company is sponsoring it.'

'Why's a pharmaceutical company sponsoring a surgical conference?'

'Even cutters prescribe drugs, you know.'

'Yes. Sorry.'

'They'll pay all the hotel costs if we take a husband or wife with us.' She smiled. 'They won't ask for a marriage certificate. All you'll have to do is pay your own air fare. Harry, do come. I'm sure it'll do you good.'

'Thanks, Jenny, but I don't think I can get away.'

'Oh, come on! I know you: I bet you've got weeks of back leave owing.'

'It's not that. The investigation's still going on.' He smiled bitterly. 'I mean it's got to get started again. I can't simply swan off and leave everything.'

'If your Superintendent Harkness is as intelligent as you say he is, I'm sure he'll think it's a good idea for you to have a break, get away. Let's make the most of the opportunity while we can: they're clamping down on drugs companies' lashing out expensive gifts and providing junkets.'

'I should bloody well hope so.'

'This one's genuine,' she said sharply. 'Otherwise I shouldn't be going.'

'Yes, of course. Sorry, darling. But you don't want me along. I'd be a terrible wet blanket.'

Jenny Long rose. 'Well, if you're absolutely determined to slosh around in a slough of despond, it's up to you. You've got till Tuesday to change your mind.' She started to go out, then stopped at the door like a female Colombo to deliver a final thought. 'You wouldn't be committing yourself to anything.'

That she had understood his motivation better than he had himself was the last blow that made his misery total. But his decision would have an unexpected bonus.

The lie came much more easily than Anthea Wightman had expected. When she asked her husband if it was true that he had been charged with rape his immediate reaction was to counter with, 'Who told you? Was it that policewoman?'

She gave him the answer she had prepared. 'No. It was a man; an anonymous phone call.'

'Some bloody policeman trying to stir things up, obviously.'

'So it's *true*. Ross, why didn't you tell me?'

'Oh, God! A dozen reasons. First of all, it happened before I met you. And what was I supposed to do? Just casually say one evening over dinner, "Oh, by the way, I was charged with rape in Norfolk a couple of years ago. It's all right. The case was thrown out."?'

'What happened?'

He sighed. 'It doesn't put me in a very good light, but if you

175

know that much, I guess you're entitled to know the whole thing – the old story: it was at a party and we'd both had too much to drink. And . . . well, we did it. On the bank of one of the broads. I suppose there's a funny line there somewhere, but I don't feel like trying to be flippant. From what I could gather later, when she got home she had grass and mud on her clothes. Her boyfriend was waiting for her – he'd been working late and couldn't get to the party. When he saw the state she was in he—'

'What state *was* she in?'

'For God's sake, Anthea, do I have to draw pictures? We'd been . . . having sex . . . on the grass, there was mud and everything on the inside of her skirt . . . Christ Almighty! And you ask why I didn't tell you! . . . Anyway, obviously she regretted it, and was embarrassed and ashamed in front of her boyfriend. Perhaps she thought he'd dump her. So she said I'd raped her. When it got to court it was obvious she was lying and she'd made up the rape. It was so obvious I didn't have to give evidence. The magistrate stopped the case.'

There was a long, heavy silence between them. Eventually Ross Wightman spoke again. 'I told you: it was before I met you. If I'd known you then, it would never have happened: I wouldn't have gone off with that silly bitch . . . I can't even remember what she looked like.'

He made a tentative step towards her. Seeing that she did not move back, he carried on and took her into his arms, holding her close to him.

'Forgive me?' he said softly, his mouth close to her ear.

'We'll have to see,' she said, in a voice that told him as plainly as if she had said it outright that she believed him. In fact if Sarah Lewis had witnessed the whole scene she could well have believed him herself and begun to have doubts about his guilt. Ross held Anthea more tightly, her head on his shoulder.

Outside the house it was dark and the window reflected the room behind her. In the reflection she could see a second reflection in a large mirror.

The expression on her husband's face made Anthea feel an icy hand grip her heart.

'Guv,' Sarah addressed Bob Farmer as winningly as she could manage, 'the Emma Leyland rape case—'

'Yes, I'm sorry, Sarah,' he replied, jumping two-footed to the wrong conclusion. 'No need to apologize. I know you've tried your best, but—' Sarah silently gritted her teeth, imagining she was sinking them into his throat. He went on, 'But we've run out of suspects, and there aren't any new lines of enquiry on the horizon. So, I'm afraid we're going to have to start running it down now.'

'That's not quite what I had in mind,' she said. 'What I'd like to do is ask Wightman if he'd be prepared to take part in an identity parade.'

Farmer stared at her as if she were an extra terrestrial. 'Oh, for Christ's sake! There's absolutely nothing to connect him to the woman whatshername, Leyland, and his wife's given him a brass-bound alibi. There's not the faintest justification to ask him to stand in a line-up. Go away and forget it.' The tone of this last sentence carried an unmistakable coda: '. . . you silly little woman'.

Sarah stood still for a moment before turning away, her mouth full of bile.

Although life is chaotic and unpredictable, there are times when a certain symmetry occurs in the lives of people who have some sort of relationship. When this happens, it may seem that the law of averages has been repealed, as when red comes up on the roulette wheel ten times running, or the England cricket captain loses the toss in all five test matches. This is illusory: the law is immutable and will prevail over a longer period.

In the meantime, however, the lives of Sarah Lewis and Harry Timberlake had taken on a similar form. Sarah's depression hardly deserved the same name as Timberlake's black *cafard*. Nevertheless, it was more than having the hump, and the causes of her dejection were much the same as his: the bottom had fallen out of her confidence when she was on the point of successfully concluding a difficult case. There was no hint of a reaction from the Wightmans after her last visit to Anthea, and Bob Farmer had shot her down in flames.

Like Harry Timberlake, she sat at home, staring at a wall, wondering what the hell to do next.

It was then that the phone rang. It was Julian Tabard, inviting her to dinner. Sarah tried to put him off, but he was as persistent as a carpet-seller in a souk faced by an American tourist. And gently persuasive with it.

He was sensitive enough to gather from the way Sarah answered his invitation that she was in no mood for a Savoy Grill or Quat' Saisons evening. So he said it would be an informal do and she could wear slacks and a tee-shirt if she felt so inclined. Sarah felt more like wearing sackcloth and ashes, and as she got ready to go out she wondered how the hell Julian had talked her into it.

They went to a place called Mother Carey's, which, despite its name, was paradoxically celebrated for not serving chicken in any sort or form whatsoever. Eggs might sneak into things like mayonnaise, custard and flans, but that was all. Mother Carey, a woman of stupendous proportions, hated, loathed and detested chickens. Her dream was to meet Colonel Sanders alone in a dark alley one night. She prepared meals from a necessarily limited menu on a giant black stove in the restaurant itself, as in some provincial restaurants that still survive in untouristed parts of France. She was assisted by her husband, who looked like an unfrocked bank manager. Nobody called him Father Carey. He uttered probably not more than a hundred words in a week.

The restaurant had only five tables, which meant the prices were high to make the place a viable concern; but the food was so good, the ambience so uplifting – people actually *talked* to each other, almost unheard of in an English restaurant – that diners paid up without pain.

Normally the restaurant was fully booked weeks in advance, although specially favoured customers who were willing to brave having Mother Carey kiss them would be squeezed into a sixth table, brought out in an emergency like a life raft. Julian Tabard was one of Mother Carey's very favoured clients.

Sarah's life now continued on its parallel course with Timberlake's.

'I'm off to do a rush job, a three-day shoot in the Caribbean,' Julian said. 'I'd love you to come.' He praised the exotic attractions of the West Indies in language that outdid travel brochures for extravagance. 'Seventy-eight hours' sun, sea and sand, plus anything else you might care for,' he concluded, hinting at pleasures not usually mentioned in polite travel literature.

She was almost overwhelmingly tempted. God knows I need a holiday, she told herself, for she had been working hard for months before this present major case. If she went, it would mean abandoning the Emma Leyland/Ross Wightman case, but everyone at Terrace Vale had virtually done that already. And what was one more unsolved case in the mountain of them already?

'I'm willing to bet you have some leave owing,' Tabard went on seductively. 'If you haven't, I have a tame Harley Street man who'll give you an impressive not-fit-for-work medical certificate.'

That was a mistake. It made up Sarah's mind for her. It was the old male attitude that a woman's work wasn't important, and she had no real dedication to it anyway.

'No, thanks, darling,' she said. 'Of course I'd like to come. But it's not on while things are as they are.'

Something in her manner, in her regard, told him she would not change her mind. He shrugged. 'If you have second thoughts—' But they both knew she wouldn't have. They both wondered if they were drifting apart.

Chapter 25

The Metropolitan Police have an excellent internal information network. If there is a major armed robbery by four men wearing ski masks and using a stolen BMW for the getaway in London SE5, and there is another major armed robbery by four men wearing ski masks and using a stolen BMW for the getaway in London NW10, very quickly the two groups of investigating detectives will be put into touch with each other.

That is why Detective Superintendent Harkness received a telex message from Scotland Yard informing him that there had been a murder in the area that came under Manchester Row police station. What linked Manchester Row and Terrace Vale was the name of the murder victim.

Lucinda Pusey.

Since it was highly probable that Lucinda Pusey's murder was connected with Charles Pusey's – if by no other way than by family – the overall strategy in the investigation of both crimes would be Harkness's responsibility, because his case had been the first one.

'You'll have to represent me,' Harkness told Timberlake. 'I've got a promotion board at the Yard today.'

Timberlake's reactions to this were mixed. He had a great deal of admiration for Harkness and thought he deserved promotion. At the same time he would miss having Harkness as the head of the AMIP team in his area. 'Well, good luck, sir,' he said.

'I'm not a candidate. I'm on the selection panel. I'll be back by this evening. You can bring me up to date then.'

Although Manchester Row detectives were assigned to the AMIP team, it was logical that Harry Timberlake, representing Harkness, would be the senior officer in charge of tactics for the time being. In any case, he had the advantage of having interviewed the victim a matter of a few days before her death.

By the time Timberlake and Webb arrived at the Eaton Square the SOCOs had done their thorough sweep of the flat and taken fingerprints from various pieces of furniture, and the police surgeon, Dr Don Houghton, had certified Lucinda Pusey dead. Apart from his duties as a police surgeon Dr Houghton had a lucrative sideline as medical adviser to a TV medical series, which seemed to have gone to his head. Although he never appeared on the screen himself, he always seemed to be looking surreptitiously for the camera to make sure he was in shot, and he had begun to articulate like Charles Laughton, whom he resembled. According to the DI from Manchester Row, he was a right pain in the left iliac fossa.

As the Terrace Vale detectives were entering the flat, Professor Mortimer, whose hospital was close by, was leaving with Gertrude Hacker trundling on behind. 'Subject to the post mortem examination, death by asphyxiation caused by a pillow forced on her face. Time of death, plus or minus an hour, nine o'clock last night.'

'What he didn't bother to tell you,' Dr Houghton said confidentially, 'was that we agreed it's not certain whether she died of suffocation or whether the shock caused a heart attack. The p.m. should settle it.' Timberlake thanked him.

The local DI was Dougal Frazer, who had studiously preserved his Glasgow accent despite being in London for the past twenty years. He was bandy-legged, gap-toothed and had the craggiest face Timberlake had ever seen. He had bags under the bags under his eyes.

'Sorry we have to come barging in on your patch,' Timberlake said politely, 'but you know how these things work.' If he was going to have to work with Frazer it was best to establish friendly relationships with him from the outset.

'Och, you're welcome to this one. It's got trouble written all over it.'

'Oh, God. What sort?' Timberlake asked.

'First things first,' Frazer said with a certain relish. 'She was found by a Mrs Padmore. She's a nurse, companion and daily help. There's another couple of them, Pauline Buck – unmarried – and Mrs Vickers. They work one week on, two weeks off; four hours in the morning, four hours in the evening.'

'Not at night?'

Frazer shook his head. 'Padmore turned up as usual at eight o'clock and let herself in, and found the old biddie dead in that armchair.'

'So she has a set of keys.'

'Right. But there's only two sets: Lucinda Pusey's own keys and a set for the dailies. They hand them over at the end of their week's duty. Padmore swears her set never left her possession. And I believe her. Still, see for yourself. She's in the kitchen.'

'I'm sure you're right,' Timberlake said politely. Just the same, he decided to question her when Frazer was out of the way.

'Any chance of duplicate keys being made?'

'No. There're three locks, and in each case you have to get duplicates from the manufacturer, delivered personally to whoever signed the original certificate. I've got a man checking. I'll give you a bell as soon as he's finished, but I'll bet you a pound to a pinch of shit there haven't been any extra keys made.

'Now,' Frazer went on, 'Lucinda Pusey was famous round here. When she was on her own it was easier to get into Hitler's bunker than get in this flat if she didn't know you, and often even if she did. Sometimes we had to send a couple of uniformed officers with the men to read the meters. So how did you manage to get in?'

'Her solicitor phoned to say I was coming to talk about her nephew's murder. I turned up with a uniformed WPC and I held up my warrant card so she could see it through the peephole.'

'She must have thought you had an honest face.'

'I think it was more basic: she *wanted* to talk to me.'

'Anyway, the big problem is why she opened the door to her murderer. And that's just the first part.' He seemed to be enjoying himself. 'She had one of those geriatrics' distress call gimmicks round her neck. A lot of old folk on their own have them in case they fall down, or have a bad turn. It's like a wee radio. Press a button and it triggers the telephone to send a recorded message to a control centre. They send round paramedics.'

'How do they get in?'

'They pick up the keys from the duty nurse. It's part of the nurses' deal: they have to be available at home during their week of duty.'

'And I take it the centre didn't get a distress call.'

'Right in one. Well, I'm away to the Manchester Row nick if you want me for anything, or any more troops. Good luck, Jimmy.'

Timberlake didn't bother to tell him his name was Harry. Frazer, it was obvious, was a stage Scotsman who called everyone Jimmy. And underneath his apparently willing co-operation Timberlake sensed a certain maliciousness.

The poisoned dart came when Frazer was at the door. 'Oh, aye. There's the other problem,' Frazer said with a faintly superior smile.

'How did the murderer get through the front door without a key?' Timberlake said quietly. 'I've already thought of that.'

Frazer's face fell slightly. 'It's a Steelguard security lock. You can only get a key from the company with an authorization.'

'I assumed as much. D'you live in a house or a flat?'

Frazer looked at him blankly. 'A house,' he said at last, pronouncing it 'hoose'.

'I guessed you did. Getting in downstairs wasn't difficult,' Timberlake said blandly, and left it at that.

'Och, aye,' Frazer replied, like one of those irritating people who say, 'I know, I know,' or, 'I was about to say that,' when they are taken by surprise. He hesitated, then went out like someone who had just been given a knee in the sporran.

'Darren, have a word with Mrs Padmore in the kitchen,' Timberlake said. 'You know the drill: any odd phone calls, letters, recent changes in Miss Pusey's behaviour; the usual things.' He escorted Webb to the door. Quietly, out of earshot of a detective constable from Manchester Row, Bill Letterman, who was still in the room, he added, 'Make sure she was here until eight o'clock, and press her about not letting her keys out of her possession.' Webb nodded. He realized that Timberlake didn't want the local detective taking stories back to Frazer. 'While you're at it, get the keys from her,' he added.

Timberlake turned back into the room. 'Right, Bill, isn't it? You and I are going to give people in the other flats a call.' Although Bill Letterman looked like Mr Mole he was out of much the same spiritual mould as Nigel Larkin. Ever since Frazer had left he was bursting to ask a question. 'Guv, how did the killer get in downstairs?'

'One of three ways. More like two and a half. We're going to find out about the first one right now.'

The man who opened the door to the top flat – the one immediately below Lucinda Pusey's penthouse – was vaguely familiar to

Harry Timberlake. He was shortish, had straggles of grey hair and a lot fewer teeth than nature had originally issued. Although it was approaching midday, he was wearing only a dressing-gown. He had legs as hairy as a cat's. Timberlake introduced himself and Bill Letterman. 'May I have your name, sir?'

The question clearly irritated the man. 'Simon Bond,' he said ungraciously.

'Thank you. We're investigating the incident in the penthouse last night,' he said.

'What incident? And what's all these people tramping about the place?' the man asked.

'In one moment, sir. At any time last evening did you get a call on the Entryphone and you pushed the door release button, but no one came to your flat?'

'What would they buzz me for if they didn't come up?'

'Did that happen, sir?'

'No, of course not.'

'So you didn't let anyone into the building you didn't know?'

'I just told you.'

'Did you go out of, or come into, the building between eight o'clock and eleven o'clock last night?'

'No. I left for work at six, and got home after midnight. What *is* this all about?'

'Miss Pusey was killed here last night.'

'Who's she?'

Surprised, Timberlake answered, 'The woman who lived in the penthouse above you.'

'Oh, the mystery! I call her Mrs Rochester. You know, Rochester's mad wife they kept locked in the attic. *Jane Eyre.*'

'Fancy,' Timberlake said in a tone that would have penetrated rhinoceros hide.

'I've been here five years and I've never seen her,' Simon Bond said lamely.

'You said you left to go to work at six o'clock. What work is that, sir?'

Bond glared at him. 'I'm Clarence in *Richard Three* at the Regent.' Timberlake was tempted to say he didn't care for *Richard III*: it gave him the hump, but he felt it wasn't the occasion.

Bond slammed the door.

Light dawned on Timberlake. He had seen Simon Bond on

184

television – once or twice – playing a captain of industry. With all his expensive teeth in, his dark hairpiece in place and lifts in his shoes he was, almost literally, a different man. 'Well, that explains a lot. As a TV director warned me once, you can't expect actors to be concerned with anyone else.'

'That's a bit hard, guv,' Letterman said.

'Perhaps,' Timberlake agreed.

They called on the other flats. The residents were, in descending order – geographically and not socially – a retired senior army officer; the wife of a barrister; and a rather attractive and enigmatic woman of about thirty-five years of age. Unlike Simon Bond, all of them had been at home between 8 p.m. and 11 p.m. the previous evening, and all of them insisted that they had not carelessly let anyone into the building.

'Well, they would, wouldn't they?' Letterman observed later.

'Did you go out yourself, or have any visitors who arrived or left between those times?' Timberlake asked them all. The former army officer had a caller: a retired officer like himself who had arrived at 8.30 p.m. and left at 1 a.m. in a taxi. The barrister's wife had entertained three women friends who had arrived at that time for a bridge party. Letterman dutifully took down all their names and addresses.

The enigmatic woman on the ground floor was rather hesitant when the same questions were put to her. She admitted that a visitor called for her at about 8.45 p.m., and they left together at about 9.30 p.m.

'What time did you get home?'

'I didn't come home last night,' she replied levelly, looking Timberlake straight in the eyes. He forced himself not to look her up and down with an undressing glance. Even so, his peripheral vision was enough to make him envy her companion of the previous evening. When it came to giving him the name of the man – she did not deny it was a man – she was plain evasive. At last she said she would make a call and if she could pass on the man's name she would phone Timberlake.

'If he's a married man we'd make sure not to cause any embarrassment at home,' Timberlake assured her.

'It's not that,' she said. 'I'll phone you.' She made it sound promising.

The addresses of the four known visitors to the Eaton Square house fell neatly into two groups. Two of the women guests were in the Manchester Row area, the army ex-officer and the third woman were nearer Terrace Vale.

'It's pretty obvious what I want you to do,' Timberlake told Letterman, who nodded wisely to conceal a blank mind. 'Find out if anyone entered the house as the visitors went in or out.' He studied the younger man. 'You live in a house, too, don't you?' He admitted that he did. 'Well, if you live in a block of flats you sometimes turn up at the front door as someone is going in or coming out. You say, "Thanks very much," and the other person holds the door open for you. If you're a villain all you have to do is look decent and walk up to the door confidently, maybe with a key in your hand, and give the other people a smile. Happens all the time.'

'Even if they don't know who you are?' Letterman asked incredulously.

'The people who let you in don't necessarily live there. And residents in flats themselves don't see much of each other, apart from coming in and going out. If you're in a house you see your neighbours in the garden, or cleaning the car, or painting the place. There's much more contact. Right, off you go.'

Darren Webb had nothing encouraging to tell Timberlake. Mrs Padmore had answered all his questions unhesitatingly and directly; Webb was certain she had stayed until eight o'clock and had never let the keys of the flat out of her possession. 'She had them on a chain round her neck like one of those superior wine waiters in a posh restaurant.'

'A sommelier.'

'Is that right?' Webb said. 'I wouldn't wonder she wore the keys in bed at night.' He didn't explain this mysterious theory.

Up to now Timberlake had been feeling quite cheerful – not madly lighthearted or over-optimistic, but not downcast. At least they were doing something positive about Lucinda Pusey's murder in trying to find someone who had seen the murderer entering the Eaton Square house. The chances were . . . well, reasonable.

Without warning he was hit by a sudden wave of depression and physical tiredness, like someone coming down from a drug-induced high. Somehow he had managed to push to the back of his mind the enigma of why Lucinda Pusey had opened the door to her murderer and let him into the flat – Lucinda Pusey, who

186

knew no one but her nurses, never went out and was pathologically suspicious of callers. The thought opened the floodgates of memory to the facts that he was precisely nowhere with the Charles Pusey murder, the reason for Thérèse Chardet's suicide and Princess Tozharska's disappearance.

He couldn't remember ever having been so depressed and help-less. 'Maybe it's time to chuck it all in,' he said, not realizing he was thinking out loud.

He was so obsessed with his own wretchedness and the question of how the killer got into Lucinda Pusey's flat that it did not occur to him that there was a more important problem: one that held the key to all the mysteries.

Chapter 26

Whether Sarah Lewis had chosen a good or a bad day to take Bob Farmer and Ted Greening head on would not be clear until the end of the affair. The first cloud on the horizon had been Ted Greening's being called in to the office of Chief Superintendent Gregory Marlow, Terrace Vale's senior officer. It was, Marlow said, an informal chat; but Greening was not invited to sit down and was addressed as Chief Inspector, not Ted, or Mr Greening. It is true that Marlow smiled a few times, but the expressions were evocative of famous lines in the ballad *Eskimo Nell*:

> And although she grinned
> She put the wind
> Up the other thirty-nine.

The chief superintendent's smiles were definitely disquieting. He was relatively new at Terrace Vale, but it had not taken him long to suss out Greening as a master leadswinger, buck-passer and slick sycophant with a rare talent for coming up with the smooth answer. Marlow had been a good street policeman and a successful detective. He could smell out a bullshitter at a dozen paces upwind quicker than a sniffer dog.

Greening did a minimum of paper work on the private principle that if it wasn't written down they couldn't put any blame on him – for whatever it was. Marlow was too shrewd to be taken in by this, and he was moved to remind Greening of the duties and responsibilities of a DCI.

As a result, Greening had decided to make a few waves, for a while at least; and if possible put somebody in the wrong to distract attention from himself.

On this particular day Greening, Farmer, a couple of detective sergeants and a posse of detectives including Sarah were reviewing a number of current cases. Greening would write a report of the meeting, including hints and lies to the effect that he had given the troops encouragement and advice based on his considerable experience.

The previous night Sarah had been brooding over her case and her treatment by Farmer in particular. She had built up an inner pressure of resentment that was liable to burst at any second. Some anti-feminist quips by her male colleagues on the way to the meeting had made the explosion inevitable.

When the Emma Leyland rape was raised she said in a voice that cut through the clouds of tobacco smoke, 'Guv, I want to have another go at Mrs Wightman.' She added, hoping her voice wouldn't betray her rapidly evaporating confidence, 'I'm sure another little push'll make her change her mind about giving her husband an alibi.'

Someone called out, 'I'll give you a little push if you like, darling.'

'From what they tell me it *would* be a little push – a *very* little push,' she replied in a flash.

The laughter was half-hearted. While the macho men enjoyed the rapid comeback, they weren't enthusiastic over a young woman squelching a male colleague.

'All right, all right, that'll do,' Greening said to no one in particular. He turned to Sarah. 'What makes you think so?'

'She found out about the Norfolk case.'

'How did she do that?' Farmer asked with an edge.

'It must have been something I said,' Sarah said with transparently false innocence.

Greening was considering more angles than Pythagoras. 'You sure Wightman did her . . . it?' he said, going for a cheap laugh.

Sarah nodded, not trusting herself to speak.

'I'll think about it,' Greening said at last. 'Bob'll let you know.' He had covered himself. If things went wrong, he could say it was all Farmer's fault. 'But in the end I suppose I must take the responsibility as DCI,' he would say nobly. Farmer, a fair hand at buck-passing himself, looked at him, well aware of the trenches Greening was digging.

Timberlake's gloom, like English weather, persisted overnight and right into the next day. Detective Superintendent Harkness had not returned to Terrace Vale the previous evening. He had telephoned Timberlake to say he had been delayed at the Yard, and they would meet the next morning. This had been followed by another call to say that he had to attend a consultation with a QC who was going to prosecute in another murder case at the Bailey. It looked like being a long meeting. He'd see Timberlake tomorrow, Harkness said. Timberlake had been dreading having to tell Harkness of the total lack of progress he had made, while another part of him would have appreciated the catharsis of confession. The mental conflict darkened the clouds and there was no sign of sun anywhere.

The ringing of his telephone broke into his introspection.

'Inspector Timberlake?' came Sergeant Rumsden's voice in its formal, polite mode. 'The desk sergeant here. There's a gentleman here to see you . . . on official business.'

'I'm on the way down,' Timberlake said, wondering what new catastrophe was waiting for him.

The visitor was a neatly dressed young man in a civilian uniform of bowler hat, rolled umbrella, dark grey suit and an Old Etonian tie. He introduced himself as Edward Parker and produced an official pass which identified him as an official of the Foreign Commonwealth Office. He looked placatory rather than intimidating. Timberlake led him into an interview room. Parker surveyed it as if it were a Mongolian slum.

'How can I help you?' Timberlake asked, deliberately sounding as cockney as Michael Caine in his early days, and ready to be as difficult and obstructive as possible. Parker was the epitome of everything Timberlake disliked in the civil service.

'You interviewed a young woman at a flat in Eaton Square yesterday.' He waited, but Timberlake said nothing. 'As I understand it, you were enquiring about a visitor who had called on her the previous evening.' Still nothing from Timberlake, but Parker was unperturbed. 'We should be most grateful if you would not press the matter – in the public interest, of course.'

' "We"?' said Timberlake.

'The Foreign Office.'

'I see. And in which public's interest would that be?'

'The national interest, detective inspector.'

Timberlake looked as cynical as he could manage, which was on a par with a boxing promoter explaining how brain damage was good for you. 'What about the interests of justice?'

'I see I shall have to be frank with you,' Parker said, with the smile of a prefect about to beat a fag. 'The visitor was a foreign diplomat in this country on a most important trade mission.'

'You mean he's buying arms. And why was his visit to this woman so . . . sensitive for the Foreign Office to be concerned?'

Parker was at last becoming slightly frazzled. He cleared his throat a couple of times. 'When influential diplomats from certain countries visit the UK, they occasionally feel a need for company during their moments of relaxation. We want to ensure they are not involved in, ah, any incidents. My department can sometimes provide escorts for them: women who are totally reliable, experienced, intelligent, can pass in every level of society and who are, most of all, discreet. The young lady you interviewed is one of them. You can imagine that it might be embarrassing for her companion to be interrogated about his association with her, and he could well lose confidence in the discretion of one of the departments of Her Majesty's Government.'

He pronounced the last three words in the tones of an archbishop at a coronation.

'Pause for a short chorus of *Land of Hope and Glory*,' Timberlake said to no one in particular. He thought hard. Even if he managed to winkle out the diplomat's name and get to talk to him the man was unlikely to be co-operative. And it was hardly likely that he had murdered Lucinda Pusey.

'All right, Mr Parker. I won't press it. I don't suppose he'd be very helpful anyway.'

Parker's manner changed; he gave a brilliant smile. 'I was sure you would understand the realities of the situation when I explained them to you. Good day, inspector.'

The young man's patronizing manner thoroughly got up Timberlake's nose. As Parker started to leave the room Timberlake said, 'You know, I never knew it was part of the Foreign Office's duties to provide tarts for foreign VIPs. We have a funny name for that sort of thing in the police.' The back of Parker's neck turned slightly pink.

Somehow the encounter and his own Parthian shot cheered up Timberlake. The brief moment of very mild euphoria soon vanished in the prevailing gloom. DC Letterman phoned from Manchester Row. He had interviewed the two women bridge players

191

who had visited the barrister's wife at Eaton Square.

'They arrived together and they reckon they saw a dodgy looking man coming into the building after them.'

'Any description?'

'It depends what you mean by a description. He was either five foot seven or eight or over six feet, clean-shaven with a moustache; fair hair and dark hair, a bare-headed man wearing a hat, about twenty-four or forty-five, wore glasses, and didn't wear glasses, and had piercing eyes.'

Timberlake sighed. 'In other words, as usual. Thanks, Bill. You'll let us have a report, won't you? I'll be in touch.'

It was Darren Webb's turn to bring negative news to Timberlake. 'I interviewed those two people, guv,' he said. 'The people who visited the house. The ex-army officer – a brigadier – practically had me doing jankers for suggesting he might have let somebody in.'

'Where did you get that word?'

'Jankers? My dad did National Service in the army. Anyway, the old boy went on about how security conscious he was, and had started in on giving me a full history of the war when his phone rang. I scarpered. Rhyming slang, guv: scarper from Scapa Flow, go.'

'I'm not King Dick, young Darren. Rhyming slang. King Dick, thick. What about the woman?'

'She kept bumping into her own furniture. Then she put on her glasses. Like bottle tops. When I asked her, she said she wasn't wearing them when she went into the house. If King Kong had been in the corridor she wouldn't have seen him.'

'How did she get there?'

'Private hire cab. I got the number in case the driver saw someone come out. It's local: I could nip round there.'

'Good show, Darren,' Timberlake said. 'Off you go.' He wrote up his latest report as he waited for Webb to return.

It was not going to be his day. Webb's face told him everything before he opened his mouth.

'I found the driver, guv. No luck, I'm afraid. He whizzed off before his fare went into the house, and he didn't see anyone hanging around. Sorry.'

'I'm not going to do much good here, Darren,' Timberlake said. 'I think I'll go home and let the subconscious work on the case. You can get me there if I'm needed.'

'Fair enough, guv. Have an early night. Is there anything you'd like me to do in the meantime?'

'Yes.' He took his keys from his pocket and unlocked his middle desk drawer. He took out Mrs Padmore's keys to the Eaton Square flat which Webb had given him for safe keeping. 'Go round to the flat and have a good look at all her papers. See if there's anything there that'll give us a lead.'

'Right, guv. Er, suppose Mack the Knife, or one of his lot, turn up?'

'They won't: not without clearing it with the superintendent here first. But if they are trying it on, tell them you've come from the AMIP Incident Room and the guvnor has sent you.'

'Er, he's not here.'

'Yes he is. I'm your guvnor, aren't I? On top of that, I'm in charge while Harkness isn't here.'

'Very true. I'll pull rank if there's any trouble.'

'When you've done, go round to Manchester Row, be very nice to the jock, and ask how the uniforms are doing with the door-to-door.'

Timberlake tidied his desk – it didn't need much, he always kept it neat – and walked downstairs to the back door giving on to the station car-park. He opened it before he remembered his car was at his local garage, being serviced. Wryly he told himself the incident typified his present mental state. He turned back and walked out of the nick towards the nearest Underground station. He was halfway there when he heard someone call his name.

Sarah Lewis was at the wheel of her car next to the pavement. Timberlake went over. Their lives, which had been moving parallel for a while, now converged and meshed.

'I might remind you, madam, that kerb-crawling, importuning innocent pedestrians, is now an offence,' he said.

'In the first place I'm miss, not madam, I'm not importuning, and Christ knows you're not innocent.'

He laughed. 'Where're you off to?'

Her Welsh accent became increasingly prominent as she spoke. 'I'm going home. I've got a headache banging it against a brick wall and two dickheads. If I'd stayed in the nick much longer I'd've kicked somebody. What about you?'

'I'm off home too. I've got a severe case of mental atrophy. My mind's working like the Mad Hatter's watch.'

'*Whose?*'

'The Mad Hatter's. In *Alice in Wonderland*. The March Hare put butter into it to lubricate it. It was the *best* butter.'

'You're babbling. Get in. I'll give you a lift,' she said, what passed for her London accent returning to place.

'Stop gabbling, Hedda,' Timberlake said inconsequentially.

'I'll call for the men in white coats if you stand out there rabbiting on like three widows.' He got in.

Whether they both knew at that point how the evening would end is uncertain; but if they had, neither of them would have fought the inevitable. Certainly the signs were loud and clear when Sarah drove her car into his parking place at his block of flats, got out and locked it. He made no comment, but stood back when he unlocked his front door for her to go through.

There was enough food in the fridge for a reasonable meal, and he always had a bottle or two of his – their – favourite Rhône wine. They lingered over the meal, talking quietly, unhurriedly. Anyone overhearing them would have thought it an aimless conversation about trivialities – other meals, places they had visited, snatches of remembered conversations and odd, inconsequential phrases; even the silences were significant . . . But below the placid surface there were strong, deep-running currents which bore declarations that there was still love between them.

Eventually, 'Don't you drink too much,' she warned him as he poured himself another glass of wine.

'And you make sure you drink enough,' he replied.

They judged the quantities perfectly.

At first they were slightly hesitant; apprehensive, perhaps, that gestures, words or movements might appear to be evocative of their relations with other partners, but they soon fell into the old familiar, but inventive practices that made it seem – almost – that they had never separated. He put on a tape of an Albert Hall concert by a trio of virtuoso jazz guitarists, John MacLaughlin, Paco de Lucia and Larry Coryell. Their total rapport, intricate musical patterns and breathtaking, insistent rhythms heightened Timberlake's and Sarah's desire: their blood raced and their hearts beat faster.

What Harry Timberlake had forgotten were how marvellous Sarah looked naked, and the abandoned, but not disconcertingly loud, sounds from throaty moans to prolonged squeals she made in ecstasy. For her part, she had not remembered the way his whole frame shuddered as he held her tight against him.

At last they lay back exhausted, and then dragged themselves to the shower before preparing for sleep.

She whispered a tired 'Good night, darling,' before she turned on her side with her back to him. Very quietly he said, 'Sarah, whatever happens in the future, I'll never, ever, forget you.' She made a small sound, but he couldn't be sure whether she was already asleep.

Timberlake woke quite early, before it was fully daylight outside. He slid out of bed carefully so as not to wake Sarah, put on pyjama trousers and went to the kitchen. He set the percolator going, and poured two glasses of freshly pressed orange juice.

He took the juice and coffee on a tray and returned to the bedroom. Sarah was sitting up in the bed, still not fully awake, her eyelids slightly lowered. She looked twice as sexy as Marlene Dietrich after two hours' preparation by a make-up artist and an expert lighting cameraman.

'What did we do last night?' Sarah asked rhetorically.

'You mean you can't remember?'

Of course, her true meaning was 'Where do we go from here?', which was a question Timberlake knew he couldn't answer.

Chapter 27

Ted Greening swivelled his chair to turn his back on the door of his office in case someone came in without knocking, and took what he would call a healthy swig from a bottle of whisky, then returned it to the bottom drawer of his desk. He sighed with satisfaction, an exercise that set him coughing. Quickly he lit a cigarette and took a deep draw on it to smother the irritation. Now thoroughly prepared, he went to the door and called out across the corridor to Farmer's office. 'Bob, got a minute?'

Farmer rose from his desk and began to reach for his jacket on its hanger, then changed his mind. He had noticed that his own neat clothes often clearly disturbed Greening, who frequently looked as if he lived in Cardboard City.

'Shut the door,' Greening said with what was meant to be a friendly smile. The effect was ruined by another bout of coughing. When he had recovered he said, 'I've been thinking about the Welsh Rarebit and the Emma Leyland case. I think we ought to let her have another go at whatshisname, Wightman.'

We, Farmer noted. He was being rowed into the decision by Greening. They batted responsibility backwards and forwards like badminton players.

'You think so, guv?'

'What do *you* think, Bob?'

'A lot depends on how good Lewis's gut instincts are, and you know her a lot better than I do.'

'Yes, that's true, that's true.' Greening coughed, this time voluntarily, to give himself time to think. 'But you interviewed Wightman, and you should have some idea about the man.'

'He's not the problem, guv. The key to it is the wife: she's giving him the alibi.'

'So you reckon Sarah's probably the best one to deal with it?'

'Like I said, you know her better than I do.'

Greening kept his calm, although he could feel a growing need for another whisky.

'Let's suppose we let her have another go and she manages to get the Wightman woman to retract the alibi for her husband—'

We again, Farmer thought.

'. . . credit all round, right?'

'True,' Farmer said after consideration.

'If she falls flat on her face, we warned her of the dangers, right?'

'Seems reasonable to me, guv.'

'That's settled, then. Go and give her the green light. Well done, Bob.' Greening picked up a thick file, opened it and studied it intently, putting an end to the discussion. The buck was safely out of his hands.

Sarah Lewis was in the CID office with a number of other detectives.

'Sarah,' Farmer called out loudly from the doorway. Sarah and the others all looked up. 'The DCI says it's okay for you to have another go at Mrs Wightman.' Farmer was learning. The buck had been returned . . . and in front of witnesses.

Greening heard him in his office, and cursed. He took another drink. Sarah had no idea of the irony of the situation. Greening would be hoping now that she would be successful with the Wightmans.

Timberlake knew that a number of prominent sportsmen – mainly tennis players, for some reason – had admitted publicly or privately that after a night of satisfying sex they played superbly the following day. (Of course, it is highly unlikely that anyone who played wretchedly would confess it was due to enthusiastic humping the previous night.) The morning after his night with Sarah Lewis his mind seemed clearer and sharper, but he put it down to coincidence. He at least woke up to the fact that had been staring him in the face since Lucinda Pusey had been murdered. There *was* someone she would have opened the door to. He reached for his phone, but changed his mind. Better to turn up unexpectedly, he decided. 'Anyone know where Darren is?' he asked the detectives in the CID office.

Almost inevitably it was Nigel Larkin who answered. 'He said to tell you he hadn't finished going through Miss Pusey's papers last night and he'd do the rest this morning. He also left these for you.' Larkin produced another bunch of front door keys for the Eaton Square flat. 'They're Miss Pusey's set. Darren – Sergeant Webb – said he didn't want them falling into the wrong hands.' He looked as innocent as a cherub on a church's stained glass window. Timberlake had a fair idea that the young aide had guessed whose Scottish hands might be the wrong ones. 'And there was a message from Superintendent Harkness. He'll be here late this afternoon.'

'I'm going to see someone. I think you'd better come along with me.'

Nigel Larkin got up from his temporary desk so quickly he knocked over his chair.

After a great deal of thought Sarah decided that it was pointless trying to plan her next, and probably last, interview with Anthea Wightman. There were so many ways it could go, depending on what effect their last meeting had had on Mrs Wightman. In fact there was no certainty that she would talk to Sarah at all, if she was in at all, that was. So, once again she had to rely on instinct ... and good luck.

To Sarah's considerable surprise Anthea Wightman was not in the least hostile when she opened the door to her. She tried to gauge her mood, which seemed not so much tranquil as apathetic. She looked rather tired.

'Would you like some coffee?' Anthea asked listlessly. 'I felt like a cup myself, and then I couldn't be bothered, but now you're here—'

'Thanks. You all right? You look a bit peaky.'

'No, it's nothing. I just haven't been sleeping properly lately. And I don't like taking pills for that sort of thing.'

'Mmm, it can get you into bad habits. I know it's an old Welsh wife's cure, but a glass of hot milk always works for me.'

'Perhaps I'll try it, although ... it's not me. It's—' She broke off.

'Your husband? Yes, men can be thoughtless bastards some-times.' But that wasn't what Anthea meant, and Sarah knew it. 'Anthea ... I came to apologize.'

'Apologize? What for?'

'For letting the cat out of the bag. It didn't occur to me you didn't know. I hope I didn't cause any trouble between you and your husband.'

Anthea turned away to look out of the window so Sarah wouldn't see her face. She shrugged. 'I suppose I'd've found out sooner or later.'

'Well, I'm sure you'll both put it behind you when we've got the swine.' She paused, knowing the risk she was taking and that it was her last card. If it failed, there'd be no chance of ever convicting Ross Wightman. 'And we will get him,' she concluded. 'We've got evidence.'

Anthea turned back sharply. 'What evidence?'

'Look, Anthea, I shouldn't tell you this, and for God's sake keep it to yourself. It's not been in the papers or on TV. The woman who was raped said the man had a red scarf, probably woollen, over his face, and he threatened her with a bone-handled knife that had a blade with a sort of wavy engraving and a broken tip. He's not aware we know about them, so we're hoping he hasn't got rid of them. When we identify him, if he's got the scarf and the knife at his home, that'll be that . . . I only pray we get him before he rapes someone else . . . or kills them.'

Anthea Wightman's reaction to this information was the key to the whole case. If she found them in the house and destroyed them to protect her husband . . .

It didn't bear thinking about.

Jonathan Mellick received Timberlake with even less warmth than on his previous visit. Larkin he managed to treat as if he were silent and invisible. In fact Mellick's attitude to Timberlake was like that of a snob householder, conscious of his neighbours, who had reluctantly called in a rat-catcher at night, and then was dismayed to find the rat-catcher back on his doorstep in broad daylight.

The solicitor could hardly refuse to see them as they were on a murder case and he did have a professional relationship with the victim's family, if not the victim herself.

'It would save a great deal of time if you would be good enough to give us some idea of the provisions of Miss Pusey's will,' Timberlake said politely.

Mellick considered this gravely for some time. 'Of course, it has

199

not yet been admitted for probate.' Timberlake nodded. 'And I am, as yet, unaware of the total value of the entire estate, including the unexpired lease of the Eaton Square apartment. The trusts established by her brother pay the income directly into her bank. However, I believe that Miss Pusey was, ah, very, ah, frugal.'

For 'frugal' read 'stingy', Timberlake thought.

'Who are the principal beneficiaries?'

For once Mellick seemed almost cheerful. 'The entire estate, real and actual, is divided equally between three charities: the RSPCA, NSPCC and Salvation Army.'

Timberlake was taken aback. 'No individuals?'

'None.'

'Not even the nurse-companions?'

'No.'

'Who are the executors?'

'I am one; the managers of the trusts are the others. And this firm's charges for being executors will be to scale.'

There was no mistaking that Mellick was enjoying himself.

'Mr Mellick, when did you last see Miss Pusey?'

'I haven't seen her for some years.'

'As a matter of routine, will you tell me where you were between 8 p.m, and 11 p.m. on the ninth of this month?'

Mellick's mild pleasure increased. He turned to a leather-bound desk diary and opened it, as if he actually had to check. 'Oh, yes. I was in the Royal Masonic Hospital. Earlier that day I had undergone an endoscopy.'

And I bet you enjoyed it, Timberlake thought savagely and unjustly.

'May I ask a question, sir?' Nigel Larkin said modestly to Timberlake, who nodded. 'Mr Mellick, do you have a set of keys to the Eaton Square flat?'

All the lights went out on Mellick's face. He seemed to shrink in his high-backed, padded chair. His 'Yes' was almost inaudible.

Larkin looked an unspoken question at Timberlake, who inclined his head.

'May we see them, please?' the Eager Beaver requested.

Mellick prised himself out of his chair and went to an unimpressive tapestry on one of the walls. He pulled it back to reveal a safe which looked as if it had been made by craftsmen who had worked on building *The Rocket* with Robert Stephenson. When Mellick opened the safe with a large key among several on a key-ring and chain Timberlake would not have been surprised to see bats fly out.

The safe contained several files, a cashbox and four drawers. Mellick reached for one, pulled it out and put it on his desk.

In the centre of the drawer was a bunch of keys on a ring with a label. The solicitor was about to pick them up when Timberlake stopped him. The keys, like the bottom of the drawer, were covered with a thin layer of dust. Timberlake took a pencil and lifted the keys out by the ring. Beneath them was a clean, dust-free outline of where the keys had been.

'Thank you, Mr Mellick,' Timberlake said neutrally. 'By the way, when the body is released, what will be the funeral arrangements?'

'I shall make them in consultation with the other executors.'

'What about Madame de Gaillmont? They are – were – sisters-in-law.'

'I have already spoken to her on the subject. She says she has absolutely no interest in the funeral.'

Predictably, Timberlake thought.

'I hope you didn't mind my asking that question, guvnor,' Larkin said anxiously on the way back to Terrace Vale. He still couldn't bring himself to use the familiar 'guv'.

'If you hadn't asked it, I was going to.'

'Oh, sorry. I didn't—'

'It's all right. I'm pleased you thought of it.'

Nigel Larkin almost pulsated with pleasure, then his brow furrowed. 'Why d'you think he looked so worried when I asked him?'

'Natural nervous disposition. He's probably scared by violent TV commercials. It's almost certain he wasn't the killer who got into the flat, or that he lent someone the keys. The dust on them was genuine. No, he's not involved, more's the pity. What's interesting is that he hadn't seen Lucinda Pusey for some years.'

'Why's that?'

'If someone phoned and said he was Mellick and he was coming to see her on a vital matter, maybe she wouldn't realize it wasn't Mellick when the killer turned up at her door.'

He glanced at the clock on the car dashboard. 'Oh, damn, I've just remembered.' Jenny Long had sent him a picture postcard of the Coliseum with the date and time of her return flight from Rome. He assumed she wanted him to meet her at the airport. 'You don't have a date or anything, do you?'

'No, sir – guvnor—' he lied loyally.

'I have to go to Heathrow to meet someone off a flight. D'you mind coming? It'll only take us an hour and a half there and back.'

'Fine.'

For once the traffic on the M4 was moderate and Timberlake made good time, even though he drove his cherished Citröen along the M4 at no more than the legal 70 mph. He didn't want to be recorded speeding by the closed circuit TV cameras on the motorway. He cheated when he got to the airport by parking on double yellow lines in an area forbidden to private cars. Within minutes a couple of airport police came up. Timberlake showed his warrant card and spoke politely to them: Met officers weren't always popular with policemen from other forces.

One of the men was belligerent and said that detective inspector or not, he would have to move the car, or it would be towed away.

'Very well,' Timberlake replied calmly. He looked at the man's number on his epaulettes. 'Can I have your name, please, constable?' he said with a voice like broken glass.

'Greenaway,' came the reluctant answer.

'Larkin, make a note of this man's name and number, please.'

'Yes, sir,' the Eager Beaver replied with the exaggerated respect of a Brigade of Guards sergeant-major. He whipped out his pocket book.

'Wait a minute, please sir,' the second constable said. He turned to his companion. 'Fred, I think we can overlook this, as a professional courtesy—'

'That's very good of you.' He addressed Larkin, concealing a wink from the constables. 'If there are any problems while I'm in the terminal, use the car radio to call the Yard and have them contact me on my mobile phone and I'll come and move the car.'

The two constables were on their way to harass a taxi driver before Timberlake had finished speaking.

The arrivals board was showing that the passengers on Jenny's flight were already in the customs hall when Timberlake entered the terminal. Within minutes she came through the swing doors into the waiting area. She looked great, and was wearing a dress he hadn't ever seen before. Its undoubted chic made him guess she had bought it in Rome. Strangely, she didn't have a baggage trolley nor was carrying any bags. She turned, the doors opened and the doctor who had replaced Timberlake in Jenny's affections and bed during the year she had been separated from him came through pushing a baggage trolley with two people's suit-cases on it.

Jenny spotted Timberlake. She gave him a hesitant smile and a small wave as she approached him. He made no move to kiss her or even take her hand. He nodded coldly to the doctor, who remained several paces behind her, out of earshot.

'I see you weren't short of company after all,' Timberlake said. 'I'm sure you two will want to travel back to London together.' He spun on his heel and walked out.

As he stamped to his car, he mentally ran through the dismal list of his reverses professional and personal: no success in the Charles Pusey murder case, no idea why Thérèse Chardet commit-ted suicide, no idea what had happened to Caterina Tozharska, no hint of a solution to the Lucinda Pusey killing ... And now this.

It most certainly wasn't Timberlake's day.

Chapter 28

Long before they got back to Terrace Vale Timberlake had regained full self-control. His driving for the first couple of miles out of Heathrow had made Larkin raise his eyebrows and clench his buttocks. Eventually the traffic forced Timberlake to slow down. It also gave him time for self-appraisal. He admitted to himself that his behaviour at the airport had been juvenile, and the fact that he was having a bad time of it at the moment was really no excuse. So, he forced himself into a conscious effort to think and to conduct himself like an adult. He knew that if Harkness had seen him at the airport, he would have had reservations about his competence.

Harkness, who had arrived an hour or so earlier, was waiting for him with Darren Webb in the AMIP incident room.

'Sorry, sir. I didn't expect you back from the Yard for another hour.'

'It's all right, Harry. I've been going through the last couple of days' reports.'

'Sergeant Braddock not with you?'

'He went down with appendicitis rather suddenly.' He smiled. 'I'll have to carry my own bag for a while.'

'I'm sure Larkin here will be pleased to do it for you.'

Larkin lit up like a Christmas tree; Darren Webb looked slightly sour. Keen young men following in one's tracks are never popular, although only a paid-up ratbag could actively dislike Larkin.

'Right. Darren?' Harkness said.

'I went through Lucinda Pusey's papers and records, sir. There wasn't a lot of them. She had more than a million and a half quid in a current account! The bank manager wrote to her a couple of times telling her she should put most of it into a deposit account, but apparently she took no notice. There were no unusual withdrawals or payments. The executors of the trusts dealt with her tax, and paid the nurses. There were direct debits for things like gas and electricity, service charges. I think the biggest cheque she wrote out was for a hundred quid.'

'In brief, nothing suspicious or out of the ordinary.'

'No, sir, apart from the fact that she made Scrooge look like a philanthropist.'

'What about letters from friends?'

'There weren't any. Letters, or friends, I shouldn't think. I found an address book. There weren't many names in it in the first place, and most of them were crossed out anyway. I rang the others. They were mostly old people. None of them had seen her or talked to her for months. While I was at it I got on to British Telecom to see if I could get a printout of her calls for the past year or so. I wouldn't mind betting she hardly used the phone.'

'Did you have time to go to Manchester Row, see if the uniforms had any luck with the door-to-doors?'

'Yes, sir. Nothing.' Webb shrugged resignedly.

'Very comprehensive,' Harkness said. 'Well done.'

Next, Timberlake reported his fruitless visit to Jonathan Mellick, finishing with, 'It's asking too much of coincidence to believe that Charles Pusey's and Lucinda Pusey's deaths aren't connected. The only common denominator is the de Gaillmonts ... And Caterina Tozharska is directly connected with them, too.'

'Not forgetting Thérèse Thing. I know she topped herself, but the odds are that Sophie de Gaillmont pushed her to it,' Webb interjected.

'*Faute de mieux*, I think we'll have to make another visit to Towers Court,' Timberlake said. He stopped and shook his head helplessly. 'What I can't get over ... What I still can't imagine is how the hell anyone got into that flat.'

'Just a minute, Harry,' Harkness said. 'Perhaps that isn't the real question.' Timberlake looked at him. 'You're fixed on *how* the murderer managed to kill Lucinda Pusey. Maybe what you should be asking is ... *why* did he kill her.'

Were it not so serious, it would have been comic. Timberlake – and the others – sat as if they had been instantaneously petrified with their mouths open.

'That's if it was a he,' Harkness added almost as an aside. 'Once you know the motive, *then* you can start working on how.'

'How could I have been so bloody stupid,' Timberlake said bitterly.

'You're not being fair to yourself,' Harkness said firmly. 'It's always easier for someone to come up with a suggestion after someone else has done the groundwork.'

Timberlake was not consoled. He frowned with concentration. 'There was something Lucinda Pusey said to me when I interviewed her. It struck me at the time, and I was going to ask her about it but something distracted me and it went out of my head ... Something about her flat, I think.'

'Then go back. Have a look round, see if it jogs your memory.'

'I might as well. What else have we got?'

Sarah's and Harry Timberlake's lives, which had run parallel before converging explosively, now began to run parallel once more, although they were not aware of it.

Julian Tabard had returned from the Caribbean and had phoned her at a moment when she wanted to forget work for a while. He suggested supper at his apartment at his studio.

'I didn't know you could cook,' she said.

'I can't. But I know people who can.'

By the time she arrived, there was a small table laid for two: flowers, candles, three sets of wine glasses ... and a cold meal ready on a side table.

'A local caterer does it for me,' Julian said.

He looked marvellous – bronzed, fit and wearing a silk shirt and trousers that were probably the work of one of the more expensive fashion houses who were his clients. He somehow reminded her of Leslie Howard, or maybe it was Paul Henreid. She saw a lot of old movies on late-night television.

'I thought that having money was supposed to make you miserable,' Sarah replied.

'It's a rumour put about by people who've got it and don't want other people to take it away.'

It was a casual throwaway line, yet it left her vaguely uneasy for a moment.

'Can I have a look at some of the photographs?'

'Don't you just know how to talk to a man,' he said. 'I was afraid you'd never ask.'

He took her through to a room he used as a gallery. There were, she guessed, a hundred photographs on the walls, some half life-size.

The pictures were of a summer collection, and Tabard had made the most of the Caribbean light and backgrounds to present the clothes to the best advantage.

'Some people like to do summer collections in Iceland, or up Mont Blanc or somewhere, and winter clothes in the Sahara. Frankly, I think that's too tricksy, and murder for the poor models.'

That made Sarah look at the young women rather than the clothes. There were five different ones in all – 'More expensive, taking so many with you, but if you use only one girl and for some reason she doesn't appeal to most of the public, you've laid a very expensive egg.'

Sarah hardly heard him: she was carefully examining the pictures. There was no mistaking that Julian was good, very good, at his job. He had made the most of the exotic backgrounds, which could have overpowered the subjects of the pictures, to enhance the clothes. His work was brilliant.

In most of the photographs the models were pouting, belligerent – positively threatening. In other words, in the modern idiom. All except one. The exception was the solitary blonde of the group. She smiled, looked happy, *flirted* with the camera, seemed to share secrets with it. The more Sarah studied the photographs the more obvious it was to her that the blonde had been Julian's mistress during the shoot – if not before, or since, or both.

She felt her heart beating faster, but she was not certain what emotion was causing it. Nevertheless, Sarah kept her head. She asked the names of two of the other models and trivial questions about them before mentioning the blonde.

Julian Tabard, with a fine insouciance, nearly successfully completely disguised his relationship with the blonde, named Velanne – nearly, not quite. Sarah's Celtic blood might have been expected to boil over at this point, but she was much more collected than Timberlake had been with Jenny Long at Heathrow.

A few minutes later she excused herself to go to the loo, carrying her bag with her. She took out her new portable phone and called Harry Timberlake's number.

'It's me, Sarah,' she said softly. 'Have you got my mobile phone number? . . . Right. Will you call me on it in five minutes and say I'm wanted at the nick?'

Nine minutes later her mobile phone rang. Sarah and Timberlake performed their small telephone sketch. Julian Tabard called her a taxi, and half an hour later she was home. She took off her shoes and prepared to throw one of them at the wall, and then decided it wasn't worth it. With some astonishment she discovered she wasn't that angry. And she didn't want to cry, either.

Timberlake arrived early at Eaton Square, driven there in a Terrace Vale panda so he wouldn't have to worry about parking. Most of the local inhabitants hadn't stirred or started to read their *Financial Times* or *Daily Telegraph* yet.

He found it slightly unnerving to be alone in Lucinda Pusey's flat, and for some time he moved about carefully to avoid disturbing the non-existent tenant. Darren Webb had explained to him where Lucinda Pusey's documents were, and he began a careful, methodical examination of them. While he did this he had the weird sensation that someone would come in and demand to know what he was doing reading private papers.

It took him most of the morning to go through the bank statements. However, he did it only from a professional obligation to be thorough rather than because he believed he would find anything relevant to the murder in them.

After some time he became aware that he was hungry. He looked at his watch and learned with a shock that it was well past lunchtime. He put away the last bank statement, and decided to go through the correspondence after he had eaten something. There were a number of restaurants and cafés within walking distance in Buckingham Palace Road, where most of the pedestrians seemed to be Japanese tourists. Anyone who didn't have a camera or camcorder wasn't Japanese.

When Timberlake returned to the house he took out the front door key. Before he could use it a man came out, and held the door open for Timberlake to enter. Timberlake assumed he was the barrister resident, for he was an important-looking man who carried an important-looking briefcase. He wished DI Frazer from Manchester Row could have seen the incident.

Lucinda Pusey's letters, such as they were, reflected a lonely and arid life. He found it difficult to believe that a woman who had lived so long could leave such meagre traces of her passing behind her.

He looked carefully at the writing desk. It had a familiar air about it, yet he had never been in the flat before his interview with Lucinda Pusey, and the memory the desk stirred was a distant one. Why the thought should persist niggled him, and he finally decided it was because he was bored and subconsciously seeking a distraction from the tedious job of reading the dead woman's letters.

And then it struck him.

The desk – more properly an *escritoire* – was of much the same type and period, although not a copy, as the desk that had been in the Newman house.*

He took out the small drawers one by one. He had already examined the contents, which were trivial: a man's penknife, a thimble, an old box of matches and, curiously, some glass marbles . . . There was even a bank card that had expired ten years previously.

The drawers were all the same size, so he knew nothing was concealed behind them. He examined the spaces left by the drawers without success: there were no concealed knobs or catches in them. At last he found it, a device so simple that he had overlooked it. There was a knot in the wood at the side of the desk. He pressed it, and a long, shallow drawer sprang out a few inches beneath the large central drawer.

Timberlake paused a moment before pulling it out fully.

The contents were banal: two bundles of letters, tied with a ribbon of indeterminate colour, faded and discoloured with age. The handwriting was the same on all the envelopes, but the post-marks were different, some of them from foreign countries. For all his experience of the world's underside and man's beastliness to his fellow man, Timberlake had not been made insensitive. When he began to read the letters he was moved to sadness and a sense of prying into someone's soul, although the person who had received them was dead. Probably by now the writer was, too, Timberlake thought.

They were letters which revealed a blazing, passionate, sexual love, yet not without tenderness. The letters were signed with a monogram that Timberlake could not decipher. Because they were posted in different towns and sometimes countries, he thought

*See *Elimination*, the second Harry Timberlake story.

209

they were written by a soldier, perhaps, or a diplomat. Puzzlingly, they were all on plain paper with no address.

They covered a period of some years, beginning when Lucinda Pusey must have been quite young. The lovers did not appear to have gone out anywhere together, nor was there any reference to friends of either of them. Their relationship seemed to have been purely sexual, and almost obsessively so.

Later letters had strange hints of the need for keeping their relationship secret. Timberlake wondered if the man was already married, or perhaps – fancifully, he admitted to himself – was a member of a royal family. Next came warnings that their great love must inevitably end, for both their sakes. Almost the last letter revealed that there had been a terrible scene between them. The man had spoken of their both marrying other people, and having families, which had driven Lucinda into something like a frenzy of grief.

The final letter was blotched with tears – whether they were the writer's or Lucinda's it was impossible to say. It was a farewell letter full of anguish that touched Timberlake's heart. He was sure that it was after this letter that Lucinda had begun her life as a virtual hermit.

The last paragraph of this letter revealed the secret identity of the writer of the letter – a secret that took Timberlake's breath away.

Lucinda's secret lover was her brother Charles Pusey Senior.

No wonder she hated Sophie de Gaillmont with such incandescent intensity.

Timberlake reflected for a long time. Finally, he put the letters into his pocket and pushed shut the hidden drawer. He turned to the leather-bound scrapbooks and began to leaf through them.

They contained newspaper cuttings, all about Charles Pusey: financial columns, news pages, gossip columns, some of them from foreign newspapers. Many of the items he had already seen in the file that his journalist friend Claud Salter had sent him. There were other items as well: engraved invitations to formal dinners, weekends, bread and butter letters from guests who had stayed with him, photographs taken at official functions. The scrapbook showed the life of a prominent, successful man.

Now Timberlake had read the letters, he looked at the newspaper stories and their accompanying photographs with different eyes. In a few, very few, of the photographs Lucinda appeared. It was impossible to relate the image of the beautiful young woman to the old woman he had seen once in life. Trying to imagine that demure-looking Lucinda of long ago being involved in an abandoned sexual relationship was equally inconceivable.

Doggedly he scrutinized the articles that were new to him. He could see nothing of value to his investigation. He finished the last one, and rubbed his eyes. He was tired, yet there was still something niggling at him, something he couldn't quite get hold of. He decided to call it a day. In his present state he might easily miss an important detail.

Back at Terrace Vale he reported to Harkness, without mentioning the letters. He said he'd have another go at the flat tomorrow.

Within minutes of his return home the phone rang. Jenny Long asked him if he would be in if she called round in half an hour. Her manner was unrevealing. In a mixture of tiredness and indifference he said, 'If you want to.'

She didn't use her key to his flat when she arrived. He opened the door to find her standing there looking cool and like Joanna Lumley in an early *Avengers*. Staying in the doorway, she pitched into him with a calm, measured, quietly delivered dressing down that took his skin off in thin strips. The gravamen of her criticism was that he had embarrassed her in public at the airport, behaved childishly, not given her a chance to speak, and assumed rights over her to which he had no claim. And she didn't like his tie, either.

Before she left him standing with his mouth open she said, 'My colleague was invited to the conference by the pharmaceutical company in his own right, not as my companion. Not that it's any of your business, but we had separate rooms.'

For what that's worth, Timberlake said to himself. She countered the unspoken thought with, 'And were you celibate while I was away?'

He hoped his face didn't give him away.

'Sarah?' said a timid voice on the phone. Sarah was getting ready to go to the nick. She had got out of the shower to answer the call and was feeling chilly wearing only a thin film of water. She instantly forgot her discomfort when the caller went on.

'It's Anthea Wightman. That night my husband said he was at

home with me, watching *Coronation Street*. He wasn't. He didn't come home until nine-thirty. But I won't make a statement about it while he can get at me. He's changed recently, and keeps asking about you. I'm frightened.'

'Don't be,' Sarah said firmly. 'I'll make sure you're quite safe before we do anything. Just act naturally, okay? Trust me.' She wondered how many policemen had said those words in good faith and had pangs of conscience afterwards.

'I've got to go,' Anthea said. She sounded as if she was beginning to regret it already.

Despite the finality of Anthea's last sentence, something stopped Sarah hanging up.

'Sarah?' Anthea said tentatively.

'I'm still here.' She could almost hear the sounds of Anthea's internal struggle.

The words came out with a rush. 'I've found them. The knife and the red scarf.'

Sarah's heart beat so fast for some seconds that she could hardly breathe. She forgot how cold she had been feeling. 'Did you touch them?'

'God, no!' The tone of those two short words told Sarah everything. It was not concern for the quality of the scientific evidence that had restrained Anthea, but revulsion.

'Good. Leave them there. We'll be along as soon as we can.'

Harry Timberlake turned up at Terrace Vale the next morning after having passed a restless night and feeling puzzled. It wasn't the slating Jenny had given him that was the main cause of his disorientation. At first he wondered whether what she had said meant that their relationship was over, but he soon decided it was not what she was planning. She was forthright and would have told him outright. More significantly, she would have given him back the key to his flat. Her reading of the Riot Act was, he decided in a mixture of metaphors, a warning shot across his bows.

The real confusion was that he wasn't jealous of her possible adventure with her doctor friend. Was this because he cared for her enough – even in his thinking he tried to avoid the use of the word 'love' because of the implied commitment – to ignore what was a minor incident while she was away from home, or was it because he plainly did not care for her enough, and so was

212

indifferent? ... That was the question. Like Hamlet, he couldn't make up his mind.

'Good morning, Harry,' Superintendent Harkness greeted him. 'Are you all right? You don't look your best.'

'Very minor personal problem,' Timberlake said. 'I'll be all right.' Harkness had enough respect for him to leave it at that.

'Are you sure it isn't a waste of time to go back to the Eaton Square flat?'

'Sure? No, not really. But what else have we got? And I can't help feeling there's something Lucinda Pusey said that'd give me a pointer if I could only remember it, something that it tied up with the flat. Being there and looking round again is the best bet I have.'

'If you think so, then. Would you like Darren Webb with you, or that keen young CID aide who always seems to be around looking for a job?'

'No thanks, sir. I'll be better off without distractions. Particularly from the Eager Beaver. I think I may give him a Valium sandwich next time I'm with him.' He smiled. 'That's unfair. Actually, he's a promising young officer, and he's been quite helpful. It's simply that this morning's job is something that has to be taken slowly, with maximum concentration. I don't want to be distracted by a human dynamo whirring away beside me.'

Sarah Lewis arrived for duty looking unusually frazzled and in a state of high excitement. On her way to Terrace Vale she had been working out how to proceed with the Wightman case, and had come to the unpleasant conclusion that she would have to speak to Bob Farmer about it. However, she was soon to find there was good news and bad news.

The good news was that Bob Farmer was out for the day giving evidence at Knightsbridge Crown Court; the bad news was that Ted Greening was in for the day. She looked around the CID offices. The only detective inspector in sight was Harry Timberlake, who was involved in conversation with Superintendent Harkness; and anyway, she wouldn't have wanted to involve him in her case. She gritted her teeth and approached Greening's office.

Greening was off women this morning. In fact he was rarely *on* women, except in a purely topographical sense, and only with a particular class of women. The previous evening he had called on one of his informants, a tall, handsome black prostitute who rarely had any worthwhile information to offer but reluctantly granted him other services free of charge because of his rank. Greening was unaware of the fact that she was looking forward to his retirement almost as much as he was.

Despite having a high degree of the skills of her calling, an admirable ability to conceal her aversion to Greening and a lot of hard work, she was unable to overcome his terminal case of brewer's droop. As she was a shrewd young woman she poured sympathy and not scorn, told him he was working too hard, carrying too much responsibility. He conned himself into believing her, but it didn't make him feel any better. This morning he had a sort of unfulfilment hangover. The last thing he wanted was a problem that called for a decision on his part.

Sarah explained the Wightman situation in detail, and ended, 'I'd like to get a search warrant from our tame magistrate, turn over Wightman's drum and bring him in for questioning, guv. *Now.*'

'It's really Bob Farmer's case,' Greening said judicially. 'I don't want to go over his head by giving you the okay myself.'

'It's urgent, guv,' she replied. 'I'm afraid that if we don't nab him and quick, Mrs Wightman might do a wobbly and back up his alibi again.' She thought for a moment and said slyly. 'Perhaps if you got the warrant and then brought him in yourself—'

The last thing Greening wanted to do was become involved in anything contentious. Or not contentious, for that matter. He had an aversion to involvement that matched a vampire's dread of crucifixes.

'How solid is all this?' Greening asked superfluously.

'Gibraltar,' she said. Mentally she crossed her fingers and spat three times.

'Where're you going to pick him up?'

'At work. I don't want his wife there.'

Greening disliked the sound of this more and more. On the other hand, he remembered the chief superintendent's recent acid little lecture. 'Better take someone with you,' he said.

He got up and peered into the CID offices. By now they looked like the *Marie Celeste*, except for one person. 'Whatshisname Larkin's here. Take him. He's always hanging about scratching his arse and doing fuck-all. If he wants to get into CID he can do something

214

for a change,' he said slanderously. 'Get going, then. I've got a call to make.'

He returned to his desk, trying to look important, picked up the phone and dialled three numbers.

'At the third stroke it will be nine ... four ... and twenty seconds,' came a voice. Greening was nothing if not unoriginal. He belched into the mouthpiece. 'Pardon,' he said automatically. Sarah had already gone and missed the performance.

She went over to Nigel Larkin. 'You busy?' she asked, which was tantamount to asking a worker bee if it had anything on at the moment.

'Nothing that can't wait.'

'Get your skates on, then.'

'What's up?'

'Have Sergeant Rumsden fix us some transport with a couple of PCs. I'll brief you on the way.' What she told him made Larkin vibrate like a tuning fork. Sarah was so wound up herself she totally overlooked the implications of a relatively junior WDC taking so much responsibility off her own bat. She was aware that if anything went wrong, Ted Greening would drop her right in it up to her neck. Cold fingers ran up and down her spine. 'This had bloody better work out,' she told herself.

In the street outside it was warm and sunny by English standards: inside the Eaton Square flat it was as cold as the interior of a marble mausoleum. Harry Timberlake had begun by looking again at all rooms other than the main sitting-room, but he was convinced that the clue, the hint, the indication – whatever it was – which would point him in the right direction was in this room. But *where*? He had looked everywhere, twice at least.

He could have kicked himself for his own incompetence. He had found a concealed drawer and learned the long-kept secret of Lucinda Pusey and her brother Charles, yet he hadn't seen what was staring him in the face.

The piles of old magazines, neatly stacked and without a speck of dust. He had been looking for something subtle, hidden. They seemed so banal, so irrelevant – and so *obvious* – that subconsciously he had dismissed them.

They were in the style of the *Tatler, Country Life* and *Hello!*, full of 'personalities' and the upper classes at play. They had to be at play: they did little else, Timberlake thought darkly. The magazines covered the period from immediately post-war to the mid-seventies. Some of the publications had gone out of circulation some years ago, like their subjects.

He went through the magazines carefully, with increasing disquiet. If he found nothing in them he most certainly would be defeated. Page after page of gilded trivialities... The Puseys appeared occasionally, at parties, at balls, but there was nothing that possibly could have been of help in solving murders forty years later. Cold fingers began to touch Timberlake's heart. He wondered whether he had simply hoped so fervently there was something significant to be found in the flat that he had persuaded himself he had a gut feeling that there was.

He was nearing the end of the last pile with the scales going down heavily on the fears side, outweighing the hopes, when he stopped half-way through a magazine. In a previous copy he'd noticed something at barely above a subliminal level. He started looking through the last three or four magazines.

He almost missed it again. It was a photograph of Charles and Sophie Pusey – as she was then – at a Christmas house party in Scotland. In the background was a face that was familiar to him, yet he instinctively knew he had never met the man. Timberlake asked himself what was so special about this particular man that made him try to identify him. He racked his brain and tried free association techniques to recall where he had seen his face before. And when at last he made the connection it almost made him dizzy when he realized the possible implications.

Timberlake's opening remark to Superintendent Harkness was economical with words, but even a small atomic bomb can make a lot of noise.

'Sir, I know how the killer got into Lucinda Pusey's flat, and why she was killed; and I'm almost certain I know where Caterina Tozharska is.'

Chapter 29

'So far, so good,' Sarah said hopefully to herself as she and the Eager Beaver were driven to Ross Wightman's place of work. Sarah glanced sideways at Nigel Larkin. He *seemed* calm enough, but so does a wire carrying a thousand volts. She looked at him again, more carefully. 'Are you growing a moustache?' she asked.

'I was thinking about it,' he admitted, surreptitiously fingering his upper lip to see if it had started to feel rough yet. In fact he'd been thinking about it for some time, hoping it might give him some mature presence. He had to admit to himself there were times when he looked almost young enough to get into football matches half price.

'What d'you want me to do?' he asked.

'Nothing,' she said. 'The quieter you are and the less you fidget the more it'll worry chummy.' Nigel practised looking enigmatic. Sarah glanced at him. 'You feeling all right?' she asked.

'Fine. And thanks for asking me to come along.'

She didn't say anything.

When they arrived at the massive building where Wightman worked Sarah looked at it with disdain. 'Just look at that bloody place. When you think that all they do is add up other people's money and shuffle pieces of paper around all day. They don't help *make* anything, or grow anything, or do anything constructive, just consume enormous quantities of paper. And it's other people's work that pays their wages. Makes you sick, doesn't it!'

She deliberately parked in an area marked 'Staff Parking Only', and when a commissionaire came out ponderously and told her she couldn't park there, she produced her warrant card and said 'Police officers'. Nigel simply looked enigmatic. Sarah, he could see, definitely meant business, and was feeling bloody minded.

They entered the building with the commissionaire, who clearly didn't want to talk with the Bill in public. 'Can I help you?' he asked uninvitingly.

'We want to see Mr Ross Wightman, please,' Sarah said.

We *want* to see, not We *should like to see*, Larkin noted. Well, at least she said 'please'.

'I'm not sure he's in on a Saturday,' the commissionaire said ungraciously.

'So ask,' Sarah said acidly.

The commissionaire fought a losing rearguard action.

'Names?' he asked, mechanically following laid-down procedures. Sarah and Larkin stared at him. He picked up his phone.

'There are two detectives in reception to see Mr Wightman . . . I'll tell them.' He hung up. 'He's on his way down.'

Ross Wightman came out of the lift looking as innocent as a new-born infant; even more so, if you believed in original sin. Sarah reached for her warrant card, but Wightman said, 'It's all right, I remember you.'

'Mr Wightman, there have been certain developments in the Emma Leyland case, and I should like you to accompany me to the station.'

'Oh, you've got him, have you?'

'It's to help us with our enquiries.'

He considered this for a while. 'I'll just get my things,' he said at last and went back to the lift.

'D'you think he'll do a runner?' Larkin said quietly.

'No. It'd be half-way to a confession. Besides, he still thinks he's bomb-proof with that alibi.'

Wightman was back within a matter of minutes.

'Will you be able to give me a lift back?' he asked.

'As soon as we're finished,' Sarah replied without hesitation. A faint smile played round Wightman's lips. I'll make you smile, you bastard, Sarah thought furiously, heroically keeping a straight face. Nigel Larkin was preserving the silent inscrutability demanded of him. He was gratified to notice that Wightman furtively gave him an occasional puzzled glance.

At Terrace Vale Sarah told Sergeant Rumsden, on duty at the desk, that she was interviewing Mr Ross Wightman. 'What interview room is available?'

'Number two.'

'You go on,' she said to Larkin. As the two men went to the room, Larkin heard Sarah say, 'Sergeant, I'd be grateful if you'd

218

make a call for me.' What the phone call was, Larkin was too far ahead to hear.

Police interview rooms can be daunting places with their minimum of stark government furniture – a table, three or four chairs – and the twin-track cassette recorder which is a forbidding reminder of the indelibility of words once spoken. And there is the smell. Furniture polish and air fresheners cannot completely obliterate it. Many – if not most – CID officers smoke, and so do most villains. Interview rooms can smell like old railway carriages in the days of steam.

As they sat, Sarah and Nigel Larkin opposite Wightman, Sarah pushed a packet of cigarettes across the table. 'Have a cigarette,' she said encouragingly. Nigel Larkin was surprised: he didn't think she smoked – which she didn't.

Wightman took a cigarette and smoked it. During the interview he smoked two more.

Sarah switched on the recorder and spoke the classic prologue to an official interview, beginning with the time and date. She went on, 'This is an interview with Mr Ross Wightman at Terrace Vale police station. I am Detective Constable Sarah Lewis, four-seven-three. Also present is PC Nigel Larkin, five-one-eight.

'Mr Wightman, will you give your full name, address and date of birth.'

'Is all this necessary?'

'It's standard procedure.'

'Oh, very well.' He gave the information.

'I have to tell you now that I suspect you of raping Emma Juliette Leyland near White Hart Lane, Terrace Vale, on the eleventh of last month.' She continued with the new standard caution, ending with, 'Do you understand?'

'This is ridiculous. I've already—'

'Do you understand the caution I have just given you?'

'Yes, of course.'

'Do you want a solicitor present?'

'I don't need a solicitor. I've not done anything wrong.'

'Very well. Will you tell me where you were between seven-thirty p.m. and nine-thirty p.m. on the eleventh of last month. It may help your memory if I tell you it was a Monday.'

'I know what day of the week it was, and I know where I was! I've been through this with you before!'

'Will you answer the question, please?'

'You know very well. I was at home with my wife.'

'Have you ever been on the waste ground by the railway tunnel between Churchyard Walk and White Hart Lane?'

'Never, to my knowledge.'

'Were you there on the night of the eleventh between—'

'How many more times, for Christ's sake? I was with my wife!'

'Your wife has since informed me that you didn't return home that evening until after nine o'clock.'

'She's lying! The lying bitch—' He gathered himself. 'She must have got the evenings mixed up. I told you when you came to my house: I saw *Coronation Street*. That's on from seven-thirty to eight.'

'That episode was repeated, Mr Wightman.'

'Well, I didn't know.'

Sarah had a small bomb prepared that even Nigel Larkin was unaware of. 'Mr Wightman, your wife has told me that you explained your late return home as being because you were with a Julia Strang, a colleague at your office. Do you have any comment to make?'

Wightman remained silent.

'I also have to tell you that I have interviewed Miss Strang and she denies that she was with you on that evening.'

'Of course she does! I wasn't with her. It's my wife! She's making all this up! She's lying!'

'Why should she want to do that?'

'Get me in trouble! You know what bloody wom—... couples can be like when they've had a row.' He regained some part of his self-control to become smooth again. 'I did something I'm heartily ashamed of, even though I was provoked. The other day I hit her. She's lying to get her own back.'

'Do you own a red woollen scarf?'

'I may do. I've got a lot of clothes I don't wear very often.'

'What about a bone-handled knife with engraving and a broken tip on the blade?'

'No.'

Sarah stared at Wightman, before saying, 'Have you finished with these?' She drew the ashtray towards her.

Puzzled, he said, 'Of course.'

Sarah gathered up the cigarette stubs, put them into a small plastic envelope, sealed it with a label, signed the label and passed it to Larkin, who countersigned it.

'What're you doing?' Wightman asked. Sarah reached across the table. She appeared to pick up something from the surface and put it into another bag. Neither of the men could see anything at first. She held it up: there were two hairs in it. They weren't Sarah's or Larkin's, they were the wrong colour.

'What the hell are you doing?' Wightman demanded.

'I shall send these hairs from your head and the cigarette ends for DNA profiling of the saliva on them to compare with specimens left on Miss Leyland's clothing. Now, is there anything you wish to change in the statement you have made so far?'

'No.'

Sarah reached into her large handbag and took out two evidence bags of transparent plastic. She said clearly, to make sure the tape recorder got every syllable, 'I am showing Mr Ross Wightman two exhibits: a red woollen scarf and a bone-handled knife with engraving and a broken tip on the blade, to which I have attached labels and signed with the time and date. Mr Wightman, have you seen these before?'

'No.' It was so futile. Sarah wondered why he bothered to struggle.

'I have to tell you that earlier today I obtained a search warrant for your home where DCI Larkin and I, accompanied by two uniformed officers, found these items in the bottom of a wardrobe containing your clothes. Do you have any explanation?'

Wightman sat silent and motionless in his chair.

Sarah addressed the recorder. 'No reply. Interview concluded at—' She glanced at her watch and added the time. She switched off the machine, took out the cassettes and passed one to Wightman.

'Come with me now, please.'

Sarah and Larkin led Wightman to the custody sergeant, Thomas Goodchild, where he was formally arrested by Sarah and charged with the rape of Emma Leyland on 11 September, at Terrace Vale, contrary to the Sexual Offences Act 1956 1 (1). After that he was fingerprinted and photographed.

Sergeant Goodchild and PC Rambo Wright escorted Wightman to the cells with Sarah following. On the way they passed another interview room, where a uniformed WPC was showing in Anthea Wightman.

'What have you said, you cow!' Wightman shouted at her. 'You wait! You just wait!'

'Wait about ten years, I should say,' Sarah commented.

Wightman took a pace towards his wife. Rambo laid a hand on his arm, apparently without force, but Wightman winced and moved on, mouthing threats.

Sarah went to Anthea. 'You've done the right thing, you know. I'm sure he's attacked other women. We'll check the dates and places he was away from home to see if they match up with any unsolved cases.'

Anthea nodded. 'Are you sure I'll be all right?' she asked anxiously.

'It's all over. You're safe.'

'Safe, but it's not all over,' Anthea said sadly.

'Don't worry; you won't have to give evidence against him. You're not allowed to, because you're his wife.'

'I know. But what's going to become of me now?'

Sarah struggled for an answer, but couldn't find one. She settled for, 'Wait for me in the front hall. I'll get my car and drive you home. You can give me a monster cup of tea.'

As Sarah opened the door to the station's car-park Bob Farmer was coming in. He was patting his hair into place.

'Hello, guv,' she greeted him. 'The Leyland rape case and Ross Wightman—'

'Don't ruin my day by going on about that again.'

'Oh, I shan't,' Sarah said sweetly. 'It's over, more or less. I've arrested him. He's stitched up better than Michael Jackson, *and* with physical evidence. So I haven't ruined your day after all.'

They both knew she'd devastated it.

Timberlake placed the magazine on Harkness's desk, open at the page with the photograph that had so fired his imagination. Darren Webb, Nigel Larkin and other detectives of the AMIP squad all strained to get a look at the picture. Harkness studied it for a few moments. 'What's the point?' he asked.

'That man there, just behind the Puseys. I knew I'd seen him somewhere, and then it came to me. There were photographs of him, as an older man, all over the place at Towers Hall. It's Comte Pascal de Gaillmont.'

Harkness saw the significance almost at once. 'Do the dates match?'

222

Timberlake nodded. 'To the week. I checked. Lucinda Pusey put me on the track when she said that Sophie would spread her legs for anyone with a title. And Lucinda Pusey said she had proof at the flat, in black and white. I've got a pretty good idea that's what she meant.'

'So you think Sophie Pusey, as she then was, had an affair with Pascal de Gaillmont at the house party?'

'I'm absolutely certain of it. And there's no doubt in my mind that de Gaillmont senior was Charles Pusey's father. There's an added bitter twist to the story as far as Sophie de Gaillmont is concerned. Charles Pusey, the son of Pascal de Gaillmont – his biological son but legally Pusey Senior's legitimate offspring – Charles was born a month before Jean-Louis.'

'Pascal seems to have had a busy month,' Webb commented.

Timberlake was so wound up with his theory that he almost didn't hear it. 'In her mind, *her* son should have been the Comte de Gaillmont. The whole thing fits now, the substitution, everything.'

'Perhaps,' Harkness said. 'But it's going to be difficult – if not impossible – to prove.'

'Not if he admits to the murders,' Timberlake said.

'Why would he do that, guv?' Webb asked.

'There might be a way, if we time things properly . . . and we're lucky,' Timberlake said.

Chapter 30

Timberlake didn't want any problems of getting through the gates at Towers Hall, so he phoned Jonathan Mellick, the solicitor, to arrange it with Jean-Louis and Sophie de Gaillmont for them to be interviewed at once on a matter of some importance. Mellick did not like the idea at all, but he really had no alternative: he called Towers Hall. When he put the phone down there were beads of sweat on his upper lip, and his hands trembled.

'They'll be in to receive you,' he said. 'It's all right.' It was very far from being all right.

Timberlake and Nigel Larkin arrived at Towers Hall escorted by a jam butty police car manned by Rosie Hall and Rambo Wright. They stayed in their car outside the house, while a newly engaged servant opened the big iron gates for the detectives.

The man calling himself Jean-Louis de Gaillmont was badly disconcerted when Timberlake asked him to accompany him to Terrace Vale to help them with their enquiries. Sophie de Gaillmont was outraged. However, they were both more accustomed to French procedures, where a *juge d'instruction*, an examining magistrate, can order witnesses to turn up for questioning and compel them to answer his questions on oath; and the police are less considerate of citizens' rights. Reluctantly Jean-Louis de Gaillmont agreed to go to the nick. Sophie said she would arrange for a solicitor to be present when Jean-Louis was questioned.

'But not that *crétin* Mellick,' she said in French. 'I shall have him find someone who is used to this sort of affair. Do not say anything until he arrives.'

The solicitor who arrived in a powder-blue Rolls-Royce to advise de Gaillmont was a high-profile, well-fleshed lawyer whose profile was even higher when he was horizontal than when he was vertical. He wore a suit that probably cost enough to feed three

Chinese families for a year. Jean-Louis de Gaillmont was no less elegant. He no longer had his damaged hand in a sling, but it still had a protective bandage round it.

Were Sir Ffoulkes Harbing not so stridently English, it could easily be imagined that there was a Sumo wrestler somewhere in his ancestry. His full-moon face had eyebrows like camel-thorn bushes over eyes like small currants, hooded by heavy eyelids, which gave him a completely false air of having a brain that never got out of bottom gear. In fact he was as sharp as a scalpel and as rapid as a mongoose. His lips were a more accurate indication of his character: he had none to speak of, only two thin brownish-pink lines set in a downward disbelieving curve. It was said of him that if you asked him the time it would cost you £50, plus VAT. His personal rates were never less than £500 an hour.

The team to question Jean-Louis de Gaillmont and his formidable legal adviser was Detective Superintendent Harkness and Detective Inspector Timberlake. Darren Webb had disappeared, sent somewhere on a mysterious task by Timberlake, accompanied by the Eager Beaver and a couple of uniforms.

De Gaillmont and Harbing sat at one side of the table in Interview Room No. 1, Timberlake opposite de Gaillmont, Harkness facing Harbing. Timberlake switched on the cassette recorder and made the formal statement of time, date, place and those present. Sir Ffoulkes Harbing immediately said, in a voice matured by port and cigar smoke, 'I want it made plain that my client agreed voluntarily and readily, without coercion, to come to the station and help the police with their enquiries into a matter or matters as yet unspecified.'

'Agreed,' Harkness said.

'Will you state your name, date of birth, and address, sir?' Timberlake addressed de Gaillmont.

'Jean-Louis Pascal Henri Honoré, Comte de Gaillmont, 29 September 1959. At present living at Towers Hall, Terrace Vale.'

'That is your correct name?'

'Of course.' Sir Ffoulkes looked curiously at Timberlake.

'Then I shall address you by that name.'

'Monsieur de Gaillmont, I now have to inform you that I suspect you of conspiracy to murder a man at Towers Hall on the eighteenth of September. There may be other matters that concern you to be considered later. Anything you say will be recorded, taken down in writing and may be used in evidence. Do you understand?'

'One moment!' Sir Ffoulkes Harbing said sharply. 'Who is this man you say was murdered at Towers Hall?'

'As yet his identity has not been completely established,' Harkness said smoothly.

'I can only suppose that the inspector is referring to my stepbrother Charles Pusey. He was murdered at Towers Hall on that date.'

The detectives made no comment. Timberlake took up the questioning again. 'Did you know the late Lucinda Pusey?'

'What has this to do with the murder at Towers Hall?' Sir Ffoulkes demanded.

'There is a connection which I shall come to later. In any case, I did say that there may be other matters to concern your client.'

'I'm not sure I can allow my client to continue to answer any more questions.'

The two detectives were unruffled. 'Very well,' Harkness said. 'Of course, our enquiries are continuing, and we may require Monsieur de Gaillmont to answer questions or make a statement. If he fails to do so, perhaps you will advise him that under the new legislation attention can be drawn to this in any subsequent proceedings, and that adverse comment may be made on his refusal to speak.' Harkness stood up, and Timberlake followed his example.

'Wait a moment.' Sir Ffoulkes considered for a moment. 'If Monsieur le Comte de Gaillmont wishes to continue to assist you he will do so, but I reserve the right to intervene on his behalf.'

'Of course.' The detectives sat down again.

'I repeat the question, Monsieur de Gaillmont. Did you know the late Lucinda Pusey?'

'I knew of her, vaguely. I never met her.'

'Did you ever visit her flat?'

'No, never. I don't even know where it was.'

'Will you tell me where you were between 8 p.m. and 10.30 p.m. on the ninth of this month?'

'I've no idea at the moment. When I've had time to think about it . . . There may also be something in my diary. I should think I was at home with my stepmother. I rarely go out in the evenings. Now I should like to go to the lavatory and then have some tea or something.'

'Interview suspended at 2.48 p.m.' Timberlake switched off the recorder. He took out one of the cassettes and handed it to Sir Ffoulkes Harbing.

Darren Webb stamped his feet in a vain attempt to get them warm. The afternoon had turned raw and cold for the time of year. It reminded him of when he was on emergency point duty in his days as a uniformed PC standing in the middle of a cold road. Now, as then, he wished he was somewhere else.

Two constables, sweating despite being in shirt sleeves, were digging in the soft ground. A spade hit something that wasn't earth. 'There's something here, skip,' one of them said. The one who had spoken was scraping earth with the edge of his spade. The second one helped him, and a hard, rectangular shape became visible.

'It's a suitcase,' the second one said.

'HT was right,' Webb said. 'Keep going . . . gently does it.'

Fifteen minutes later two suitcases were on the surface next to where the men were digging. At the bottom of the neat trench could be seen the body of a young woman, face down. In the back of her head, at the base of the skull, was a hole which needed no expertise to recognize as being most probably a hole from a large calibre bullet.

The interview of Jean-Louis de Gaillmont was in session again. Timberlake's questions had become harsher, more rapid. Twice Sir Ffoulkes had to warn him he was harassing his client, and now he looked ready to ask how much longer this questioning would continue. Timberlake knew he had to make the plunge now, or it might be too late.

'I have told you that I suspect you of being party to the murder of a man at Towers Hall. I now say I believe that the murdered man was Jean-Louis de Gaillmont, and you are, in fact, Charles Pusey.'

'That's preposterous!' A shrillness in his voice betrayed his tension.

'We have done blood-grouping tests,' Timberlake went on. Jean-Louis turned pale. 'Has your mother ever told you that Pascal de Gaillmont was your father and not Charles Pusey?'

'Of course he was! That's—' He stopped, his face ghastly. He made a courageous attempt to recover himself. 'You're confusing me with your questions . . . I misunderstood—'

'I have already warned you that you were harassing my client,' Sir Ffoulkes boomed. 'I shall advise him to conclude this interview.'

'As you wish,' Timberlake said. 'I think your client has told me all I want to know.'

There was a knock at the door. Darren Webb opened it gingerly and gestured to Timberlake.

'If you'll wait just a moment, please,' he said, and went out.

Harkness said, for the benefit of the recording, 'Inspector Timberlake leaves the room at 3.20 p.m.'

Timberlake was outside for less than a minute. Harkness noted his return.

'Mr Pusey, or Monsieur de Gaillmont if you prefer, I remind you of the caution I originally gave you that anything you say may be used in evidence. Mr Pusey, the body of Caterina Tozharska has been discovered in the grounds of Towers Hall, in the same place where the hundred-year-old corpse of a young woman was buried.

'I am now arresting you for conspiracy to murder Jean-Louis de Gaillmont and Caterina Tozharska,' Timberlake said quietly. 'There may be a further charge. Mr Pusey, do you wish to say anything?'

'Not at this point,' Sir Ffoulkes Harbing said on his behalf.

'Yes, I want to make a statement,' Pusey said wearily.

'I think you should take time to gather your thoughts,' Sir Ffoulkes warned him.

'Oh, what's the point? It's over. I helped kill them. And I killed Aunt Lucinda. She was always fond of me, and she let me in when she saw me through the spyhole in the door. I told her the police had made a mistake and it wasn't me that was killed. But I could never have passed myself off as Jean-Louis. She would have known . . . It was a pity, really. I rather liked her.'

A small convoy of cars arrived at Towers Hall, led by Timberlake driving Harkness. Behind them came a police car with Rosie Hall driving Darren Webb. Coming up in the rear was the powder-blue Rolls Royce with Sir Ffoulkes Harbing.

A butler whom Timberlake had not seen before showed the police and Sir Ffoulkes into the usual reception room. While they waited Harkness studied the photographs of Comte Pascal de Gaillmont, and nodded at Timberlake. 'Yes, it was him all right.'

Sophie de Gaillmont entered as white and strained as Lady Macbeth, but with her head up. For the first time in his life Timberlake really had some idea of how the French nobility approached the tumbril.

Timberlake glanced at Harkness, but the superintendent gestured to him to do the talking.

'Madame la Comtesse,' he began, using the formal address for the first time since the early days of her arrival, 'as you must be aware, the body of Princess Caterina Tozharska was found buried in the grounds of this house earlier today. I must also tell you that your son Charles Pusey, who has been using the name of de Gaillmont, has confessed to his part in the killing, the murder of Comte Jean-Louis de Gaillmont and the murder of Lucinda Pusey. As a result of that, I arrest you for the murder of Jean-Louis de Gaillmont. Other charges may be preferred later.' He recited the usual caution.

'Very well,' Sophie de Gaillmont said. 'If you will be good enough to wait a few moments, I have some small matters to attend to, some toilet articles to collect.' She turned and walked out of the room.

'Rosie,' Timberlake said. Rosie Hall, who seemed hypnotized by Sophie's performance, started, then hurried after her.

Before she could stop her, Sophie de Gaillmont entered the small lift and closed the door behind her. The lift moved up, leaving Rosie Hall stranded. 'Sir! Sir!' she called out.

Timberlake, Harkness and Webb came hurrying out. They took in the situation at a glance. 'Butler! Butler!' Timberlake shouted, feeling awkward because he didn't know the butler's name. The butler arrived with a butler's dignified gait. 'Where is madame's bedroom?' Timberlake demanded.

The butler was taken off-balance.

'Quick, man!'

'Second floor, sir. Centre door.'

Timberlake and Webb set off at a run and took the stairs two at a time. At the second flight Timberlake stumbled for no apparent reason, and brought Webb crashing down. The two men struggled to their feet, Timberlake hampering Webb as he again seemed to miss footing.

They were a few yards from Sophie de Gaillmont's bedroom

door when there was the unmistakable report of a heavy hand-gun.

Madame la Comtesse Douairière Sophie de Gaillmont lay dead on her bed, a dark hole from which a little blood trickled in the centre of her forehead. Her dead left hand held rosary beads with a crucifix. A foot or two from her right hand lay a .455 Webley and Scott revolver.

'We were just too late,' Webb said. Timberlake just looked at him.

'Guv, you didn't—'

He was about to say, ' – you didn't fall down deliberately to give her time to—' when Harkness entered, and Webb didn't finish his question. Ever.

Much later the three principals in the investigation, together with Sergeant Braddock, out of hospital minus his appendix, were having a quiet drink in a private room of the Terrace Vale nick's local pub. 'Did we ever find out why Thérèse Chardet committed suicide, guv?' Braddock asked Timberlake.

'Yes. It was in Charles Pusey's statement. Apparently Chardet was hopelessly in love with him and was his mistress—'

'The two don't always go together,' Harkness interrupted with a rare shaft of cynicism.

Timberlake paused, wondering about his own situation for a moment before continuing. 'She went along with the whole scheme for his sake. But when Charles Pusey had become Comte Jean-Louis de Gaillmont and Thérèse started talking of marriage Sophie killed that stone dead. She wasn't going to have some little bour-geoise employee as the future comtesse. Pusey, of course, didn't stand up to his mother—'

'The whole scheme was hers, and Pusey was totally dominated by her,' Harkness said.

'Well, it was all too much for Thérèse, and—' He shrugged, then turned to Harkness with a smile. 'At least my trip to Saint-Rémy-de-Provence was worthwhile, sir.'

'How's that, Harry?'

'It was Capitaine Lapollet who gave me the idea where Tozhar-ska was buried. He said Pascal de Gaillmont, Sophie's husband, was a legend in the Resistance. One of his ruses when the Gestapo were after him was to wait until they'd searched a house, and then

230

nip into it. It wouldn't occur to them to go back to a place they'd already looked at. Sophie would know about that.'

'Oh, by the way, the gun's been traced,' Harkness said. 'It was part of a batch that was parachuted to the Resistance during the war.'

Timberlake was silent for a moment. 'In a way her son was a much nastier character. Sophie was Lady Macbeth writ large. She pulled the trigger on Jean-Louis and Caterina Tozharska herself.' He smiled wryly. 'But even Lady Macbeth couldn't bring herself to kill. As for Pusey . . . he was keen enough to be the *comte*. Though when it came to the crunch, he blamed everything on his mother. He never stopped talking, trying to make himself out to be a victim of her mad ambitions. I might have believed there was something in that if he hadn't killed poor old Lucinda Pusey.'

'I agree with you, Harry,' Harkness said. 'Of the pair, I think the son was the more repulsive. And Sophie, well, prison life would have been unendurable for her. Privately, I'm not sorry that she managed to kill herself,' Harkness admitted.

Timberlake and Webb didn't look at each other.

As the French say, the de Gaillmont–Pusey case caused a great deal of ink to flow. Newspapers kept it alive for days after Charles Pusey was sentenced to life imprisonment, and television companies brought out instant documentaries.

In a Shepherd Market flat a woman of thirty-two years of age, who managed to appear seven or eight years younger in the careful light of her bedroom, switched off her television with some irritation. 'Christ, I'm tired of hearing about that case,' she said. An older woman, whose battered face was a Dead Sea scroll of a vast sexual history, came in.

'Your next punter's due here any minute now, darling.'

'Who is it?'

'That skinny wine merchant. I've got a new video for him to have a look at.'

'Oh, God,' the younger woman groaned. 'Another couple of years of this and I'll pack it all in. I'll have enough to retire to Bournemouth, or somewhere. Or maybe get married. Two of my regulars keep asking me. No, on second thoughts, no.'

'You ever been married?'

'Once, very nearly. Lucky I missed it.' The doorbell rang. 'There's old skinny. Let him in.'

231

The older woman went out, and Betty Lock, who once was nearly Mrs Charles Pusey, got off the bed and smoothed it down ready for her next client.

Emma Leyland came to see Sarah at Terrace Vale. Without preamble she said, 'You've got him, then.'

'Yes. To rights. Firmly stitched up and bagged. Scarf, knife, genetic fingerprint evidence matching him up with the stains on your underclothes.'

'Good. Congratulations.'

'What does your mother say?'

'Nothing. It's as if it never happened.' Emma said wryly. 'You know, the first time I'll actually see him will be in court.'

'Does that bother you?'

'Absolutely not.'

'I have to warn you again: giving evidence won't be easy. It could be very dirty.'

'How?'

'His only possible defence is that you led him on, agreed to have sex, and then claimed he raped you because you were ashamed your boyfriend might find out. His counsel will try to show you're sexually promiscuous.'

'Maybe I am. Does that give anyone the right to rape me?'

'Of course not. But that's how things are.'

Emma looked steadily at Sarah. 'Don't worry. I won't lose my cool. I'll be all right.'

Sarah returned her gaze. 'Yes, I'm sure you will be.'

Emma shook Sarah Lewis's hand. 'Thanks. Now I'll try to put my life together again.'

Harry Timberlake looked at the imposing black marble headstone. Beneath the inscription in gold *Charles Everett Pusey* and dates *1922–75* there were newly carved letters:

And his loving sister, Lucinda Anne Pusey, 1924–95.

He took a bronze urn from inside his coat and placed it carefully on the grave. It was the sort of urn used for the ashes of cremated bodies.

This one contained ashes, but not human ones. They were the ashes of burnt letters.

He turned away, wondering what on earth had made him make this gesture.

232

At the gate of the cemetery was the familiar figure of a woman.

'Hello,' he said. 'How did you know I was here?'

'Darren Webb told me.'

'Big mouth.'

'Well, it was *me*.'

'Aren't you on duty today?'

She shook her head. 'Day off.'

They were both silent for a while.

'Well,' she said at last. 'Is it on again? Us?'

'What about *him*?'

She shook her head again. 'Finished.'

He looked at her for a long, long moment. 'Shall we get out of here?' he said. 'Cemeteries depress the hell out of me.'

'You know the best cure for depression?'

They both laughed.

'Your place or mine?' she said with one of her wicked looks.